D0371991

NCPL
DATE DUE
07 02 93
NCPL
DATE DUE
07 27 01

WHY DO BIRDS

Also by Damon Knight

A for Anything
CV
The Observers
A Reasonable World
Rule Golden / Double Meaning

WHY DO BIRDS

Damon Knight

A TOM DOHERTY ASSOCIATES BOOK
NEW YORK

WHY DO BIRDS

This book is printed on acid-free paper.

A Tor Book
Published by Tom Doherty Associates, Inc.
175 Fifth Avenue
New York, N.Y. 10010

Tor® is a registered trademark of Tom Doherty Associates, Inc.

Library of Congress Cataloging-in-Publication Data

Knight, Damon Francis
Why do birds / Damon Knight.
p. cm.
"A Tom Doherty Associates book."
ISBN 0-312-85174-X
I. Title.
PS3561.N44W47 1992
813'.54—dc20 92-28382
CIP

Printed in the United States of America

0 9 8 7 6 5 4 3 2

Tell of the day when We shall blot out the mountains and make the earth a barren waste; when We shall gather all mankind together, leaving not a soul behind.

The Koran: "The Cave,"
translated by N. J. Dawood

"Well, there's certainly something screwy going on around here."

The Marx Brothers, *Room Service*

CHAPTER 1

"Well, Mr. Stone, what seems to be your problem?"

"I think I was kidnapped from nineteen thirty-one and brought here, and I think the aliens sent me back to put the whole human race in a box."

"And why do you think that?"

"Because I'm crazy."

The psychiatrist blinked and looked more closely at the detainee. He appeared to be a man in his late twenties or early thirties, clean-shaven, with a round cheerful face. He was wearing a brown suit and necktie, and carried a fedora.

The psychiatrist and the detainee were sitting on opposite sides of a chipped gray acrylic conference table with a mandala of coffee rings on it. The panels overhead were humming and buzzing in an irritating lack of rhythm.

"Mr. Stone, can you tell me what year it is?"

"Twenty ought two."

"And who's the President?"

"Tennafly."

The psychiatrist scribed a note. "So, then, you believe you're here because you're crazy?"

"Don't you?"

The psychiatrist blinked again. "Let's go back a little. When did you first realize that you had been kidnapped by aliens?"

"When I woke up on their spaceship."

"And when was that?"

"April fifteenth, nineteen thirty-one. Or the next morning, maybe. That would be the sixteenth."

"What happened then?"

"They hypnotized me and told me to come back and put everybody in a box."

"I see. And so you came back?"

"Well, they *brought* me back. I got in trouble in the hotel because I wasn't registered, and I didn't have any ID, the kind you use now. All I had on me was some money with old dates on it, and an expired driver's license. The cops took the money."

"I see. Where were you when you were kidnapped by aliens?"

"Right here, Trenton. I was staying in the same hotel, but it's all different now."

"How is it different?"

The detainee gestured vaguely. "Wallpaper, lights. All the new buildings. Holos, and those gadgets like the one you're using."

The psychiatrist looked at his memopad, scribed in a comment. "And when did your driver's license expire?"

"Thirty-two."

"Nineteen thirty-two?"

"Right. I mean, it was good when I *had* it, but it ran out the next year, because I was on the spaceship. I was wearing this suit and hat when they arrested me, and the dentist said I have the kind of fillings they used then."

"That would be the correction center dentist?"

"Right. They arrested me for suspicion of felony, and

then the judge ordered me to see you, to find out if I'm crazy."

"And you think you *are* crazy?"

"Well, what else could it be? I think I was born in nineteen ought one, but that would make me a hundred and one years old, right? And I have these ideas about aliens and spaceships, so I'm crazy."

The psychiatrist cleared his throat. "How do you account for the fillings?"

"I can't. The dentist couldn't figure it out either."

The psychiatrist scrolled through the documents in his file. No previous record, no prints. "Tell me, how do you feel about the aliens?"

"I love them, but they scare me."

"Why do they scare you?"

"Because I don't know what they're going to do with us after they get us all in a box."

"What do you *think* they're going to do?"

"Well, they say they're going to take us to another planet before the Earth is destroyed, but I'm not so sure."

"What is the name of this other planet?"

"I don't know. The aliens don't use words like we do."

"How do they use words?"

"I mean, they don't use them at all. They have these symbols, kind of like Chinese writing, that flash on their foreheads."

The psychiatrist nodded several times. "And is that how they told you about the other planet?"

"No, they used a telepathy helmet when they hypnotized me. Are you going to tell the judge to send me to a nut-house?"

"Is that what you want me to do?"

"I don't care. I can get out all right, but I don't want this charge hanging over me."

"You mean you can get out of the mental health care facility?"

"Oh, sure."

"What will you do, just walk out?"

"No, I'll tell the head doctor to certify me sane, and he'll let me go."

"Why will he do that?"

"Because I'll touch him with my ring."

Guardperson Eldon Wiggan, forty-six, anglo, five feet eight, two hundred fifty pounds, took the detainee back to the tank. "Hey, do you have to grab me that hard?" the detainee asked.

Wiggan slammed him against the wall. "That hurt?"

"Oh, yeah."

CHAPTER 2

Patrolperson G. W. Griffin, thirty-four, male, anglo, blond, six feet one, one hundred eighty pounds, drove the detainee from the County Correctional Center across town to the New Jersey State Mental Health Care Facility.

It was a bright November day; a wind was whipping the tops of the bare trees, and all the smog from New York had blown off to the east.

The patrol, whose eyesight was 20/20, watched the detainee now and then in the rearview mirror. Stone appeared to be curious about everything he saw. As the cruiser whispered down a residential street, he turned around to look at a yard enclosed by a white picket fence where a boy was struggling with a cat under a spruce tree. The cat was biting him in the stomach, and the boy couldn't pull away. Something dark was hanging from the tree, possibly the tail of another cat. Stone kept watching until they were out of sight; then he straightened around and sat quietly behind the mesh, with his wrists Velcroed.

A moment later the patrol saw a contrail streaking overhead; there was a deafening concussion.

"What was that!" Stone shouted in the ringing silence.

"Sonic boom. Concordes fly too damn low."

"Are they propelled by detonite?" Stone asked. The patrol didn't answer. He turned in to the drive in front of the Facility, unlocked the rear door and pulled the detainee out.

"Do you like being a cop?" Stone asked.

"Sure. Do you like being a coo-coo?"

"No. Thanks for asking."

Two white-coated attendants were waiting outside the door. The patrol stripped the Velcro and turned the detainee over to them. "Have a nice day," he said, and walked back to his humming cruiser.

Early Tuesday morning, when attendants opened the main entrance of the Facility, they found Stone shivering in his pajamas under the roof of the portico. He offered no resistance when they restrained him and took him back to his room.

Dr. Gary Lipshitz, the Chief of Psychiatry, visited him there on his morning rounds. "Edwin," he said, "how did you get outside last night?" Stone was in a straitjacket, but seemed cheerful and talkative.

"The aliens came and got me," he said. "They can go

through walls. They knew I wanted to get out of here, but they don't understand about clothing."

"They don't understand what about clothing?"

"That you have to have it. They gave me mine back, but they gave me a lot of other stuff too, that I had with me, and I think they just don't understand how things work down here."

"How do things work down here, Edwin?"

"By the rules. You have to have clothes on, and you have to have the right papers."

Dr. Lipshitz made a note. "What will you do if you get clothes and the right papers, Edwin?"

"I'll go to New York and look for somebody to build the box."

"What box is that?"

"The box big enough to put the whole human race in."

"Isn't that going to be a pretty big box, Edwin?"

"You bet, Doc."

CHAPTER 3

Edwin, I'm Dr. Wellafield, the Director of the Facility. Sit down, please. You can go now, Harris."

"Glad to know you," said the detainee, extending his hand. The Director took it, and felt a slight sting of coldness. He sat back, massaging his finger absently, while the patient arranged himself in the visitor's chair. The patient was four inches taller and thirty pounds lighter than the Director, and he had no mustache.

"Now, Edwin," the Director said, "it seems that you were examined under sodium pentothal, and you stuck to your story about leaving the Facility on Monday night. The aliens came and got you."

"That's right."

"But you decided to return, because you knew you couldn't get far without ID and clothing."

"Correct. And money."

"Yes. And Dr. Lipshitz tells me that your intention is to go to New York and find somebody to build a big box. Do you have any idea who that somebody might be?"

"No, Doc, I don't. I was wondering if you could give me some ideas."

"Well, there are a number of good architectural firms in New York. Yallow and Moore are said to be one of the best. Now, Edwin, you realize that if we believe you're a danger to yourself or others, it's our duty to keep you here and treat you. On the other hand, if we decide you're mentally competent, we have to return you to the Municipal Court for trial. Is that clear?"

"Yes, Doc. Can I ask you a question?"

"Certainly, Edwin."

"When you say treat me, does that mean you could clear up my delusions if I stayed here?"

"No, I couldn't promise that."

"Is there any chance?"

"Well, frankly, in terms of a *cure,* no. In this particular disorder, there are some experimental therapies, but basically all we can do is confine the patient and keep them from harming themself or other people."

"I get it."

"All right, now because you're not violent, in my judgment it would serve no purpose to keep you in the Facility, but on the other hand it wouldn't help to stand trial, either. I'm going to make a call to the courthouse and see if I can straighten that out. Who was the judge who sent you here?"

"Judge Sloat was his name."

"Oh, yes, I know him. I don't think there'll be any difficulty. Now about money, you'll get that back as soon as they dismiss the charges. How much was it?"

"Over fifty bucks."

"That won't be enough." The Director looked in his wallet. "I don't have a lot of cash, but here's a thousand." He folded the bills and handed them to the patient.

"A *thousand?* That's too much."

"No, you'll need more than that. About papers, the best thing would be to get a job as soon as you can, and open a credit account and so on. What was your occupation in your former life, Edwin?"

"I was a kitchenwares salesman in Harrisburg, but the company went broke. I tended bar part time in a speakeasy for a while; that didn't pay enough. See, my wife left me, and I couldn't get the family back together unless I had a decent job. So I thought I'd drive down to New York and see what I could do. Trenton was the farthest I got. I went to sleep in the hotel that night, and when I woke up I was in the spaceship."

"Uh-huh, uh-huh. Well, a good salesperson or a bartender can always get a job, I'm sure. Just one thing, Edwin, when you apply for work, I wouldn't tell your employers about the aliens."

"Gotcha." The patient stood up. "I don't know how to thank you, Doc. I'll send this money back as soon as I can. Could I borrow your pen and a piece of paper?"

"Certainly." The Director handed him a scriber and a pad from the desk. "But don't worry about paying me."

The detainee shook his head. "Dr. Wellafield, one thousand," he said, writing. "I won't forget this, Doc." They shook hands again, and once more the Director felt a curious cold sting. "I'd do more than that for *you,* my boy," he said, with a catch in his throat.

CHAPTER 4

One leather suitcase, with contents." The sergeant put it on the counter. "One wallet and contents, fifty-three dollars. One key ring. One pocketknife, legal blade. One handkerchief. One packet of cundrums. Twenty-seven cents in metal change. One magazine. Sign here."

The detainee picked up the magazine and looked at it. "Sure glad to see this again." It looked like nothing much: a lurid thing with some kind of monster on the cover. The detainee signed. "Thanks a lot, Sergeant."

"Go on, get out of here."

It was a slow afternoon in the KoffiShop. The holo in the corner was displaying scenes from the destruction of Accra, but no one was watching. Two lawyers sitting at a window table got up and left, and a man in a funny hat came in.

"Yes, sir?" the counterperson said. It was a holo in a glass case, a digitized healthy young man with a boyish hairdo and perfect teeth.

The customer was staring at the menu. "Are you kidding with these prices?"

"What's wrong with the prices, sir?"

"Ham sandwich, fifty bucks?"

Alerted by the tone of the customer's voice, the counter flickered and went into alarm mode. It said, "Don't make any trouble, sir."

"No, I won't make any trouble. Judas Priest. I'll take the ham on white, french fries on the side, and a cup of java."

"A cup of what, sir?"

"*Coffee,* for Cripe's sake."

"Sixty-two fifty, please," the counter said.

"Right now?"

The counter flickered again. "Yes, sir. Don't make any trouble, or I'll have to call for assistance."

The man looked for a way through, or around, the glass case that contained the holo. "Where do I put the money?"

"Put it in the slot, sir."

The man put a hundred into the machine; it revolved, and plastic coins tinkled back. A minute later, when the packages thumped down the chute, the customer was watching the holo and muttering.

"They bombed Ghana," he said. "Where the hell is Ghana?" He looked at the packages suspiciously, unwrapped one, took a bite of the sandwich and looked up with his mouth open. "Hey," he said, half strangled.

The counter looked at him and said nothing.

"What's in this sandwich?"

"It contains soya ham, sir."

"What's soya ham?"

"Soybeans, with enhanced ham flavoring."

The customer spat a mouthful on the floor. The counter flickered again. "I am calling for assistance," it said.

"Never mind, I'm leaving. Judas Priest." The customer stood up, took a sip of his coffee, and spat that out too.

"Sixty bucks," he said, with coffee dribbling down his chin. "You guys ought to be *ashamed.*"

In the gray afternoon, a Rollaway bus drifted up the Interstate through the industrial area of east New Jersey: mile after mile of tall concrete towers, about half of them belching gray, brown and yellow smoke. The young man, who had got on at Trenton, was coughing and holding a handkerchief to his face.

"Jesus, it never used to be like this," he said to the fat man beside him.

"Yeah? How long since you been through here?"

"Seventy years."

The fat man, who thought he must have misheard, said, "Wait till we get in the Lincoln Tunnel, you think this is bad."

"What's that?"

"You never heard of the Lincoln Tunnel?"

"No, it must of been after my time. What's so bad about it?"

"It can't handle the pollution. You bring a mask?"

"No."

"Well, here, I got a spare." He rummaged in his briefcase and brought out a white rectangle of padded gauze. "Better put it on now, if it's bothering you already."

The young man looked at the mask as if he had never seen one before. "Is it like this in New York, too?"

"Depends on where. It was bad in the financial district until they roofed it last year. Downtown is bad. The East Side is okay, but watch out for guys in running shoes."

"Their shoes smell bad?"

The fat man laughed. "That's right, their shoes smell bad. That's a good one. Where you from, son?"

"Harrisburg."

"I guess you don't get to town much, huh?"

"Not lately. Is there anything else I should know?"

"Well, always carry at least five hundred bucks in cash. If those muggers grab you and you haven't got any money, it makes them mad and they cut you up."

"They do?"

"Oh, yeah. Read about it all the time."

"The cops don't do anything?"

"Listen, the *cops* travel in armored cars."

CHAPTER 5

The information clerk in the main data room of the New York Public Library looked up from his reader to see a young man in a funny hat standing there. "Yes, sir?"

"Say, can you tell me where to find the phone books?"

"Phone books? For what year?"

The young man looked puzzled. "Well, the current one."

"I don't understand you. The last telephone book published in New York was in nineteen ninety-seven."

"Well, how do you look up a number, then?"

"Use one of the terminals."

The young man looked around at the booths that lined all four walls. "You mean one of those things over there?"

"Yes. Haven't you ever used one before?"

"No."

"Well, it's quite easy. What number did you want to look up?"

"Yallow and Moore. They're architects."

The clerk tapped keys on his console. "The number is 788-8456. Did you want the address?"

"Yeah, please."

"Two oh seven Park Avenue."

The young man took a pad from the desk and wrote it down, but he still looked puzzled. "Listen, if I want to make a phone call do I have to come here?"

"No. Why do you think that?"

"Because I asked in a drugstore in the bus station, and they said try the library."

"Try the library for what?"

"Phone books."

"We don't use phone books anymore."

"So where do you make phone calls?"

"Use any terminal."

The young man looked around again. "Those things over there, right?"

"Right."

"So if I want to make a phone call, I have to come here?"

"Why would you have to come here?"

"To use the terminal."

"These are no different from any other terminals."

"*Forget* it," said the young man. "Judas Priest." He turned and walked out.

Four dudes in plastic Levi's and watch caps, with dirty sneakers on their feets, saw the young man entering the uptown pedestrian stream on Park. He looked like a yoke, wore a mask but it was hanging crooked; he had a funny suit on and a *hat.*

They followed him halfway to the corner, then crowded him into an alcove in front of a boarded-up jewelry store.

The pedestrian stream moved past them. Rong said, "Hey, dads, you got any crappo?" He let the pilgrim see the knife.

"I don't know what you mean." The yoke's eyes looked scared, but not enough.

"I *mean,* do you have any currency, any coin of the realm, any hundred-dollar bills, any five-hundred-dollar bills, do you know what I'm explaining about now? Do you understand my meaning?"

"Oh, money. Yes, I sure do. How much do you want?"

"Well, how much do you *have?* That's the question I'm asking you. Give the leather, and we'll *see* how much we want."

The yoke got his leather out, handed it over. Rong pulled the bills and flipped them. "Well, by sheer amazing coincidence, this is just about what we want right here. Thank you, pilgrim."

"You're welcome." The yoke stuck out his hand. "No hard feelings?"

"No, none on our part whatsoever." Rong pressed the flesh, felt a funny cold sting in his finger. He dropped the leather on the sidewalk and turned away, followed by the other three, but he never took two steps before he begun to feel sort of weird. He swung around. The yoke was just straightening up with the leather in his hand.

"Hey, pilgrim," Rong said, "I don't want to rob you. Was you counting on this crappo for any reason?"

Elvis nudged him in the elbow. "What the matter with you?" Rong shook him off and walked toward the pilgrim. "Do you need some of this crappo? How much do you think you need?"

"Well, I gave you six hundred there, right? Suppose we split it, and then I'll stand you guys a beer or something."

"Sounds all right to *me,*" said Rong. He peeled off half the bills and handed them over. Elvis was poking him again. "You crazy?" he whispered.

"Listen, this man is my friend," said Rong. "Shake hands with my friend." But Elvis backed off, and so did the other two. "Give us our havvies and we'll zoom," Elvis said. "I'm not running with no crazy man."

"Bug your havvies, then. Go zoom, see if I give a puke." He had his knife out again. After a minute Elvis said, "Come on, he's crazy." They high-stepped away with their hands in their pockets.

The pilgrim watched them go. "Listen," he said. "I'm sorry if I got you in trouble with your friends."

"No trouble, man, and no friends neither. What they call you?"

"Ed. Ed Stone."

"I'm Rong. Give me five." The young man reached for his wallet again.

"*No,* man, I mean press the flesh."

"Oh." They shook hands. "How do you spell that, w-r-o-n-g?"

"Wrong!" He laughed. "I spell it with an R, but you're right, I'm Rong. My mama named me Wright, but I knew that was wrong, do you catch my drift?"

"I guess so. Well, how about that beer?"

"I *hear* that suggestion. Will you kindly follow me?"

Rong led him around the corner to Tony's; they went through the airlock into the warm room and pulled their masks down. The holo over the bar was tuned to a sumo wrestling match.

"Hello, Rong," said the bartender. "What'll it be?"

"Shot and a half for me and my friend. Dick, this here is my friend Ed."

"Glad to know you, Dick," said Stone. He reached across the bar and shook hands. The bartender, with a goofy smile, poured two beers and two shots. "Where you from, Ed?"

"Harrisburg, but I've been in a spaceship since nineteen thirty-one."

"Is that right?" A customer at the other end of the bar rapped with his glass, and the bartender reluctantly went away.

"First one with this hand *today,*" said Rong, raising his shot glass. He poured the liquor down, then sipped from the beer.

Stone took a drink of his beer but did not touch the shot glass. "Hey, Rong, can I ask you something?"

"Sure, man."

"Well, is this the only thing you can do to make a living—rob people?"

"What you want me to do, be a college professor?"

"There's no jobs, huh?"

"No jobs, no school that's worth puke, no nothing. You live where I live, you can rob people or you can deal, or sell your pussy. I don't hurt nobody unless they do something stupid, you understand?"

"How long has it been like this?"

"Been this way *forever,* man. You really been in a spaceship, huh?"

"Yeah."

"All right, now I want to tell you something for your own personal good. I don't give a flying puke where you come from, you are *not* suppose to walk around in a outfit like that, you know what I mean? Elvis and them, if they see you one more time they going to cut you, and if *they* don't some other puker *will.* Listen to what I'm telling you."

"I'm listening, but I've got to wear this suit. It's kind of a trademark."

"It is? It is, huh? Well, that's a problem." He drank half his beer and gestured to the bartender with two fingers.

Dick came over and poured another shot for Rong.

Stone put his hand over his untouched glass. "Hey," said Dick, "what was it like in that spaceship?"

"Never mind spaceship," said Rong, "we got some heavy thinking here. Like, how is this man going to walk around in those clothes and not get hisself killed?"

The bartender's brow wrinkled. "Why can't you change your clothes?" he asked Stone.

"I could, but then people might not believe I'm from nineteen thirty-one."

"Oh, I get it. Uh-huh. All right, how's this? Say you walk over to Fourth and buy yourself a raincoat like the winos wear. Nobody mugs a wino, am I right? Lie it down in the street, let a couple cars run over it. The hat you can put in your pocket. Then when you go in an office, you take the raincoat off and put the hat on. What do you think, Rong?"

"Yeah, you got it. I don't know about that haircut, though. Maybe better to keep the hat on. Hey, Ed, you going to drink that shot?"

"No, I have to stay sober for when I talk to the architects."

"Well, no use letting it go to waste."

CHAPTER 6

The holo in the glass case in the lobby of the Mitsubishi Building was a sturdy Sikh with a white turban and black beard. It said, "What office are you visiting, sir?"

"Yallow and Moore. The architects."

"Are they expecting you?"

"No."

"Tell me your name, please, and the purpose of your visit."

"Ed Stone. I want them to build something for me."

The guard fell silent. "They say they don't know you, sir, and they are not accepting any new clients."

"Well, could I just go up and talk to them?"

"No, sir. Step to one side, please."

The young man moved, and watched in bewilderment as two other people walked up, spoke to the guard, and were admitted.

The third was a young black man in a Greek fisherman's cap, who showed the guard a clipboard and a parcel. The guard let him in. Then there was a lull. The guard rotated to face the young man and said, "Sir, may I speak to you, please?" The young man came forward eagerly.

"You cannot remain here, sir," the guard said. "Go away now, or I will have to call for assistance."

The young man said, "Okay, but can I ask you a question?"

"Certainly, sir."

"That last guy, the one in the cap? How come you let him in without even phoning?"

"He is a messenger," the guard said.

"He is, huh? Listen, did you know I'm a messenger too?"

"May I see your ID, please?"

"I must of forgot it. I'll be back."

"Thank you, sir."

Rong saw the pilgrim coming out of the building, and fell in beside him. "Hey, my man," he said. "You talk to them architects?"

"No, I couldn't even get past the guard. Hi, Rong. Listen, uh, how do you get a job as a messenger?"

"They take anybody, because it don't pay puke, but they check your record first."

"Oh. How long does that take?"

"I don't know, man, a couple weeks?"

They stopped at the corner and turned their backs to the gritty wind that was blowing down 44th Street under the bottom of the dome. "You need to get in sooner than that, huh?" said Rong.

"Yeah."

"Well, this'll take some thought. That three hundred is all the crappo you got, right?"

"Right."

"Well, the way I'm thinking, we need more than that. If I lend you the other three hundred that you give me, can you pay me back sometime real soon?"

"Yeah, I guess so. Sure."

"All right, come on."

They walked back to the building entrance, and Rong

leaned against the wall beside it. "Do like I do," he said, putting a toothpick between his teeth.

"What are we waiting for?"

"A messenger. Might take a while."

"And then what?"

"Depends what kind of messenger. Some you got to talk to one way, some another way, you know what I mean?"

Stone said, "You got another toothpick?"

"Sure, man." He handed it over; Stone put it in his mouth and leaned against the wall beside him.

"Here come one," Rong muttered after twenty minutes had passed. "Don't look, fool. Hang loose, be *casual.*"

The messenger was a young white man in a checkered shirt. His face was carmine, and so was the bare hand that held the envelope and clipboard. As he started to enter, Rong stepped in front of him, turned him, and pushed him against the building.

"Hey, what's this?" The messenger looked left and right.

"No problem, we just want you to do us a favor, okay?"

"Yeah, what favor?" said the messenger. He looked at Stone, then away.

"We want to borrow your puke for half an hour, you know what I mean? The ID, the clipboard, the envelope."

"No way," said the messenger, holding the clipboard to his chest.

"Three hundred bucks, half an hour," said Rong. He took out the bills and fanned them where the messenger could see.

The messenger shifted his weight a little. "Nah, I couldn't do it for that."

"How much could you do it for?"

"I might consider, say, a thousand."

"No way, ofay. Five hundred."

"Eight."

"Six," said Rong, holding out his hand sideways. Stone got out his wallet and gave him the money.

"Seven," said the messenger.

"Six is all we got," said Rong, "and either you take it *or,* me and my friend are going to be real disappointed with you. You hear what I'm saying?" He slapped the money into the messenger's palm.

"Okay." The messenger handed over the clipboard and envelope. He took a plastic card out of his shirt pocket and gave it to Rong, who passed everything over to Stone. "Where do I get it back?" the messenger asked.

"Tony's, around the corner," Rong said. "Hey, I'll even wait there with you, my man, and *you* can buy the drinks."

"What office are you visiting, sir?" asked the Sikh in the cage.

"Bernice Fashions." The young man held up his parcel and ID.

The Sikh flickered. "Sir, the photograph in your ID does not appear to match your face."

"What do you mean, it doesn't match? Sure it matches."

"Sir, the photograph has dark hair and your hair is light."

"So I had it dyed."

The Sikh flickered again. "Your eye color is also different."

"Uh, I had an operation?"

The Sikh flickered and said, "I am calling for assistance."

"Ah, hell. That's all you guys know. Forget it, I'm leaving."

CHAPTER 7

The messenger, Sherman Cohen, was sitting with Rong at a table near the bar; Cohen was finishing a corned beef sandwich and Rong had just swallowed the last of his beer when Stone walked in, looking glum.

"No good, huh?" said Rong.

Stone sat down and put the clipboard on the table. "No, the ID didn't match. The guard noticed that he has dark hair and I don't. And the eye color is different, too." He looked at Cohen and put out his hand. "Hey, thanks anyway."

Cohen shook hands and pulled the clipboard closer. "Well, sorry it didn't work out."

Stone said, "I was figuring once I was in, you know, I could borrow some money to pay you back, but I couldn't get in the door."

"Don't worry about it, man. Hey, this guard, was he a real person or a holo?"

"A holo, I guess. One of those things in glass cages?"

Rong reached over and took the ID card from the clipboard. He looked at the picture, then at Stone. "Looks the same to *me,*" he said.

The bartender was hurrying over. "Hey, Ed, good to see you. What'll it be?"

"I don't want anything right now."

"Yeah, he does. Bring him a shot and a half, Dick, and two more for me and him, and it's on my friend here." Sherman smiled and waved.

"Right back." The bartender brought the drinks, then pulled up a chair and listened. He said to Stone, "Suppose your hair was the same color as him, would that do it?"

"I don't know. There's the eyes, too."

"Well, what if we take a picture of you and paste it on this guy's ID?"

"Hey," said Cohen. "I don't think that would work. Those holopix on the ID cards, they're supposed to be made of signature plastic. You put another photo on there, the signatures don't match."

"Well, it's worth a try. Hey, Mary." He beckoned to a youngish woman at the bar.

"Me?" She picked up her drink and came over to the table.

"Mary, you got any hair dye in your purse?"

"No, I don't use it no more. This is a wig."

"It is? Let's have a look."

Mary took off the wig, revealing a head covered with mousy hair, unevenly cut and standing out in tufts. "Jesus," said Dick, "give her a hat, somebody."

Cohen passed over his Greek fisherman's cap and Mary put it on. "Hey, I ain't *that* bad," she said.

Dick set the wig on Stone's head and they all looked at it critically. Dick tugged it forward a little, then back. "What do you think?"

"Pass the cap back," Rong said.

"You got a cap yourself. I'm suppose to keep this on."

"Okay, I'll trade you." They exchanged caps, and Rong put the messenger's cap on Stone. "Who got a pair of smokes?" he asked.

"I do, behind the bar." Dick got up and came back in a

moment with a pair of dark glasses. Rong slipped the ear-pieces over Stone's ears and sat back to study the effect.

"I don't know, I seen better faces on dead guys," said Dick.

"Let's look at the problem," said Rong. "One way it's bad that this guard is a holo, see, because if he was a guy you could pay him something, maybe, or you could just wait till he goes to lunch, and then you're talking to somebody else, but with a holo, they don't never go to lunch."

They thought about this. "That's sad," said Cohen.

"*But,* the other way it's good that he's a holo, see, because a holo is not as smart as a real person. Now a real person would *never* go for that wig, am I right? But a holo maybe would, and especially if you confuse it."

"Confuse it how?" Stone asked.

"Man, how do I know? Do something crazy. What have you got to lose?"

CHAPTER 8

The young man walked into the lobby of the Mitsubishi Building and held up his clipboard and ID.

"Sir, were you here earlier?" asked the Sikh in the cage.

"Who, me? No."

"Is your name Sherman B. Cohen?"

"That's right."

"A person named Sherman B. Cohen was here earlier today. His hair was light, and yours is dark."

"Oh, that's my brother Sherman. He has different color hair."

"Sherman B. Cohen is your brother?"

"Right."

"And your name is also Sherman B. Cohen?"

"Yeah, that's right. See, his middle name is Bill and mine is Bob. That's how they tell us apart." The young man reached up and lifted his cap, snatched the wig off and replaced the cap.

The Sikh flickered. "Sir, were you here earlier today?"

"I just told you, that was my brother Bob."

"Your brother is named Bob?"

"Right, and I'm Bill."

The Sikh flickered again. "Sir, was your brother here earlier today?"

"That's right." The young man lifted his cap, replaced the wig, put the cap on again. "Listen," he said, "I think there's something wrong with you. Are you supposed to keep flickering like that?"

The Sikh flickered violently. "One moment. Diagnostic complete. Reset. What office are you visiting, sir?"

Stone held up the clipboard. "Thank you, sir," said the Sikh. The door clicked open. Beyond it was the row of elevators.

Carrying the parcel, the clipboard, and his shabby raincoat, the young man entered the reception area of Yallow and Moore.

"Yes, is that for us?" said the receptionist, and held out her hand for the parcel.

"It is, yeah, but I have to give it to Mr. Yallow or Mr. Moore."

"Mr. Yallow passed over several years ago. Give me the package and I'll see that Mr. Moore gets it."

"Uh, that's nice of you, but I have to talk to him about a project."

"What project would that be?"

"I want to build a box big enough to put the whole human race in."

"I see." The receptionist reached under the desk and buzzed for assistance. "I'm afraid Mr. Moore is much too busy to see anyone today. If you'll leave your name and number—"

"Ed Stone. I haven't got a telephone, I just got here."

"Well, the best thing would be, call later in the week, or better yet, make it next month."

"Okay, thanks." Stone put out his hand. "Nice to meet you, Miss—"

She took the hand and felt a curious cold shock. "Kathy McCarthy," she said without intending to. She felt a little dizzy. "Wait a minute, let me— I can at least let you talk to Mr. Moore's secretary."

"Could you? That would be swell."

A uniformed guard came in and approached the desk. "That's all right, Ken," said McCarthy. "It was a mistake."

"Yes?" The guard looked at Stone. "What's your business here?"

"I'm waiting to see Mr. Moore. My name is Ed Stone." He put out his hand.

"It really is all right, Ken," said McCarthy. "I hit the button with my knee."

"Okay." The guard shook Stone's hand. "Sorry about that, but we can't be too careful." He grinned. "There's so many almondcakes around—you understand."

"Sure. Well, nice meeting you."

"Same here." They smiled at each other; the guard left with visible reluctance.

"He *liked* you," said McCarthy.

"Yeah, I guess he did."

"Well, I'm going to take a chance and buzz you in to see Mrs. Rooney, Mr. Moore's secretary. Through there, turn right, and it's the last door on the left."

"Say, thanks a lot."

"Good luck."

Florence Rooney looked up as the young man entered her office. "Yes?"

"Miss McCarthy sent me in. My name is Ed Stone." They shook hands; he sat down in her visitor's chair and put his funny hat on his knee. "Mrs. Rooney, I need to see Mr. Moore about a big project."

"Well, perhaps I could squeeze you in— What sort of project is it?"

"I want to build a box and put the whole human race in it."

"You do? That will be quite a costly project."

"I know."

"Well, let me see." She pressed a button. "Mr. Moore, a young man named Ed Stone is here to see you. Can you give him ten minutes?"

"What's it about?"

"A very unusual project. He can explain it better himself."

"Okay."

CHAPTER 9

Sit down, Mr. Stone," Thomas Moore said. The two men shook hands and seated themselves. "My secretary told me I ought to see you, but I'm not sure why. I understand you have some kind of unusual project."

"That's right, I want to find somebody to build a cube big enough to pack the whole human race into it."

"You do?"

"Uh-huh, and I guess the first thing is, how big would it have to be?"

The architect scratched his nose. "Well, the world population is around six billion now. Can I assume—"

"Wait a minute. *Six* billion? Back in the thirties, it was about *two.* How could that happen?"

"Natural increase, I suppose. Anyway, am I right that you want to pack them in there dead? They don't have to have room to move around?"

"Not dead exactly, but yeah, just pack them in."

"Okay, fine. Well, suppose we figure about twenty-five cubic feet per person. That's high, because some of them will be children, but if you want to standardize it—You're going to put each body in a casket, and then just stack them on some sort of structural grid?"

"Right."

"Okay, let's go with twenty-five, then, and let's take a wild guess that you'd need another thirteen cubic feet apiece for structural members." He tapped keys on his desktop. "That would give you a cube just over sixty-one hundred feet on a side—about one and two-tenths miles."

"Okay."

"But now you want the whole population, is that right? Every man, woman and child?"

"Uh-huh."

"All right, you've got to figure that you're dealing with an exploding population. How big is it going to be when you get this thing built? Suppose it takes twenty years. By that time you'd have a world population of maybe six and a quarter billion, unless we get another wave of famines. Okay, but now you've got the thing built and you're packing them in. How long will that take? Let's say you can load a million a day." He tapped keys again.

"That's going to take you about sixteen and a half years," he said, "but the more you load in, the less there are outside to propagate, so you're budgeting more space than you need. You really want a computer program for this, and it's sensitive to all kinds of factors."

"Where could I get a program like that?"

"That's easy, you could use a standard population generator or even a spreadsheet, but you don't know yet what numbers to put into it. You have to make some assumptions about population growth. You need to know how long construction will take. Can you load them in while construction is going on? That might be the easiest way, in fact. How do you organize transportation, and so on? I assume you realize that this is a bizarre idea."

"Yes, I do. Well, one more thing I wanted to ask you, is it a practical proposition, just to build something that big?"

"Depends on what you mean by practical. Frank Lloyd Wright drew plans for a mile-high tower in the thirties, and Paolo Soleri had some plans for even bigger structures, but they never came to anything."

"Why not?"

"Well, anything that tall would be a hazard to planes, especially if it was near a major airport. And there just never seemed to be any good reason to do it. It doesn't make economic sense to build high except in the core areas of big cities, where the land costs so much that you can't afford to build low. Even there, when you get above about a thousand feet, the wind load problems multiply, the damn thing sways like a flagpole, and you get more headaches than you're paying for."

"So, anyway, if there was a real good reason, you could do it?"

"It could be done, sure."

"Could your outfit take it on?"

"No, we don't do anything on that scale. You want somebody like Norman Chang, or Richter Associates in Chicago."

"How much would it cost, do you think?"

"Just for the design? I'd say about ten million."

"Thanks a lot," said Stone. "Say, I hate to bring this up, but I wonder if you could lend me three thousand dollars."

"Three thousand? Well, it's unusual—"

"I'll pay you back as soon as I get on my feet."

"All right. I'm feeling a little bizarre myself." The architect took some bills out of his wallet.

"Thanks a lot, Mr. Moore."

"Happy to be of help. Keep in touch, will you?"

Mrs. Rooney smiled as the young man came out of the inner office. "How did it go?" she asked.

"Swell. Say, have you got a business card I could take, and have you got an envelope and a stamp?"

"A stamp?"

"You know, a postage stamp?"

She shook her head. "Don't you remember, the post office went out of business? Do you want to send a fax?"

"No, some money. You mean to say I can't mail a letter anymore?"

"Afraid not. We use fax and electronic transfer now. Give me the money and I'll take care of it."

"Would you? That's swell." He handed her a bill and wrote on her desk pad: *Dr. Wellafield, State Mental Health Care Facility, Trenton, New Jersey.*

"There's my man," said Rong when Stone walked in. They were at a different table, and there were more of them now, two women besides Mary, and two men. Dick was there too; Paul was behind the bar. They all crowded aside to make room for Stone. "You made it, huh?"

"Yeah." Stone took the wig out of his pocket and handed it to Mary. "Hey, thanks a lot." He took some bills out of his pocket. "Here's three hundred for your trouble, and here's the three hundred I owe you, Rong, and here's another three hundred for you, Sherman. You been buying all the drinks?"

Cohen waved his hands. " 'S all right," he said. "Good folks."

Rong said, "Okay, this is Cindy and this is Loella"—two young black women, one fat and one slim—"this is Shirley"—a large white male—"and this here is Julio"—a gray-haired Hispanic. Stone shook hands with all of them.

"Listen," he said to Cohen, "I stopped off at Bernice Fashions on the way out and left your package, okay? Here's the receipt."

"Won-der-ful," said Cohen. "That was won-der-ful."

"You think we ought to get him home?" Shirley asked. "Where at do you live, Sherm?"

"Ho-bo-ken."

"Me and Julio will take him over. "What's the address, Sherm? Where's it at?"

"Hunnerd fifty-two."

"Hundred fifty-two what?"

"Look on his ID, on the clipboard," said Stone.

"Okay, we got it. Come on, Sherm." They hoisted Cohen to his feet and took him away smiling and waving. The others spread out around the table with expressions of relief.

"Listen, can we get something to eat here?" Stone asked.

"Sure you can," said Dick. "Corned beef sandwich, roast beef sandwich, or pizza from next door."

"Okay, I want the corned beef, and then I got to find a place to stay tonight."

"How much money you got left, Ed?"

He looked in his wallet. "Eleven hundred."

"Well, that ain't going to go very far. You got to pay for your sandwich, and then there's breakfast tomorrow." Dick stood up and went to the terminal booth in the corner. He tapped keys, leaving the door open, and called back, "Here's the Marlin Hotel, six-fifty a night, but that's in Brooklyn. You want Manhattan?"

"Yeah, I'd better."

Dick peered at the screen again. "The Netherland, seven hundred a night? It's on Canal Street."

"Seven *hundred?* Is that the cheapest?"

"Unless you want a shelter. I wouldn't send my brother-in-law to one of them places, and besides, have you got a blue card?"

"I don't think so."

Loella said, "Listen, you can come home with I and Cindy."

"Hey, thanks, but I think I better get a hotel and get up early—I got a bunch more calls to make."

"Yeah? What's next, Ed?"

"Well, I got to talk to some banks about a loan."

"For money to live on, huh? That's smart."

"No, for money to build the big box."

CHAPTER 10

Douglas R. Pearson III had an edge office on the seventy-ninth floor of the Seemans Building; it wasn't a *corner* office, of course, but it *had* a corner because it was part of the structure that protruded from the tower and cast a shadow on the other parts. Which really was the whole point. From his desk he could look out over the East River in one direction and the gold-topped towers of lower Manhattan in the other. On some days he simply sat and watched the helicopters buzzing around the rooftop pads to the east; on other days, when the smog was too thick, he watched the smog.

"Mr. Stone is here," said the computer on his desk. Pearson dropped a half-eaten candy bar in a drawer, closed the drawer, and said, "Send him in."

The young man entered, advanced with his hand out.

His grip was firm, but Pearson felt a curious cold sensation.

"Sit down, Mr. Stone, and tell me how First Boston can help you."

Stone sat in the visitor's chair and put his curious hat on his knee. "Mr. Pearson, thank you for seeing me. Did Mr. Schoenstein tell you anything about my problem?"

"Yes, as a matter of fact, he said you want to organize a project to put the whole human race in a box."

"That's right, and I talked to some architects, they say they can design it, but before I can go any farther I have to get funding. Mr. Schoenstein says his bank isn't big enough, so that's why I came to you."

"I understand. What do you estimate the cost of this project might be?"

"Well, Mr. Chang said he thought about two trillion dollars."

"Um-hm. Now, Mr. Stone, you realize we are an investment bank. Ordinarily, when we lend money, we want to know what the return is going to be."

"Yes, I know that. I've tried to figure out how you could make money out of this, but the only thing I can think of is to charge admission."

"To visit the project, do you mean?"

"Well, that too, probably, but I was thinking, if everybody who got in the box had to pay something? I mean, if it costs two trillion dollars and there are six billion people, that's only about three hundred bucks apiece."

Pearson picked up a scriber and twirled it between his fingers. "I see one difficulty with this. If that idea works out, and I don't see why it shouldn't, the bank will have its money back, but there won't be anybody left to operate the bank, or anything to invest the money in."

"Well, that's true."

"I mean, everybody is going to be in the box. By the way, how will they breathe in there?"

"They're going to be in suspended animation."

"Oh, I see. Like the Egyptians?"

"I guess."

"Well, fine. Now, from what you tell me, I think this proposal should go to the International Development Association. McNevin Fairbairn is the man to see, and he's in town now. I'll give him a call if you like and set up an appointment."

"That would be swell. Mr. Pearson, one other problem I have is money. For myself, I mean. I've been borrowing from people, but then I have to borrow more to pay them back, and Mr. Schoenstein said what I ought to do is ask you for a line of credit."

"Well, that could be arranged, certainly. How much do you think you'd need?"

"I'd like to have enough so I could travel, and stay in hotels and so forth, until this project gets started, but I don't know how much to ask for."

"Well. When the project is funded, I imagine you'll have an official position and a salary. But I see the difficulty until then. Suppose we set you up for two years to start with, say a million four? Does that sound all right?"

Stone swallowed. "Yes, sir. I can't get used to these numbers."

"Well, you'll find it gets easier as you go along."

CHAPTER 11

From his high-rise office overlooking UN Plaza, McNevin Fairbairn could observe humanity at a convenient distance; the swarm in the plaza at certain hours was rather like an ant farm. The holomaps on the walls gave him an even more Olympian view: here was South America, a patchwork of blue, green, yellow, and brown, and here was Africa in the same colors, with flags for national capitals, per capita income, infant mortality, rollover on delinquent debt, and so on.

Fairbairn, a man in his late forties, had got where he was by hard work, application, diligence, and the wise counsel of two uncles high in the federal government. His department was running smoothly, and his workload was really not onerous, but he remained in his office for seven hours every weekday, because on the whole this was where he was happiest.

"Mr. Stone," he said to his oddly dressed visitor, "you may not realize that the IDA does not initiate projects. We merely arrange for loans from our member banks to foreign governments for projects we deem in the global interest. Now, unofficially, we might suggest this or that, but the formal proposals must come from governments. Now *I* think the best thing to do would be to go to Washington, drum up some support there and get whatever U.S. funding you can. Once you have that, you see, it will be much easier to go to other governments, get them interested, and at *that* point the IDA could become involved."

"Yes, sir, I see now. This thing is a lot more complicated than I realized."

"Well, you'll soon catch on. Let me just see if I can get you appointments with one or two people in the legislature." He addressed the computer. "Flossie, will you call Senator Givens's office and see if you can set up an appointment tomorrow for a protégé of mine, Mr. Ed Stone? And then try the Speaker, and, let's see, Senator Whelk and Congressperson Yamada?"

"Yes, sir."

"Givens is one of the most influential men on the Hill," Fairbairn explained. "He has the ear of the President, and if he likes you, he can do you a lot of good in the Senate. Now in the House—"

"Ten o'clock tomorrow for Senator Givens," said the computer. *"The Speaker is out of town, but he can see Mr. Stone Monday at three. I'm still trying the other two."*

"Thank you, Flossie."

"Does that thing work all by itself?" Stone asked.

"I don't know what you mean."

"I mean, is it a kind of robot?"

"Yes, I suppose so. A robot. I hadn't thought of that."

The door opened; a young woman walked into the office, smiled at Stone, and laid a folder on Fairbairn's desk. "The Nicaragua summary," she said.

"That's splendid, Linda. Oh, I want you to meet Ed Stone. Linda Lavalle, our assistant project review manager for South America." Stone, who had risen, shook her hand. "Ed has an international project that he's trying to get funding for. He wants to build a big box and put the whole human race in it."

"That sounds—interesting. Well, good-bye, Mr. Stone. Lots of luck with your project." She turned to go.

"Listen, if you'd like to know more about it, maybe we could have lunch?"

Ms. Lavalle looked bewildered. "Well, I've got a lot to do this afternoon. I was going to eat at my desk. Maybe tomorrow?"

"I'm sorry, I have to be in Washington tomorrow. It's my birthday, too, but this is more important. What about dinner Saturday?"

"I have a— No, never mind. Dinner would be fine. Where are you going to be staying?"

"The Netherland, but I could pick you up wherever you say."

"No, your hotel is all right. About seven-thirty?"

"Sure. Listen, I don't know the restaurants here. Could you pick one out?"

"I suppose so. All right, seven-thirty Saturday, then."

When she was gone, Fairbairn said with a smile, "You work fast, Mr. Stone."

"I have to. Thanks for everything."

"A pleasure. I mean that sincerely."

Linda Lavalle told her roommate, "I met this guy in the office today. His name is Ed Stone. He asked me out Saturday night, and I said yes."

"You did? What's Julian going to say?"

"I don't know. I don't know what I want him to say."

Sylvia poured the cocktails. "This must be some extra kind of a guy, right?"

"Yes. He's not like anybody else. For one thing, he's crazy."

"And you like that?"

"I guess so. I must be crazy too."

"Well, at least it's a change from Julian."

CHAPTER 12

"Young man," said Senator Givens of Oklahoma, leaning back in his tailored chair, "I like your style, and this is certainly an exciting concept. If we can bring this off, why, it will be one for the history books. Except, I sort of wonder if there will *be* any history books."

"I don't know about that, Senator, but anyhow, you'll have the satisfaction of doing something really swell. And besides, you and your loved ones will get off the Earth before it explodes."

"Yes, there is that, although of course I would never do anything for personal reasons, because I am first, last and foremost a servant of the people. And I know my distinguished colleagues in both Houses will see it in that light, regardless of affiliation. This has to be a bipartisan effort, in fact a multiglobal effort. Have you talked to the Speaker?"

"I'm supposed to see him Monday morning, and some other congressmen."

"Good, good. Now I want you to meet three or four other people in the Senate this afternoon, and then maybe next week sometime we could have an informal joint meeting. It's important to get these things lined up well in advance. Tell me, in your opinion, what sort of a political organization are we going to be able to put together on this new planet?"

"I don't know anything about that, Senator. I guess it could be pretty much whatever you want."

"Good, good. That's just what I was thinking."

Linda Lavalle, dressed to the nines, entered the Netherland Hotel lobby, which was about the size of a freight elevator. It didn't even have a real airlock, just a weather door. She advanced to the desk. "Mr. Stone, please. Tell him Ms. Lavalle is here."

The deskperson, a human being, spoke into his/her microphone, listened. "He'll be right down, Ms. Lavalle."

"Thank you."

"He is a *wonderful* person, isn't he?"

Lavalle raised her eyebrows. "Yes, I guess so." She turned and looked at the lobby: one polyethylene plant, a sofa, two armchairs. She crossed to one of the chairs, took a closer look at the variegated blotches on the upholstery, and decided to stand.

After a moment the elevator door opened and Stone came out, wearing the same suit. "Hi there," she said.

"Hello. Glad you could come. Listen, do you want to have a drink in the bar next door?"

"No, let's go. I've got a taxi waiting."

As the armored cab pulled out into traffic, she turned to Stone and crossed her arms. "Why are you staying in that trash can?" she asked. "The cabbie couldn't even find it, that's why I'm late."

"It's cheap," he said.

"Well, it *must* be, but if you're masterminding an international project—"

"Yeah, but I haven't got any money, until my line of credit comes through. Are you mad?"

"No, I'm not, but I'm confused. Do you like Greek food?"

"I never had any."

"Great."

There was a jam at Watts and Sixth; up ahead they could see dark figures silhouetted against a tower of flame. "What's the matter now?" Lavalle asked.

"Looks like they torch another sweeper," said the cabbie's voice.

"Can you get around by Hudson? We're in a hurry."

"Ma'am, this cab don't fly."

"What's a sweeper?" Stone asked.

"It scoops up the druggies that pass out in the middle of the street. Sometimes people throw a bottle of Flame-O at them."

"What for?"

"To tie up traffic, I suppose."

The cab inched into the far lane, and in a few minutes they were out of the compression. They rode in silence through the flaring streets until the cab pulled up at the restaurant. Stone reached for his wallet, but she said, "No, that's all right," and put her card through the slot.

"Listen, I can pay for a cab," Stone said as they crossed the littered sidewalk.

"You can pay for the next one. Let go of my arm."

"You *are* mad at me," he said.

"No, I'm not, but I can get through a door without help. Hello, Spyros."

The maître d' bowed and smiled. "Always a pleasure, Ms. Lavalle. Will you come this way?"

He led them to a table covered with a snowy white cloth, plates, silverware, flowers, and candles. "Now I think I *will* have that drink," she said. A smiling waiter appeared. "Gibson for me, Jimmy."

"And you, sir?"

"I'll have a rye highball."

"Yes, sir." The waiter did not quite make a face. He went away.

Lavalle took a pack of cigarettes out of her purse. When she put one in her lips, Stone was leaning across with a lighter. She stared at him, but allowed him to light the cigarette. "Thanks."

"Don't mention it. Say, how come all the cigarette packs have a skull and crossbones on them?"

"They're bad for you. Give you lung cancer and emphysema."

"I wish you hadn't of told me that." Stone had a pack of Camels Heavies half out of his pocket; he looked at it and put it back. "Now I've got to quit," he said mournfully.

"Why right now?"

"Because if I died before the project gets finished, I'd be letting the aliens down." He opened the menu and looked at it. "What is all this stuff?"

"It's all good, but I recommend the moussaka."

"What's moussaka?"

"Eggplant, cultured lamb, and cheese."

"You're kidding. I'll have a steak."

The waiter brought the drinks and took their orders. "I want some kampa with the moussaka, Jimmy. What about you, Ed?"

"What's kampa?"

"It's a Greek wine."

"Oh. I guess I'll have a glass of beer." The waiter went away again.

"Okay," Lavalle said, "what is this famous project anyway, and who are the aliens?"

"The aliens are the ones that kidnapped me and brought me here from nineteen thirty-one. They want me to build a box big enough to put the whole human race in it."

"What for?"

"I'm not sure."

"You're crazy."

"I know."

Lavalle stubbed her cigarette out nervously and took another one out of the pack. "Don't *do* that," she said when he offered his lighter. She lit the cigarette herself, took one puff and put it in the ashtray. "Listen, what I want to know is, why do I feel this way about you?"

He looked unhappy. "Because I touched you with my ring when we shook hands."

"What's the ring got to do with it?"

"The aliens put something in it that makes people like me and believe in me."

"They did, huh? Let me see this ring."

He held out his hand and she took it. The ring seemed to be made of some dull metal that was not silver or platinum; there was a place for a gemstone in the middle, but it was empty.

"I think they copied it out of an ad in a magazine," he said. "They didn't get it quite right. I mean, they're aliens. Listen, I think it'll wear off eventually."

"It will?"

"Yeah, and then if you still like me, it'll be because, you know, you like me."

"Well, that's a relief."

The food came. The waiter poured the wine and beer.

"Listen," Stone said, "I'm sorry about this, but I had to talk to somebody. I can't believe some of the things I've found out since I came back. All these swell inventions, but you've got poison gas in the air, these African countries are bombing each other, and you're having another depression—"

"Growth adjustment."

"Is that what they call it now?"

"Uh-huh. Before that it was 'recession,' and before that 'depression,' and before *that* it was 'panic.' Whenever we don't like something, we change the name so we can like it better."

"Well, it's still the same thing, right? And millions of people are starving— This isn't how I thought it would be."

"We don't say 'starving,' we say 'nutritionally challenged.' How did you think it would be?"

"I don't know, I thought science would solve everything."

"So did a lot of people. How's your steak?"

"Okay."

"Try a bite of this."

He accepted it, chewed. "Say! You said it was good, but I didn't believe you."

"Trust me."

"Okay, I will." He smiled, and she saw the sudden glint of a gold tooth. "Listen, I said I was sorry, but that wasn't true. If I hadn't touched you with the ring, would you of gone out with me?"

She looked at him for a moment before replying. "Probably not."

"Well, I'm glad you did."

"So am I, but let's not get squishy about it."

"Okay. So. What do you do, at the IDA?"

"I review project analyses and make recommendations."

"I don't know what that means. What does the IDA do?"

"It loans money to Third World nations and gets them deeper in debt."

"What's the Third World? I thought we only had one."

"Pre-developed countries, mostly in Africa and South and Central America."

"Is that like poor?"

She smiled. "Yes."

"Okay. So you loan them money and get them in debt. Is that a bad thing?"

"Usually."

"So why do you do it?"

"It's a job. It pays well, and once in a while I get a chance to approve something that might do some good. The world is such a mess that nothing really works."

"Well, what's the problem, if there's all this money to throw around? Do you know what they're giving me? A million four. That's the way he said it. I just walked in off the street."

"You don't think that's fair?"

"No."

"Going to give the money back?"

"No."

"Okay, then don't complain. What was it like, in the thirties?"

He chewed and swallowed. "Hard times. Lots of people out of work, factories closing down. Breadlines, soup kitchens. But listen, I think it's *worse* now. I saw people sleeping in cardboard boxes last night. I mean, not just regular cardboard boxes, but ones that said 'PortaHouse' on them. A guy who asked me for a handout, he had burns all over his face."

He looked at his beer and put it down. "Something I never could figure out, you've got all these factories, if you opened them up people could have jobs and buy the stuff the factories make. It just goes around and around. It's like, 'If we had some ham we could make ham and eggs, if we had some eggs.' "

She laughed. "I like that."

"You do, huh? Your name, Lavalle, is that French?"

"It is, but I'm not. I was married before."

"It didn't work out?"

"No."

"Got a sweetheart?"

"It's none of your business, but yes."

He looked at her. "Do you step out with other guys anyway?"

"Not usually." She put down her fork. "Listen, I'm having a good time, and I like you, but you scare me. Do you really believe all this stuff about aliens, and putting people in a box?"

"Sure."

"And you're going to do it?"

"Oh, yeah. There's no way to stop me."

"I think that's frightening."

"Well, it's like being on a roller coaster. Once you start down, you have to go all the way."

"You sound so calm about it. How can you be so calm?"

"I haven't got any choice. You know how it is when you love somebody so much, or maybe your family, or your country, you'd do anything for them? I mean, you want them to be happy and you want them to win, so you do whatever you can, right, and as long as you're doing that, you can be calm. Well, that's how I am about the aliens. I love them, and they trust me, and I know I won't let them down, so I'm calm."

"Do you think maybe they *made* you feel that way?"

"Oh, I know they did. The first time I saw them, I wanted to run. I think they put something in my brain. I can feel it in there."

"In your brain. Well, doesn't that make a difference?"

"No. Didn't you ever love somebody, and you knew you probably shouldn't, but you just couldn't help it?"

"Yes."

"Well, it's the same thing. I have to do whatever they want me to, and besides, maybe it's all true about the Earth being destroyed."

"You don't think it is?"

"I'm a little worried about it, but there isn't much I can do about that."

After a moment she asked, "What do they look like?"

"They're about the size of a rat. They sit in a hollow space in the head of a robot, and the robot carries them around. They look—I don't know. Like a yellow octopus, except they have joints in their arms. Or legs, it's hard to tell. They have suckers on their hands and feet. Their faces are all spiny, except for the forehead. That's what they talk with. They make these symbols on their foreheads, kind of like Chinese."

She shuddered. "And you *love* them?"

"Well, probably we look awful to them too."

She said, "You're crazy."

"I know I am. Don't you think I know that? Either I made the whole thing up in my head, or else they drove me crazy, so I'm crazy either way."

The waiter reappeared. "All through?" he said.

"Yes. We'll have baklava for dessert, Jimmy, and Greek coffee."

"What's baklava?" Stone asked.

"Trust me."

He ate the baklava with an expression of delight and disbelief. "Were you married before?" she asked.

"Yeah, but after I lost my job she took the kids and went back to her mother's in Teaneck."

"How many kids?"

"Two. Boy and a girl."

"Do you ever wonder what happened to them?"

"They're dead now, I guess, or they're old people. I thought about that. What could I say to them, 'Hello, I'm your father'? They wouldn't believe me, and if they did, so what?"

After a moment she asked, "Did you love your wife?"

"I guess so, at first. What about you?"

"It seemed like a good idea at the time, but he was a sleaze."

"You kept his name, though."

"Well, it was better than Izquierdos." She looked around, and the waiter appeared. "We'd like the check, Jimmy."

Stone said, "You don't have to go right away, do you?"

"Afraid so."

"I thought you might like to take in a show or something."

"Some other time."

The waiter deposited the check on a tray. Stone looked at it and his eyes bulged.

"We'll split this, of course," Lavalle said. "Give it to me, I'll use my card and you can give me your half."

"Don't you think that's a little steep?"

"Dinner for two, with drinks and wine, seven hundred fifty? No. You want real food, you have to pay for it."

"I can't get used to that. Where I come from, nobody ever said 'real food.' That was all we had. And there was enough of it to go around, except they poured kerosene on it to keep the price up." He counted out the bills glumly. "Listen, I don't suppose you could lend me cab fare? I'll pay you back next week."

"Never mind, I'll drop you on the way home."

"Where's home? You live by yourself?"

"Never mind, and no."

They watched the street scene on the way across town: people standing around fires in trash cans, food vendors with carts, lonely guitar-players. Confetti came drifting out of the sky, turning black as it fluttered. The cab drew up in front of the hotel.

"I had a swell time," he said.

"I did too."

"I suppose you've got to go home tonight?"

"Yes."

"Can I call you when I get back in town?"

"I don't know if that's such a good idea."

"I'll call you, anyway."

"Yes, I guess you will."

CHAPTER 13

Son," said the President of the United States, "Dan Givens told me I had to see you, and that's good enough for me. But I'm not sure I understand what you're asking me for. You want to build a big box and put everbody in it, is that right?"

"Yes, sir." The visitor crossed his legs and put his funny hat on his knee.

The President leaned toward him and lowered his voice. "You really think you can get the whole human race in a box? *Everbody?* How you gone talk them into it?"

"They'll want to do it. And besides, consider the alternative."

"The world is really gone be busted up?"

"That's what the aliens told me. They didn't say by what."

"How long have we got?"

"They showed me the Earth going around the sun, and then waved their arms and legs twice. They've got six of them, so I think they meant twelve years."

"Six legs, huh? That isn't much time."

"I know it. Maybe I didn't understand, or maybe they were lying about that. Maybe we've got thirty years, but I wouldn't take any bets over five bucks. That's why I came to you, Mr. President."

"Well, you done right, you done right. Now, I understand Senator Givens and Congressperson Yamada are gone to introduce a bill to establish a international corporation, is that right?"

"Yes, sir, and the Senator tells me we'll have the votes."

"All right. Now, I'll want to sleep on this, and talk it over with Mrs. Tennafly, but I believe what I might do is declare a state of national mergency. That way we can get things done quicker, you understand?"

"Yes, sir."

"But there's just so much one country can do, even if it's the US of A. You're gone to have to run around to all the other countries and line them up too."

"Where would you suggest I go first, Mr. President?"

"Well, I'd say the best thing would be, try Germany. I get along pretty good with old Heinz. If you convince him, why, he'll probably give you a big boost with the rest of the EF. Then you've got all them little Slavo countries, and Russia, and China, that's a biggie."

"How are your relations with China, sir?"

"Pretty punk. They're not getting along too good with anybody but India right now. Well, look here. Suppose you get into Japan through Germany, then they could give you India, and India could give you China. See what I mean?"

"Yes, sir. I really appreciate it."

"And, hell, we haven't even talked about Brazil yet, or Africa. Fifty little countries in Africa."

"That's right, sir. It's a big job, I know that."

"Well, son, I wish you luck. We're having a little barbecue in the Rose Garden Saddy after next. Sure would admire to have you there."

It was Tuesday morning. Ed Stone and five senators and congresspersons were sitting at a marble conference table in Senator Givens's office.

"Now, one thing," the Senator said, "there will have to be hearings on this bill, and you'll be asked to appear before a joint committee. The hearings will be holovised, of course."

"Senator, I'm not so sure that's a good idea."

"It isn't? Why not?"

"See, when I tell people about this I can make them believe me, but I can't do it over holovision. They'd think I'm some kind of a phony."

"Now, Ed, let's be reasonable. The only *reason* we've got is that you've told *us* what the aliens told *you.* If we don't have you to back us up, what have we got?"

"Well, there's my suit and hat, and my fillings."

"The clothes could have come from a costume shop," said Representative Yamada. "I don't know about the fillings."

"Well, then there's this ring."

"Morrie, you're the expert. Do you still carry a jeweler's whatchamacallit?"

"Sure I do. May I see the ring, please?"

Stone handed it over. Senator Fine took a loupe out of his pocket and screwed it into his eye, bending over the ring. "Hm," he said.

"What do you see?"

"Well, this is unusual. It's a man's dress ring in a style that I'd say belongs to the thirties or early forties, but a ring like this would normally be made of gold, maybe platinum.

I don't know what this is. It might be some kind of stainless steel. Then the setting is empty, and not only that, there's no sign that this was ever made to hold a gemstone."

"Suppose we could get the metal analyzed?"

"Hey, you can't do that," said Stone. "Give it back." He took the ring and put it firmly on his finger. The lawmakers looked at him.

Givens said, "Maybe the only thing to do is get a lie-detector test. Would you do that, Ed?"

"To find out if I'm telling the truth? Sure."

"Okay, then, we can say, 'Here he is, he's wearing these clothes and he's got this ring . . . ' "

"And my driver's license." Stone took out his wallet and passed the card across the table.

"Expires nineteen thirty-two," said Givens. "Good. All right, and then we say, 'This man has passed a lie-detector test with flying colors, and we believe he's telling the truth. We can't afford not to believe him. We must believe him and act, for the survival of the human race. Something like that. Now, I think that would play, don't you?"

"Sure, Senator."

In the echoing hall outside the Joint Hearing Room, Senator Givens drew Stone aside. "Ed, there may be some trouble with Senator Arbuthnot. He's been away for three weeks—just got back last night—says he hasn't got time to meet you before the hearings."

"So I can't shake hands with him."

"Right, and I think he's hostile. So, just answer his questions the best you can. And don't lose your temper."

"Oh, I won't do that."

"Good for you. All right, we'd better go in now."

CHAPTER 14

After the opening statements, which consumed an hour and a half, the first questioner was Senator Arbuthnot.

"Mr. Stone, I understand that you have spoken to these alien creatures, and so on, but I'm not quite clear in my mind what it was all about. Now I wonder if you could just tell me, what was the aliens' purpose in coming here?"

"I don't know. I guess just exploring, and, you know, collecting specimens. They showed me all kinds of stuff they picked up, plants, trees. They had an elephant, but I think they were going to take it apart."

"They were? Why would they do that?"

"For parts, I guess."

Senator Arbuthnot blinked. "Mr. Stone, let me ask you this. Why don't these aliens show themselves? Why don't they come down here and meet with our elected leaders? Doesn't the fact that they haven't done that suggest to you that they have something to hide?"

"I guess they can't stand the gravity, and maybe they're shy. They're little aliens, and they're not very strong."

Senator Arbuthnot scribed a note. "What exactly did they tell you about the world coming to an end?"

"They didn't really tell me, they showed me pictures. It

looked like, the aliens come down and pick up the box, and then the Earth goes all dark."

"And this is supposed to happen twelve years from now?"

"I think that's right, Senator."

"Do you realize, Mr. Stone, that if we took this seriously, government would grind to a halt? We wouldn't be able to make any commitments more than twelve years ahead, we wouldn't be able to sell Treasury bonds, every program would have to be scaled back. That would be a catastrophe for government, wouldn't it?"

"I guess it would, Senator."

"You guess it would. Mr. Stone, is the alien spaceship out there right now?"

"I guess so."

"Why haven't our astronomers seen it?"

"Maybe they haven't been looking in the right place."

"That's possible. Where should they look?"

"I don't know."

During the lunch break, four of Stone's supporters sat together at a corner table in the Senate Dining Room.

"One thing that does seem to provide some corroboration," said Senator Whelk, "the Hubble Telescope stopped transmitting in two thousand, you remember that? NASA sent up a repair mission, and they found out that the circuits were fused. They replaced the circuit boards, but all they ever got was about a half-hour of transmission. Then the Congress cut the appropriation, so they never did send another shuttle up, and we don't know what happened."

"You're saying that the aliens zapped the telescope? What would they do that for?"

"Well, who knows?"

"Listen, what *I* want to know," said Senator Feeley, "is how we're going to pay for this project."

"Worldwide, I see two ways to go about it. One, we divide the cost of construction plus a reasonable rate of return by the number of people in the world, less the number of people who can't pay anything because they haven't got anything. Okay, that probably works out to something like a thousand dollars a head, and we collect that through subscriptions, and use it to amortize the IDA loans. Two, we levy funds directly from national governments, in proportion to their populations, and let *them* collect from individuals. The second way has less headaches."

"Ron, why not just finance the whole thing from capital reserves of national governments? They aren't going to have any use for the money after we all get in the Cube."

"That's not necessarily so, and it would be inflationary. I can't recommend any method that isn't fiscally sound."

"Are you saying that the money we have now is still going to be worth something when we get to the other planet?"

"Absolutely. You don't understand economics, Eleanor."

"I'm afraid you're right," said Senator Eleanor Feeley.

After lunch the interrogation resumed.

"Mr. Stone," said Senator Arbuthnot, "you say the aliens told you the earth is going to be destroyed?"

"That's right, Senator."

"Well, did they tell you how that's going to happen? I mean, is it going to be a meteor, or what?"

"They didn't say, Senator."

"Well, isn't that a little unsatisfactory?"

"I think so, but that's all they told me."

"Mr. Stone, is it ruled out that the aliens are planning to destroy the earth themselves?"

"No, sir, I can't rule that out. They might do it."

"They might?"

"Yes, sir. All they told me is that the earth is going to be destroyed in about twelve years. They didn't say if they were going to do it or what. Maybe we're going to do it ourselves. From what I've seen since I came back, that don't seem too farfetched."

"You think we're going to destroy the earth ourselves?"

"It seems like we've been trying to."

"All right. Let's say the Earth is going to be destroyed, whether we do it or the aliens do it. Why should we get in that box?"

"So they can take us to another planet."

"But you don't know they're going to do that?"

"No, sir."

"They might just leave us in the box?"

"They might, but I don't know why they would."

"Well, you don't know why they'd do anything, do you?"

"No, sir, I don't."

"Let's just suppose, Mr. Stone, that it's true about the other planet. And the aliens are going to take us there, and then what? Are they going to just turn over a brand-new planet? Are there creatures living there already? What happens to them?"

"I don't know the answers, Senator."

"I know you don't, and that's what worries me. Now another scenario. These aliens are far superior to us scientifically, are they not?"

"Yes, sir."

"And they might regard us, quite rightly, as inferior beings?"

"I don't know about inferior."

"Well, if they're superior to us, we have to be inferior to them, wouldn't you agree?"

"I guess so, if you put it that way."

"All right. Then how do we know they're not going to put us in a zoo? Would you want that for yourself and your descendants? If you knew that was going to happen, wouldn't you rather stay here and die proudly with your planet?"

"Senator, I guess the answer is that we're taking a chance when we get in that box. But it's the only chance we've got."

The senator looked at his memopad. "Now, Mr. Stone, according to what you tell us, there are going to be no corridors, no doorways, no means of ingress or egress in this box. We're just going to be packed in there like sardines in a can."

"Yes, sir, but we'll be in suspended animation, so it won't matter."

"All right. Then the aliens come and take the whole box to another planet. They have to take the box apart to get at us, isn't that right? They can take off the top layer, let's say, and remove however many people are in that layer. Or they can remove a few at a time as they happen to need them. What if they think of us as food, Mr. Stone?"

The chairman rapped his gavel. "These are unsavory speculations, Senator. We can imagine anything our minds are capable of, but Mr. Stone has already told us he doesn't know the answers to any of these questions, and I for one think it is uncharitable to ascribe sinister motives to these alien creatures who have come to save us from disaster."

"I have no further questions, Mr. Chairman."

When the long day was over, Givens took Stone up to Senator Arbuthnot's office to meet him.

"Senator," Stone said, "I want you to know there's no hard feelings about the questions you were asking me today. I know you're just trying to do your job."

"Well, that's very kind of you, Mr. Stone." They shook

hands. "As far as that goes, I think you're just trying to do *your* job, Mr. Stone, or can I call you Ed? I really admire you for what you're doing, Ed, and I realize you're trying to save the human race from disaster. To tell you the truth," he said uncertainly, "I don't know what got into me today. I must have been tired from my trip. And when we reconvene, I'm going to apologize to you publicly."

"Gee, that's swell, Senator, but you don't have to do that."

"Call me Ralph. Yes, I do have to do it, and I'm going to." He grinned, and they shook hands again. "You keep on doing your job, Ed, and I'll do mine."

CHAPTER 15

The taller of the two FBI agents touched the sensor beside the hotel-room door, and waited. The corridor smelled like teddy bears. After a while the agent rang again. Eventually a young man wearing nothing but a pair of flimsy white shorts opened the door. "Sorry to keep you waiting," he said. "I was taking a shower."

"Mr. Stone?"

"Right."

Delgado showed him his badge. "I'm Special Agent Delgado and this is Special Agent Smith."

"Glad to know you." They shook hands. "Hey, come in and sit down, you guys. Can I get you something? Coffee?"

"No, thank you, sir, we're on duty. This is a very nice place you have here." Delgado and Smith took one of the butterscotch-colored sofas; Stone sat in a royal blue easy chair opposite.

"Yeah, it's pretty ritzy," he said. "That gadget in the corner, I can get anything on it. Old movies, any kind of information you can think of. You know there's two wine faucets in the kitchenette? Red and white. The white comes out chilled."

"Very nice. What does a suite like this cost, if you don't mind my asking?"

"Six thousand a day. Isn't that unbelievable? I have to divide everything by a hundred, and I still can't believe it. And that's just for this place—I've got another one across town."

"You have another hotel suite?"

"Yeah, because so many people were coming to see me over there, I couldn't get any time by myself. Senator Givens told you to come here, right?"

"Well, he didn't tell us directly, but the office probably got it from *his* office. Now, Mr. Stone, or can I call you Ed?"

"Sure you can. What's your name?"

"Ramón, but my friends call me Ray. And this is Tinker, they call him Tink, or sometimes Tinsmith." Smiling, they shook hands all around again.

"Now, Ed," said Delgado, "you know, this is just a routine interview. Anybody that has to do with the federal government at a high level, the FBI has to run a security check on them."

"Sure, I understand. Go ahead, shoot."

"Okay, where were you born and when?"

"Altoona, March fifteenth, nineteen ought one."

"That would be Altoona, Pennsylvania?"

"Right. My old man was a beer salesman there. He moved to Harrisburg when I was five."

"And his name was—?"

"Charles M. Stone. My mother's maiden name was Fanny Weingard."

Delgado made a note. "Have you ever been arrested or charged with a felony?"

"Yeah, when I first came back, they arrested me because I was in a hotel room where I didn't belong, and I had this old money on me. They thought I must of stolen it."

"Where and when was that?"

"Trenton, November ninth. This year."

"When you say old money—"

"Gold certificates, you don't use them anymore."

"I see. And how did that turn out?"

"They dismissed the charges and gave me the money back."

"Okay. Now do you have any identification to prove who you are? Sorry to ask this, but—"

"That's okay. Just my driver's license from nineteen thirty-one."

"Could we see that, please?"

"Sure." Stone got up and went into the bedroom, came back with a wallet. He pulled out the card and handed it to Delgado.

"Expires nineteen thirty-two," Delgado read. "Mind if I take a copy of this?"

"Go ahead." Stone watched with interest as Delgado produced a scanner from his pocket and ran it over the license. "How the hell does that thing work, anyway?"

"It digitizes the information, and then it can be reproduced in a computer and printed out."

"I've got to get me one of those. How much do they cost?"

Delgado turned to Smith. "What would you say, Tink?"

"You can get one in any drugstore for about four hundred bucks. Net order, you might get one for three fifty or sixty."

"That's amazing," Stone said. "In the thirties, that would be about four bucks. You couldn't even buy a *radio* for that."

"By the way, Ed," said Delgado, "I notice you appear to be a man of about thirty years of age. But you say here you were born in nineteen oh one?"

"That's because the aliens kidnapped me from nineteen thirty-one and brought me here. I think I was either in suspended animation, or else I died and they brought me back to life."

"I see," Delgado said. "That must have been an interesting experience."

"Oh, yeah."

"Well, let's see. Next thing, have you ever been a member of an organization declared subversive by the attorney general?"

"Not that I know of. What would that include?"

"Communists, anarchists, that kind of thing."

"Oh, no."

"It's a dead letter now, anyway. Do you know we've got a communist senator from Connecticut? Things have sure changed."

"No, I didn't know that. I'm still trying to catch up with a lot of stuff."

Delgado cleared his throat. "Now, Ed, have you ever been confined to a mental institution?"

"Yeah, the New Jersey State Mental Health Care Facility, that time when I was arrested. They let me go."

"Why were you confined in that institution, do you know?"

"Well, the judge thought I was crazy, because I told him about the aliens."

"Sometimes it's better to keep your mouth shut," said Smith. They all smiled.

"All right," said Delgado, "now I don't suppose you've got any living relatives that we could talk to? Or neighbors, employers, that kind of thing?"

"Not anymore. You could talk to the head doctor in the nuthouse. His name is Dr. Wellafield."

Delgado wrote it down. "Well, that's it then." The two special agents stood up. "Thanks for your cooperation, Ed, and for being such a great guy."

CHAPTER 16

The President of the United States got to his feet when Stone entered the Oval Office, and so did the three others, Senator Givens, Congressperson Yamada, and Carl Jaekel.

"Come in, boy, set down, take a load off your feet," said the President. "Want you to meet Carl Jaekel. We been having a powwow about you."

They shook hands all around. Jaekel was a man in his late forties, lean and balding, with a grayish complexion.

"Bourbon and branch, Ed?"

"Yeah, thanks."

The President pushed the decanter and water jug closer and watched while Stone poured a drink. "Now, Ed, Dick and Ronnie here, they tell me the enabling legislation for the international corporation is gone go through just fine, and we can start setting you up some appointments with the high mucky-mucks over in Europe. And I know you'll do just fine, but with all you've got to do, you're gonna have to have an organization behind you."

"What kind of organization, Howie?"

"Less let Carl explain that. Carl?"

"Essentially, pretty much like a campaign organization," said Jaekel. "Okay if I show you what I mean?"

"Sure."

Jaekel put a pocket viewer on the table, popped up the screen, and displayed a chart. "Now, you see here, this is you at the top. Then right under you we have a manager, and under *him,* the way this is set up now, four departments. You've got secretarial, travel, publicity, and security."

"How many people is that?"

"Depending, it might be about a dozen, or it might be twenty or more. Then, of course, you want people to liaise with the Cube Group, with the Congress, the President, et cetera."

"To do what with them?"

"To be your liaison. Keep in touch, in other words."

"Oh."

"Now, Ed, our suggestion is to think it over, and see if you'd like me to be your manager or if you'd rather try somebody else. I don't say this because I'm modest—"

Givens smiled.

"No, because I'm not modest, that's not one of my failings, but because whoever is your manager, it's got to be somebody you can trust and get along with. And one more thing, if you hire me and it doesn't work out, you can fire me. Anytime."

"Would you take care of hiring all these other guys?"

"Yes, that's my job. But you're the boss, and if you don't like somebody, they're out."

"Well, then, sure, let's try it."

Jaekel smiled and put his viewer away. "I like a man that can make up his mind," he said. He extended his hand, and Stone shook it again.

"How soon can you get something set up, Carl?" Givens asked.

"I'll know better after I make some calls this afternoon. Maybe early next week."

"That's splendid," said Givens. Now, Ed, one more thing while you're here, there's a little problem with your passport. We sent to the Blair County courthouse for your birth certificate, but they tell us those records were lost in transit in nineteen ninety-seven. Well, in a way maybe it's fortunate, because if they *found* that birth certificate, you'd have to put down your age as one hundred and one."

"Yeah, that's right."

"So, what is your real age, not counting the years between nineteen thirty-one and now?"

"Uh, let's see. Gee, it's hard to figure, because I would of been thirty March the fifteenth that year, but it was November the ninth when I got back."

"I see what you mean. Well, it would be simpler if you kept your birthday, and then you'd be thirty-one *next* March, you see. That would be better, wouldn't it?"

"Yeah, I guess so."

"Okay, now what we can do is have the FBI construct a false identity, like they do with informers, and then the passport will go through without any trouble."

"You mean a phony name and a phony birthdate?"

"Right."

"I agree that's the best way," said Yamada.

"No, guys, sorry, but that's not what I want. Then I'd be

carrying a passport that says *I'm* a phony. I *want* the real date on there, even if it's hard to believe. I mean, it *is* hard to believe, but that's the point, you see what I mean?"

"Oh. Well, yes. All right, let me straighten it out. It will take awhile."

"So would the FBI thing," said Yamada.

"That's true. Now about transportation— When were you planning to go back to New York, Ed?"

"Tomorrow morning."

"Well, if you'll check into the federal lounge when you get to the airport, we've got a little surprise for you."

"Call from Mr. Stone," said the computer.

"Who—? Oh. Put him on."

Ed's face appeared in the holo. "Hey there, how are you?"

"Okay, and you?"

"I'm feeling great. Listen, they gave me an airplane. You want to take a ride in it?"

"They *gave* you an *airplane?"*

"Yeah, so I can go anywhere I want without worrying about commercial flights. It sleeps eighteen, not counting the crew."

"You've got to be kidding. Where are you?"

"I'm in the plane. Take a look." He moved away from the pickup, and she saw gray watered-silk walls, the top of a blue couch. His head reappeared. "I'm landing at Reagan about five o'clock. I thought we could have dinner tonight or tomorrow, and then I could take you out to see the plane and take a spin."

"I don't fly in airplanes, they scare me."

"Yeah, I know what you mean. So what do you think, is tonight okay?"

She shuffled some memocubes on her desk. "You could have given me a little warning."

"I know, but I was tied up all day in Washington, and I didn't have your home number."

"All right. I had another date, but I guess I can break it. Where are you staying?"

"The UN Plaza."

"Okay, there's a nice Italian restaurant just a block from there. I'll see if I can make a reservation and call you back. What's your number?"

"Triple O five nine five, but listen, let me make the reservation, okay? You wouldn't believe how much respect I get now. What's the name of the restaurant?"

"La Cucina."

"Okay, I'll meet you there at seven-thirty, and if there's any problem with the reservation I'll call *you.*"

Sylvia was already in the kitchen when Lavalle got home after work. "Hi, how was your day?"

"Not bad. Ed called me for another date." She dropped her bag on the table, sat down and took off her shoes.

"For tonight?"

"Yes."

"Is he the one I saw on holo today?"

"Yes."

Sylvia whistled. "Does Julian know about this?"

"I talked to him this afternoon."

"What did you say?"

"Well, I said, 'Julian, I'm very confused.' "

"Uh-huh." Sylvia drew a finger across her throat, put out her tongue and rolled her eyes.

"What am I supposed to do, stick to Julian until death do us part? We're not even married. Is there any gin in the fridge?"

Sylvia opened the refrigerator, took out the gin bottle and the cocktail onions. "I just feel sorry for the poor saps sometimes."

"Julian isn't a sap."
"No, but he's a poindexter."
"You never told me that before."
"Well, you never broke up with him before."
"I haven't broken up with him."
"Not yet, but how about Monday morning?"

CHAPTER 17

The maître d' led Lavalle to Stone's table. He was still wearing the same brown suit, except that when she looked closer it wasn't: it was a new suit, almost the same color, but it was better material and the tailoring was better. Stone himself looked clean and well barbered, like an upper-level zec.

"Hi, did you miss me?" he said.

"Sure. I saw you on the news last night. You've had a busy week, haven't you?" They sat down. She took out a cigarette but did not light it. Stone was studying the menu.

"Did you really quit smoking?"

"Yeah."

"Will it bother you if I do?"

"No. I see people smoking all the time. It hasn't been tough, I never inhaled anyway."

"You don't inhale? Then the only thing you can get is lip cancer. That isn't fun, but it isn't fatal."

"No kidding?" He looked at her cigarette, and she

handed it to him. He rolled the white cylinder between his fingers for a moment, then gave it back. "Guess I'd better not—I couldn't do my job if I was in the hospital."

"You could get in the hospital if you tripped over a personhole cover and broke your leg."

"No, I'm careful."

"You fly in airplanes."

"Sure, but I *have* to do that, and I don't have to smoke cigarettes."

After dinner and the show, a hit musical which Lavalle enjoyed more than Stone did, he said, "Anything else you'd like to do?"

"Not especially. It's been a great evening."

"Okay, let's go up to my room for a nightcap."

The cab let them off in front of the hotel. While they were at the theater, it seemed, part of the East Side dome had been opened to input precipitation; the night air was scented with gasoline fumes and wet concrete. Halfway down the block, something funereal and shapeless was flapping in the gutters.

When they entered the lobby, Lavalle said, "At least you're not staying in a fleabag now."

"No, I'm living high. I feel funny about it, but I guess it's only money."

"That's the way to look at it."

She went into the elevator with him, then down the carpeted hall. Stone opened the door with his card, turned on the lights. They entered a wide living room decorated in forest green and gold; there were mirrors, chandeliers, sconces, a wraparound sofa, a love seat, four or five armchairs with spindly legs.

"Throw your coat anywhere," Stone said. He tossed his coat on the cocktail table, went to the bar and opened it. "What's your pleasure? Rye, Scotch, gin, Irish? Cream de menthy?"

She took off her coat and moved near him, pretending to examine the bottles. After a moment she put her hand on his hip and scratched him gently through the cloth.

"Hey," he said, turning.

She grinned at him. "Yes?" She put her hand on his belt and pulled him in until his thighs were pressed against hers. All of a sudden it was hard to keep the smile, because she was incredibly horny.

His hands went to her body, but he said, "Listen, I don't know about this. If it's because I touched you with the ring—"

"Well, what am I supposed to do, go home and take a cold shower, just to make you feel better?" She stood on tiptoe to kiss him, first teasingly, then with considerable earnestness, and his arms came around her hard.

After a few minutes she said, "You have *buttons* on your fly! Oh, wow!"

The bedroom, it turned out, had a fairy-tale motif; there were Hansel and Gretel pictures on the walls, and the bedspreads were textured to look like a carpet of leaves. Lavalle and Stone lay side by side looking at the bird patterns drifting across the ceiling.

"Did you know you were going to come up here with me tonight?" he asked.

"Yes."

"What about the other guy?"

"I told him I was going to go to bed with you, and then we'd see."

"And he took it, just like that?"

"Well, he didn't like it."

"What's his name?"

"Julian. He's a securities analyst for Brown & Thorpe."

"You told him you were going to try me out and then decide, huh?"

"Don't make it sound worse than it is."

"Well, did you decide?"

She rolled over and kissed him on the eyelid. "What do you think?"

When she opened her eyes in the morning, there was a glow of daylight behind the virtual draperies. That was funny, because she knew she had dialed the windows to full opaque. Come to think of it, the window was on the wrong side of the bed, too. Then she remembered what had happened.

She got up, feeling sweaty and naked. Her clothes were on a chair; she found the toiletries pouch and carried it into the bathroom.

After her shower, she opened the connecting door and looked into the other bedroom. The bed was empty; Stone was not there. For some reason, that annoyed her. She dialed the lights up, walked in and browsed through his bureau: shirts, socks, a worn leather wallet stuffed with cash and credit cards. The photograph on the cards made him look like a mugger in a lineup.

In the next drawer she found a pair of red-and-white-striped pajamas, and decided to wear the tops. That was supposed to be sexy. She brushed her hair, put on a little lipstick and eyeliner, and went out into the sunlit living room.

Stone, in his undershorts, was sitting at the window table with a breakfast tray in front of him; he was watching holovision with the sound turned off. "Hey, sleepyhead!" he said. "What happened to you last night?"

"I had to move. You were yelling and thrashing around." She sat down across from him, feeling resentful.

"I was?"

"Yes. Is there any more coffee?"

He poured from the carafe. "Hey, I'm sorry if I spoiled your beauty sleep."

"Do you do that all the time?"

"I don't know. Are you sore?"

"Only in certain places. Just shut up until I drink my coffee, okay?"

Stone took his tray over to the kitchenette area and came back with a Danish pastry on a plate.

"Thanks."

"Is that enough, or do you want some eggs?"

"This is fine."

Stone sat down and watched her eat. "Listen, Thursday I've got to go to Europe, and I'll be gone for ten days. I know you don't like to fly, but it would be great if you could come with me."

"I *hate* to fly."

"Okay, but could you do it anyway? Could you get the time off?"

"That isn't it, I've got some vacation time coming, but you don't understand. I don't just hate airplanes, they terrify me."

"Oh. Always been that way?"

"No, it started about four years ago. That was when I was breaking up with Anton, and it was a lousy time all around."

"Okay, but you haven't flown since? Not to South America or anywhere? How can you do your job?"

"They were very nice about it; they transferred me to Project Evaluation. Now I just look at the reports."

"Well, listen, will you come out and look at the plane tomorrow? Then if you like it, maybe you could try just a short hop."

"Ed, I *told* you I can't do it."

He stood up, overturning his chair. "Dammit, won't you even try?"

She could feel the furious tears starting. She got up and headed for the bedroom door, but he caught her and swung her around. "Linda, for Pete's sake—"

"Let me go, you zink!"

He released her and looked puzzled. "What's a zink?"

"Somebody who acts the way you're doing. Do you think you *own* me, just because we slept together for one night?"

He looked away. "No, I guess I don't."

She went into the bathroom, splashed water on her face, looked at herself in the mirror. Oh, damn. When she came out again, he was still standing there. She put her arms around him and leaned close.

"Our first fight," he said. She nodded against his chest.

He pushed her away far enough to look at her. "Is it over?"

"I think so." They turned and walked back to the table.

"So, what do you want to do with the rest of the day?" he asked.

"There are some great museums. Art galleries. Do you like art?"

"Not much." He stared through the window. "Looks cold out. I guess we could just stay here."

"Okay. Where did you get that underwear?"

"I had it copied in Washington, from a Hong Kong tailor. They can copy anything. I told them I wanted it exactly like mine, and they even put on the same laundry marks. I can't tell which is which any more."

"You planning to show your underwear to a lot of people?"

"No, just you."

"That's good."

"Hey," he said, looking at a huge silvery shape in the holo, "what is that, a zeppelin?"

She glanced at it; it was cruising over Paris toward the Eiffel Tower. "Right. There are seven of them now, the *Sachsen II,* the *Thüringen,* the *Bayern,* and I forget the rest."

"Hey, that's great. I always wanted to take a ride on one. If I did, could you come with me?"

"I don't know. It wouldn't be like an airplane, that's for sure."

"Terrific. How long do they take to get to Europe?"

"They don't do that anymore, just sight-seeing cruises over Europe and part of Asia. It used to take about two days to cross the Atlantic, I think."

"Oh, nuts. I couldn't take the time now anyway, but maybe later, if we get a chance?"

"I don't know. Well, do you want me to read your fortune?"

"Sure."

She got her handbag, dumped it on the table, found a memopad and stylus. She swept the rest of the things back into the bag. "Okay, what's your full name?"

"Ed Stone."

"I'll do that one too, but what's your full name, the one you used in school?"

"Edwin L. Stone, but I don't like it. Aren't you going to use cards, or read my palm or something?"

"No, this is numerology. Very scientific." She was writing on the memopad. After a moment she showed it to him.

E D W I N L S T O N E
5 4 5 9 5 3 1 2 6 5 5 = 50 = 5

"What does this mean?"

"Every letter has a number. You add up the numbers and then add them again, like five and zero equals five. That tells you what number you are, and the number tells you what kind of person you are."

"Okay, what kind of person am I?"

"You're bright, you're restless, adventurous, you like weird things. You like to travel and meet people; you don't like to stick to any one job. You'd make a good salesman, and you're sexy. Five is a very good number for a man."

"You knew all that already."

"Sure, but it's right here in the numbers. Now we'll do the other one."

She wrote again and handed him the pad.

E D S T O N E
5 4 1 2 6 5 5 = 28 = 10 = 1

"That's a good number for a man, too. Ones are strong people who know what they want and go for it. They don't let anybody get in their way. They have their own ideas. They make good leaders and inventors."

"That's all different from the first one."

"Sure it is, but they're both you. You shortened the name because you wanted to show a different side of yourself. 'Ed Stone' sounds stronger, doesn't it, than 'Edwin L.'? But the other side is still there."

"What's your number?"

"I'm a three." She smiled. "A very good number for a woman. Now let's see what your important years are. When were you born?"

"March fifteen, nineteen ought one."

"No, really."

"That's when I was born."

"Okay, what the hell. Nineteen oh one adds up to eleven. Add eleven to the date, and you get nineteen twelve, an important year."

"My father died when I was eleven."

"And that made a big difference."

"Sure."

"Okay, nineteen twelve makes thirteen. Add that, and we get nineteen twenty-five."

"I got married that year."

She looked at him. "Too young."

"Maybe so."

"All right, nineteen twenty-five makes seventeen. Add that, and we get nineteen forty-two, another important year."

"I never got that far. Maybe it would of been important if I'da got there."

She studied him. "I can't make out if you're conning me or what. Okay, if we just skip the years between nineteen thirty-one and twenty oh two, then nineteen forty-two would be the same as twenty thirteen."

"Twenty *fourteen* is when the aliens are supposed to come. So that doesn't work out."

"Well, numbers don't lie. Something's going to happen in twenty thirteen."

"Uh-huh. Maybe I'll find out how crazy I am. Listen, do you want to go back to bed?"

She smiled at him. "Oh, all right."

"Hey, I guess we're in love, huh?" said Stone. "What do you think?"

"Maybe we are. Don't rush me."

He nuzzled her neck. "I like the way you smell."

"I smell like a cat in heat," she said.

"Sure. That's what I like."

"Well, I don't. I'm going to take another shower."

"Want some help?"

"No."

CHAPTER 18

After a while they got dressed again and went down to the hotel restaurant for lunch. Then they bought some fruit and magazines, went back to the room and put their feet up. Stone read through *Time,* with muttered exclamations, then put it down and got another magazine from the writing desk: a cheap-looking thing with a monster on the cover.

When he had been staring at it awhile, she asked, "What are you reading that for?"

"There are clues in it. Listen to this." He turned back a few pages and read, " 'He watched the slow movement of the glowing point.' This is where the hero is flying from Europe to his secret base in the Artic. He has a navigational thing in the plane that shows where he is on a map of the world."

"We have that in cars now."

"Okay, you see? How did he know that, in *nineteen thirty-one,* for Cripe's sake? But listen to how it goes on. 'The Central Federated States of Europe were behind him; the point was tracing a course over the vast reaches of the patchwork map that meant the many democracies of Russia.' "

He looked at her earnestly. "You don't call it the Central

Federated States, but there *is* a European Federation, right, and there *is* a kind of patchwork of democracies where part of Russia used to be. He knew something."

"Coincidence."

"I don't believe in coincidence." He turned pages, handed her the magazine. "Look at this picture."

The illustration, in gray ink on gray paper, showed an insectile monster holding a swooning girl in its arms. Two men, one erect, one on the ground, were looking at it in horror.

"What about it?"

"The bug has a helmet on its head, like the one they used on me. And look how many arms and legs it's got."

"Six."

"And the aliens have six. So what does that tell us?"

"The aliens are the bad guys?"

"I don't know. Sometimes I think so."

She turned the magazine and looked at the cover. The illustration, in violet, red, and green watercolor, showed a gigantic spiderlike thing with eyes on stalks and a jaw like a crocodile's.

"Another monster," she said.

"Right. It's all through those stories, but this one only has four legs."

"Maybe there's two more you can't see."

"Yeah, I thought of that."

Below the monster was a metal cylinder with portholes and a round open door. Two people were trying to get in the door, but there was a spiderweb across it. In the corner was printed:

DARK MOON
A Novelette of Strange
Adventure on a
Mysterious New Satellite

By CHARLES W. DIFFIN

She looked at the spine: it said "May, 1931."

"Nineteen thirty-one? It doesn't look that old. Where did you get it?"

"I had it with me, they gave it back afterwards."

After a moment, when he didn't speak again, she glanced at him and saw that his body was hunched over, his eyes half-closed.

"That's the Earth," he muttered. "No, not there. In the story, it's on another moon, a dark one."

"Ed?" He didn't seem to hear her. "No, not there either," he said. "It's another moon around the Earth. . . . In between the Earth and the real Moon. It's a story. . . . No, not there. It's a *story*. . . . That's right, there isn't any monster like that. . . . No, that isn't real either. There aren't any spaceships yet."

His eyes opened slowly and he straightened up, seemed to see her.

"What *happened?*" she said.

"I was remembering. Or, I don't know—it's more like the whole thing is happening all over again, or like it's happening now. I can't figure out what's real."

"What was it all about?"

After a moment he said, "They showed me the cover of that magazine, and then this robot put a telepathy helmet on my head and they talked to me in pictures. They wanted to know where that happened, where it was. They showed me different planets. I kept telling them it was a story, and I guess they finally believed me."

"Why do you think they wanted to know?"

"Beats me, unless they were scared there might be people out there in spaceships, or on other planets, that could hurt them."

She sat looking at her hands for a while. "You know, we do have spaceships now, or did. The space boom collapsed in the sixties, but we had manned landings on the Moon. And some unmanned probes that went as far as Uranus. Now it's all just satellites."

"You think that will ever start up again?"

"I don't know. Maybe if things don't keep on getting worse—"

He got up and went to the bar, poured half a glass of rye, added ginger ale. He sat down with the glass in his hand, looked at it, then took a long swallow.

"Isn't it a little early for that?"

He looked at her. "Sure it is, but what else have I got?" He raised the glass again. "Don't tell me it's bad for me, for Pete's sake. Here's looking at you, kid."

CHAPTER 19

There were six of them on the plane: Stone, Jaekel, three members of the Cube Group, and a political affairs adviser named Anthony Norton, borrowed from the British Embassy.

The stewardess, whose name was Cindy, served them drinks and munchies in the lounge. Once they were airborne, they carried their glasses to the dining room and pulled up chairs around the table. Jaekel rummaged in a cabinet and produced a pack of cards and a carousel of chips. "Five card draw, dollar ante?" he asked.

"Is that poker?" asked Norton. "I'm afraid I don't play."

Stone said, "You don't? You never played poker?"

"No, sorry. Bridge is my game."

"Bridge," Stone repeated. "Hey, you ought to learn to play poker. You want us to teach you?"

The others were smiling.

"I see I'm for it," Norton said. "All right, how do we begin?"

Jaekel spread cards on the table. "Here's the sequence of the hands. First is a pair. That's two aces, or two threes, or whatever. Next is two pair, then three of a kind." Norton began writing in a little notebook, using a slender gold scriber.

"Why does a flush beat a straight?" he asked. "I'd think it would be the other way round."

"Well, look, in a solitaire game, if you deal one card and you want to try for an open-ended straight, there are thirty-two cards that could improve your hand, sixteen lower than the first card and sixteen higher."

"Hm." Norton took his calculator out, punched keys, peered at the screen, punched again. "Oh. Yes, I see now. That's quite interesting."

"It is, huh? Well, who wants to be banker?"

Cooper, one of the Cube Group, won the first hand with deuces and fours. "Heavens, I had fives and treys," said Norton, "but I thought that wasn't good enough."

"Tony, you're not supposed to tell what you had. Somebody wants to know, they have to pay to find out."

"Oh, sorry. But how is it that you see people in holos winning with straight flushes and things?"

"That can happen, but two pair is a good hand in draw poker, nothing wild, no bug."

"Bug?"

"The joker. Now if you're playing something like deuces, threes, and one-eyed jacks wild, you might want to fold two low pairs. But that's a ladies' game."

"I see." Norton tapped keys on his calculator. "You don't mind me doing this? Working out the odds?"

"No, go ahead."

The deal passed to Jaekel. While he was shuffling, Frank Chesterton came in with his uniform jacket open. "Hey," he said, "if I'm not interrupting, you guys ought to see this. Come over to the left side of the airplane and take a look while I turn off the lights a minute."

They got up and went to the windows. When the cabin lights went out, they saw a pale violet light shivering in streamers against the moonlit sky.

"What the hell is that?"

"The aurora borealis. Northern lights."

"Holy Jesus. What causes it?"

"Ionization of the upper atmosphere."

"Oh, yeah? Hey, that's pretty amazing. Where are we now?"

"We're over the North Atlantic," Chesterton said.

"Jesus. What happens if we have to ditch?"

"Well, it's a long way back to New York, especially if you have to swim. You want the lights on again now?"

"Yeah."

Chesterton left, and they sat down again. Stone looked at his cards, then at the chips on the table. "Who didn't ante?"

Norton's play steadily improved, and he won two small pots, but after three hours he was a heavy loser. "I don't understand," he said. "I'm quite sure I've been playing the odds correctly."

"There's more to it than the odds," said Stone. "You want to cash in, guys? I'm tired."

"All right by me." Jaekel, the banker, began collecting chips and paying off. Stone was shuffling the deck meditatively while the others stood up, stretched, and left the room. "Good night," they called. "Sleep tight." "I wish I was." Somebody blew a raspberry; somebody else farted.

"You've been to Europe before, right?" Stone said to Norton.

"Oh, yes."

"What's it like over there? I mean, beside speaking different languages."

"Well, different customs, too. It varies from one country to another. By the way, I've brought some briefing papers on England, Germany, the Vatican, India and Japan, and I also have some training holos if you'd prefer those. Now, as to your question. I'd say that the principal difference is that Europeans of the upper classes tend to be more formal than Americans. They take politeness quite seriously. You may find them bowing a bit more. They won't call you by your Christian name straight away, and they'll expect you to call them Herr This and Monsieur That. If you speak any European language—you don't, do you?"

"No. Parly-voo fransay."

"Well, it would be a great help to you if you could learn. Anyhow, when you do speak their languages, you want to be careful to use the formal 'you,' not the intimate one."

"There's two different words for 'you'?"

"Oh, yes. In German, it's *'Sie'* and *'du.'* In French, *'vous'* and *'tu.'* and in Spanish, *'usted'* and *tú.'* "

"That's crazy. Why can't they have one word like we do?"

"Well, the intimate word is rather nice, in fact, between lovers."

"Oh, uh-huh."

"Now in Japanese, there are three or four different ways of addressing someone, depending on their status and relation to you. But the Japanese don't really expect Americans to speak Japanese; they think it's an affectation, in fact."

"They do? How come?"

"Well, it shows that you're trying to become Japanese, and they know you can't. One thing you should always bear in mind is that these people all believe their own language and culture are the best, and that anybody who comes from another culture is second-rate."

"Hey. That's funny, isn't it."

"Ah . . . yes, it is."

"I guess it's natural, though."

"I'd say so."

Stone shifted in his chair. "So what you're telling me is I should be polite, and use the right fork, and not dunk my doughnuts in the coffee, right?"

"Yes, that sort of thing. But don't worry. You'll find they are gracious hosts, and they'll do their best to make you feel at home. As far as the language is concerned, most of the people you'll be meeting speak fluent English, and if there's any problem, you'll have good translators."

"You speak German?"

"Yes, fairly well."

"How do you say: 'Where's the bathroom?' "

"Wo ist das Kabinett?"

Stone repeated it thoughtfully. Then he asked, "How about Italian?"

"Dove è il gabinetto?"

"Hey, it's almost the same, isn't it?"

"Yes, it is. You'll find there are a great many correspondences of that kind among European languages, even when they belong to different families. Once you learn one language, it's very much easier to learn another one."

"It is, huh? When did you start?"

"At school, with German and French and a little Spanish. And Latin, of course. I picked up other things later."

"Uh-huh. You probably think I'm some kind of a hick."

"Oh, no."

"Well, I am. But I'll learn. I've got to."

"I'm sure you will. Good night."

CHAPTER 20

At four o'clock, unable to sleep, Jaekel put on a robe and went down the long corridor, through the dining room into the lounge. It was cool there, and dark except for the amber safety bulbs. The plane was droning forward with a barely perceptible motion. He switched on the lamps and ceiling lights, turned up the thermostat, and poured himself a stiff Scotch.

On the way over to his chair he picked up a copy of *Time*. The holoprint on the cover was a picture of Heinz Rottenstern; how long, he wondered, before it would be Ed Stone?

In some ways Stone was an easier assignment than any political candidate, because he had no track record and no enemies. On the other hand, that was just the problem. Jaekel turned over in his mind all the things that could go wrong, knowing as he did so that it was pointless, because he had done it all before.

Something out of Stone's past might turn up to discredit him. The fact that he *had* no past was profoundly disturbing. Jaekel rummaged in a drawer until he found a pencil, and wrote on a page of *Time,* "Relatives?"

Then there was always the chance of a sexual scandal, although most people didn't expect public figures to be anchorites. Stone had exchanged a couple of interested glances with Cindy early in the evening. That was all right, and it was all right that he had a lover in New York, but what if it turned out that he also liked ten-year-old boys, or goats and sheep? He wrote, "Sex?"

Stone was not an educated man, and he had a lot of the attitudes you would expect, but that didn't seem to make any difference; the common people liked him, and so did the intellectuals. So far. It was still possible that he would make some gigantic unforgivable blunder. He wrote, "Foot in mouth?"

On the whole, it was a good thing that Stone was going to a lot of places where he would need translators; they were trained to turn insults into compliments whenever they could. Jaekel tore off the page, folded it and put it in his pocket. He always threw these notes away, but he had to write them.

He felt himself nodding. He finished the Scotch, left the glass on the table, and walked down the long quiet corridor. Commercial airliners were as long as this one, but they were divided into sections, and there was always somebody in the aisles, except at night, when the plane was dark; here you saw the whole length of the passenger compartment, from the lounge at one end to Stone's stateroom at the other.

As he slid open the door of his own stateroom, he turned

his head toward a motion glimpsed out of the corner of his eye. At first there was nothing; then, far down the corridor, something dark was rushing soundlessly toward him, smothering the lights as it came. It swallowed him before he could move; he was in darkness for an eyeblink, and then it was gone.

Shocked wide awake, Jaekel returned to the lounge. Everything there was as it should be. Had he fallen asleep standing up for a moment, and had a dream, or a hallucination?

He went back to his stateroom and lay staring at the dark ceiling a long time, while the plane droned through space.

CHAPTER 21

A limousine driven by a taciturn Jamaican took them from their hotel to the United States Embassy on Fleet Street. It was a bright December day; there were flags along the Embankment, and visibility on the Thames was a mile or more.

The ambassador, an effusive man named Ottoway, talked to Stone about protocol. "You don't sit until the monarch invites you to, you don't use any term of familiarity, you speak mainly when you're spoken to, you call him 'Your Royal Highness,' or 'Sir,' and that's about it."

"I don't have to wear those funny pants?" Stone asked.

"No, no. It will be quite informal, you're not being

knighted after all. Although that isn't out of the question, you know, some time in the future. Now, Mr. Stone, the King has asked to see you in private, with no one else present, not even myself. That's quite unusual, and, I may say, quite an honor."

"Is that right? What's he like?"

"Oh, quite an individual. You'll get a kick out of him."

The King of England advanced cordially and shook the visitor's hand as the equerry withdrew. "It's very good of you to come, Mr. Stone. Please sit down, won't you?" In a graceful maneuver, he himself contrived to sit before the visitor could disgrace himself by a faux pas.

"Now tell me," he continued, "what's all this about putting the whole human race in a giant building? I think it's quite fab, and so does Di."

"Well, Your Royal Highness," said Stone, "it's this way. The aliens told me we've got to do it so they can take us to another planet before the Earth is destroyed."

"Yes, and you say this event is going to take place in about twelve years?"

"I think that's what they were trying to tell me, Your Royal Highness."

"Call me 'Sir,' if you will; it's so much shorter. Now, Stone, I'm intensely curious to know, where is this other planet and what sort of place is it?"

"They didn't tell me that, Sir, but I think it must be a planet like the Earth, or they wouldn't take us there. I think it's a long way off, but that doesn't matter, because they can keep us in suspended animation for as long as it takes. That's what they did to me, I think, and I didn't know it was twenty ought two until I got here."

"Sorry, I don't think I quite follow. You didn't know what year it was?"

"No, I thought it was still nineteen thirty-one, because that was when they kidnapped me."

"How bloody extraordinary! You must wait until Di comes home; I know she'll want to hear this. Now why do you think they kidnapped you in nineteen thirty-one and then brought you back this year?"

"I don't know, Sir. There's a lot of things they didn't tell me. Maybe they were waiting till they thought we were ready to build the box. Or maybe they went away for a while and came back."

"And did you actually see these aliens?"

"Yes, Sir. They're very small, and they have six legs."

"Six legs! Are they spiders?"

"No, Sir, more like octopuses."

"But octopuses have eight, surely?"

"Yes, Sir, but I just meant they're sort of squashy."

"Squashy! How devastating. Now tell me, are we all to be allowed to see these aliens, I mean will they come down and show themselves at some point?"

"Sir, I really don't know. They might just send their robots."

"Their robots! Oh, Di must hear this. How many legs do robots have?"

"They have six, too."

"Six or two?"

"No, I mean they have six also."

"Oh, I see. Six too. Then you think we might see the robots, at least."

"Yes, Sir, I think so. The robots come into my room at night and recharge my ring, and I think they put a helmet on my head to find out what's happening."

"Do they! And do you see them then?"

"No, Sir, because they wait till I'm asleep, but I can tell because of the dreams I have."

"I must say, this gets more and more fab. So, then, we'll

all go into the building, will we, and wake up on a new planet?"

"Yes, Sir, and the reason I think we'll see the aliens, or the robots anyway, they've got to bring the gadget that puts people into suspended animation. Because we don't know how to do that."

"Oh, I see. But they might just come when everybody is asleep, mightn't they? That would be disappointing. Now about the building, who's going to do the design?"

"I don't know, Sir. I think probably there'll be a competition."

"Well, I hope you won't hire one of those architects who put up horrible square boxes without any character at all. Some plinths, at any rate, don't you think? A few columns and capitals?"

Something beeped on the royal person; the King looked at his watch. "Well, it's a pity Di isn't back, but I know you've got to go and see the Prime Minister, and I mustn't keep you." He rose. "I'm so glad we had this chat, Stone; it's been most invigorating."

"Thank you, Your Royal Highness. I had a swell time myself."

CHAPTER 22

A blackish rain was falling on Berlin, streaked on buildings and people. Attendants with umbrellas hurried the departing passengers from the plane, but even so, some of them were bespattered, including Stone, Jaekel and Norton. Other attendants wiped them down, with profuse apologies. A limousine took them to their hotel and then to the U.S. Embassy on Albert Einsteinstrasse.

"Mr. Stone," the ambassador said, "you probably know that Herr Rottenstern is a little touchy about his status as head of the European Federation."

"He is? Why?"

"Well, it's all that stuff about Hitler and so on, and I certainly wouldn't refer to it if I were you. But apart from that, I think you'll find him very easy to get along with, very genial. And of course he can be quite helpful if he chooses to."

"Hitler was the one who started the war in thirty-nine?"

"Yes, I believe that's right."

"Well, Rottenstern wasn't even born then, was he? So it couldn't have been his fault."

"That's just how he feels about it. Bear that in mind, and you won't have any trouble at all."

* * *

President Rottenstern asked, "Do you know, Mr. Stone, and gentlemen, that before I went into politics, I was a civil engineer?"

"No, I didn't know that."

"Oh, yes. For many years. So I am interested in this project from a technical standpoint. You know, German engineers and architects are the best in the world. I don't say this just because I am German, but because it is true."

"Yes, sir."

"So I think it is important that this building should be designed and built in Germany. Do you agree?"

"I'll certainly bear that in mind, Your Excellency."

"That's good, Mr. Stone. Now tell me, and you gentlemen also, do you like beer?"

Rome was overcast and cold, with a drizzle out of the northeast. The audience room in the Vatican was a bit drafty, as always, but the Pope was well wrapped up in rochet, mozzetta, gaiters and bootees.

"Mr. Stone," the Pontiff said, "we understand that you have foretold the end of the world."

"Not me, Your Holiness. The aliens told me about it."

"Yes, yes. We are not capable of believing in the existence of alien intelligences. Do you think they might have been something else?"

"Like what, Your Holiness?"

"As, for instance, angels?"

"Honestly, Your Holiness, they didn't look like angels to me. But I guess I don't know what angels look like."

"We ourself have never seen them. In our tradition, however, they are often radiant and have wings."

"They didn't look like that, but I guess they could look like anything."

"We would like to be quite clear about this. You say that you believe you were in a spaceship when this revelation was given to you?"

"Yes, Your Holiness."

"Was it a construction of metal, with portholes and rocket engines and things of that sort?"

"I don't know. I never saw the outside of it. But I knew it had to be a spaceship, because the gravity was so light."

"How is that, our son?"

"When I dropped anything, it took a long time to fall. And if I stood up suddenly, I floated up to the ceiling."

"Ah, I see. That's very interesting, isn't it? And you know nothing about how you got to this place?"

"No, Your Holiness. I went to sleep in Trenton, New Jersey, and when I woke up I was there."

"We think that is significant. And these beings told you that the world would come to an end in twelve years?"

"I think that was what they meant, but I can't be sure."

"We think that is significant also, Mr. Stone. Our Lord told us that no man knows the time or place when He will return."

"Your Holiness, I don't think they're angels."

"Well, well, our son, we can agree to differ."

Premier Prutkov said, "Mr. Stone, I know you will understand me when I say that this project will be a great work of the human spirit."

"Yes, sir."

"Please call me Kuzma. Well, and I must tell you also that it is a peculiarly Russian idea. Our czars had such grandiose ideas, as for instance constructing the railway in a straight line from Petersburg to Moscow. And of course the Soviet experiment, although it failed according to some, still was a gigantic enterprise, unparalleled, adventurous. So, too, your Cube. Magnificent! You are sure your ancestors were not Russian?"

"They could of been, Kuzma."

"Yes, certainly, because if one is American one never knows! Ha, ha! And besides, you look like a Slav! That is our highest compliment. Tell me, do you like caviar?"

"You are Kalki, come to us to save us from disaster," said Chandralingam. "It has happened many times before; it does not come as a surprise to us."

"Mr. President, I don't think I know who Kalki is."

"He is an aspect of the Lord Vishnu; he is a horse with white wings who comes to destroy the Earth."

"I don't feel like I'm an aspect of Vishnu."

"No, of course not; when you come to Earth you lose all memory of your divine nature, or you could not function as a man, you see. But others can tell. You are Kalki, please believe me, there is no doubt about it."

The Chinese Premier shook hands with Stone and Cooper and offered them tea.

"Mr. Guo," Stone said, "we came to you because we want to talk about our project to put the whole human race in a box."

The translator spoke simultaneously, but with some hesitation and false starts; she seemed to be having trouble putting the sentence into Mandarin. The Premier spoke sharply.

"I don't understand the idea of putting the human race in a box," the translator said.

"The idea is, the Earth is going to be destroyed, probably in about twelve years." Another sentence from Guo; the translator said, "How do you know this?"

"The aliens told me. They kidnapped me from nineteen thirty-one and brought me here."

"Is this true?"

"I think it is true."

"What is the purpose of putting the human race in a box?"

"Then the aliens will come and get the box, and take us to another planet."

"You have pictures of this other planet?"

"No, they didn't give me any."

"What is the appearance of these aliens?"

"They're little, and have six legs, and they talk by making something like Chinese characters on their foreheads."

"That is extremely interesting."

"Mr. Guo," Cooper said, "the reason it's so important to talk to you is that we believe the best place for the box is near Shanghai. You see, twenty-one percent of the world population is right here in China, and sixteen percent more is in India. If you look at the logistics, the only thing that makes sense is to concentrate the population here. Anywhere else you put it, there's going to be a larger number of passenger miles. So what we do, we evacuate the outlying areas first, and that means that our lines keep getting shorter. When we clean out an area, we can abandon the infrastructure there. We transfer airplanes, and in some cases rolling stock, to areas farther in. So the farther we go, the easier it gets." The translator, who had been speaking at the same time, came to a stop.

"You have thought this matter out carefully. Have you also thought of the cost of all this?"

"Yes, Mr. Guo. The World Bank and the International Development Association are interested in providing loans, and we already have the support of several European governments."

"I find that I want to do it. I don't know why. Perhaps it

is that you are so persuasive. Or perhaps it is national pride. Do you know what our name for our country means, Mr. Stone?"

"No, sir, I don't."

The Premier smiled. "It means 'the middle of the earth,' " the translator said.

Minimata asked, "On this new planet, Mr. Stone, how will the living space be apportioned?"

"I think there'll be room enough for everybody, Mr. Premier."

"Yes, and will it be divided equally, with so much for each person?"

"I'd think that would be fair, Mr. Premier."

"I also," said Minimata.

CHAPTER 23

She saw the airplane droning ahead under the stars, and the meteor coming in from outer space. The motions were very slow, like a display on a monitor. She could see the airplane inching ahead on its path, and the meteor converging, and she tried to call out but her voice didn't seem to work.

Then the meteor was so close that she could see the glow of superheated air around it, and then it collided and turned soundlessly into a ball of orange flame, and the twisted skeleton of the airplane went down toward the earth.

After he came back from Japan, Stone was in Washington for a week; when he turned up in New York again, he looked tired. "Rough time in Washington?" Lavalle asked him.

"Ah, you know, everybody wants to invite me out." He rubbed his belly. "This used to be flatter," he said ruefully. "And it's the same thing in New York. You remember that little dinner party that your boss invited me to before I left? It turned out to be thirty people, and they all wanted to invite me to dinner and lunch. I've got to cut down, but I don't want to hurt people's feelings."

"Just say no."

"Right. Something else, you know I've been getting fan mail? They showed me two sacks of it. I just brought along a few to show you. Here's one."

She looked at it. It was a folded sheet of cream-colored stationery; the writing, in purple ink, was large and round.

> Dere Ed Stone,
>
> I saw you on Holovison, I think you are supper. Plese tel me ar you Maryd. I woud like to Mary you.
>
> Your Freind
> EARLENE SMITH

"Sounds like a child," she said.

"No, here's a picture." He passed it over; it was a holoprint of a plump woman who appeared to be in her early fifties.

"Some of them are pretty steamy," Stone said. He picked up another letter and sniffed it. "Lavender," he said, and rolled his eyes.

"Do you know that cartoon characters get fan mail too?"

"What do you mean, like Popeye?"

"No, more like Dong the Barbarian, but it's the same thing. People even send them presents—flowers, cakes."

"Why do you suppose that is?"

"I guess they haven't got anything better to do."

After breakfast, Stone was looking at a simulated globe of the Earth in the holo; he tapped a key, making national boundaries appear and disappear. Red dots of light marked the cities where he had been. He tapped another key, creating yellow lines like a spiderweb.

"My folks want us to come out to Rye for Christmas," she said. "Do you want to?"

"Do you?"

"Yeah, I'd like you to meet them."

"You would, huh? What are they like?"

"Well, my mother is kind of dippy. My stepfather, Geoffrey Nero, is very smart. He's in a wheelchair, though."

"Uh-huh. Are we supposed to bring presents?"

"It wouldn't hurt."

"Okay."

Stone picked her up in a hired Cadillac Saturday morning, and they drove up the Major Deegan Expressway in brown sunlight. The Cadillac had its own air regenerator, and they kept the windows closed.

"I don't get this about Christmas," he said. "It's still the twenty-sixth, but it always falls on a weekend?"

"It's simple, they just drop a few days of the week. Like in this case, Christmas would have been on a Wednesday, and that's the dumps. You have to go back to work on Thursday? Thick. So now we make Saturday the next day after Tuesday, and then it comes out even."

"It still doesn't seem right. What happens to Wednesday, Thursday and Friday?"

"We put them back in after Christmas."

"So then you've got two Wednesdays, two Thursdays, and two Fridays?"

"Sure, and *that's* the dumps too, but you can't have everything."

They were driving past a golf course. "We're almost there," she said.

"Your stepfather is a golfer?"

"He used to be, but he's in a wheelchair now. Don't offer to shake hands with him, okay? His joints are very sensitive. Here we are."

The butler appeared as they were getting out of the car. "Good to see you again, Miss Linda. Why don't you go right in? I'll bring the luggage."

"That's fine." Lavalle dropped the card into his hand. "Henry, this is my friend Ed Stone. We'll share a room."

"How do you do, sir?" said Henry.

"Nice to meet you." Stone put out his hand, and after the barest hesitation Henry took it. Then he busied himself opening the trunk and pulling out luggage.

Lavalle led Stone into the foyer, where she dropped her coat and hat on the chest. She motioned for him to bend closer. "You're not supposed to shake hands with servants," she said in his ear.

He straightened up. "No, huh?"

"No. Come and meet my mother."

"Can I shake hands with *her?*"

"Idiot."

"Wench." He put his hand on her buttock and squeezed.

"None of that," she said, pulling away. "Let's have a little dignity here. I want them to like you." She took his hand to keep it occupied, and led him into the sunny living room.

Her mother, who had been standing near her stepfather's wheelchair, came forward with an eager smile. "Linda, how nice to see you. And this is your young man?"

"This is Ed, Sherri. He's the one who was kidnapped by aliens."

"Yes, I know, dear. Linda, I probably ought to tell you that I've put a sword in your bed."

"You *what?*"

"Yes, like the knights of old, don't you remember? They put a sword between them in the bed and lay there all night long, perfectly chaste and pure. It's your great-grandfather's cavalry sword, and it isn't very sharp, but I'd be careful anyway."

"Sherri—"

"Don't you remember what happened the last time you had a young man here, dear? Enough said." She drew them toward the bay window, where Geoffrey sat crooked and smiling in his wheelchair.

"Geoffrey, this is Ed Stone, the one I told you about," said Lavalle.

"Well, Ed, we've heard a lot about you," said Nero, clacking his jaws. "Excuse me for not shaking hands. Sit down, sit down, both of you. You'd probably like a drink, wouldn't you, Ed, or a smoke? We don't drink or smoke here, but if you want to, go right ahead."

"Uh, no, that's okay," said Stone.

"Darling, the children would probably like an opportunity to freshen up, wouldn't you, dears? Linda, it's your old room at the end of the hall. Lunch will be ready in half an hour."

"Holy crap, she really did it," said Stone, looking at the sword in the bed.

"Well, take it out."

He tugged. "I can't. Oh, boy—it looks like it's chained down at both ends. Is she crazy, or what?"

"She's been a little strange since my father died. We can wrap a blanket around it or something."

"What did she mean about the last time?"

"Well, if you must know, I got pregnant when Julian was here."

"And?"

"Well, I had an abortion."

"This trip is a barrel of laughs," Stone said.

The dining area table was covered by a linen cloth and set with china and crystal, but the knives and forks were aluminum. Geoffrey pulled his wheelchair up to the window side of the table, with the broad green expanse of the first fairway behind him.

"Now, Ed," he said, "tell me about these aliens. What sort of critters are they?" His smile exposed his gray back teeth.

"They're about the size of rats. They ride around in the heads of robots."

"Is that right! Well, well. And they told you the world is coming to an end?"

"Yes, sir."

"And you believed them, of course. Well, I can understand that. Sherri, this pork is pretty tough—I can't even cut it up, much less chew it."

"Let me help you, dear."

"No, it's all right. I'll just have some more mashed potatoes. Ed," he said, "just between us, Marilyn, our cook—she's been with us seven years and we love her, but she can't cook pork. Mashed potatoes, yes. She makes the best mashed potatoes in the world. Turkey? Well, you wait and see. Pork, no. Pass me a little gravy, would you, dear?"

* * *

"Ow!" he said.

"What's the matter now?"

"The goddamn thing is electrified."

A pause.

"We could try the floor."

"No, the hell with it. Let's get some sleep."

After breakfast, when Stone was out of the room, Geoffrey beckoned her over. "Sweetheart, you know I'm just concerned about your best interests," he said.

"And you don't approve of Ed."

"Well, the man's a lunatic, isn't he?"

"Sometimes he thinks he is."

"He does, eh? That's a bad sign. Linda, you know he might actually be dangerous."

"To me? No."

"But you'd agree that he's dangerous to the world at large?"

"Oh, sure."

"Well, you know what you're doing, I suppose. Your mother is very disappointed, you know, but of course she's always disappointed."

On the way home, Stone asked, "What did your stepfather give you?"

"Some stock certificates. Gentech. If I sold them at the market, I wouldn't have to work for a year."

"He's rich, huh."

"He's done all right. He doesn't even go to board meetings anymore, because of his heart, but he's an operator. What were you talking about in his study all that time?"

"He wanted to know what I thought about the value of real estate when we start loading the Cube. *He* thinks it'll go down, but not all the way. He offered to take me into a syndicate to sell it and then buy it back."

"Did you go for it?"

"No, I'd have to borrow the money, and I haven't got time anyway. I don't even think that was what was really on his mind."

"I don't either."

"He's deep, is he?"

"Deep and tricky. He sounds dumb sometimes, but don't ever believe that."

CHAPTER 24

In a large, well-lit conference room in Washington, Conway Kettle said, "You people all know each other, so I'm just going to begin by introducing Ed Stone, the man the aliens talked to."

There were smiles, nods, a spattering of applause.

"Now, Ed, we're the ad hoc task force to generate plans for the Cube Project, and we've all got our names and specialties on our workspaces, so you can figure out who is who as we go along, okay?"

"Sure."

"All right, let's begin with siting. Sam?"

Sam Cooper cleared his throat. "Okay, the first consideration is passenger miles. If you want to put the whole human population in one place, it ought to be a central location in or near the largest concentration of people, just to shorten the supply lines. Well, that narrows you down to China and India. Next you want a seaport big enough or expandable to handle the traffic you project. All right, by all those criteria it's Shanghai. Large port, with room for expansion if necessary, good communications by air and rail with the rest of China."

"Sam," said Joan Feuerbach, "are you proposing to build the Cube there? Shanghai?"

"Sure, why not?"

"Because it's built on alluvial soil. I was there with a trade commission in the nineties, and that whole area is a floodplain. For any structure like this you're going to need bedrock. But wait, it isn't a disaster. There's Nanjing. That's about two hundred miles away, and it's in the foothills of the Purple and Gold Mountains. So my suggestion would be, use Shanghai as your staging point for deliveries by sea and air, then truck them up to Nanjing."

"Doesn't Nanjing have an airport?" asked Conway Kettle.

"Sure, but it's smaller. You could route some of the flights directly there, take some of the load off Shanghai."

"Okay, that's good," said Cooper. "Now the next question is, which areas do you evacuate first? My thought is, take the outlying ones first, then the ones a little closer, and so on. So you're shortening your transportation lines as you go, and as soon as we clean out an area, those planes and ships, and railway cars in some instances, are released for use elsewhere."

"What about Third World problems? If we start there, won't they think we're trying to get rid of brown and black folks?"

"Not if we do the right kind of PR, but I see your point. Maybe it would be a good idea to start in the U.S., just to set an example."

"Maybe start with sister cities?"

"Yeah, Steve, that would be *great* PR. Big celebrations, live global holo, fireworks, entertainers—"

"The mayors will want to make speeches."

"Okay, but we can keep them under control. Go to another camera if we have to."

"One consideration we haven't talked about, what *classes* of people do we take first? Now, obviously, transportation people have to be last, but who goes first?"

"I'd say your nonproductive people. Undernourished people, unemployed people. Get them out of the way, then you don't have to feed them."

"You'd include all the starving people in the Third World?"

"Sure. Might give them a square meal first." (Laughter.)

"Wait a minute, I'm thinking of what Paul said before, about the brown and black folks? This could be the same kind of thing. If we start shoveling all the undesirables in there first, they're going to think it's just another scheme to get rid of them."

They thought about that a minute. "I agree with Al," said Charles Bok. "We don't want to raise any suspicions that we want to get those people out of the way because they're *in* the way."

"Well, they *are.*"

"Sure they are, and that's why we've got to pretend they aren't. How about this? We start off with famous people. Rock stars, ex-Presidents."

"In the sister cities."

"Right, and then we invite a lot of other big shots, just to drive the point home. Now here's the fun part. We make the underprivileged types suspect we're going to leave them behind, get it, and we generate a worldwide protest. Then a movement starts up, or if it doesn't, we start it, to give a fair shake to poor people. We could have a slogan, like 'Don't Let Them Leave You Behind!' And we waffle a little, then we bow to public pressure, and we set up a system where everybody gets the same chance, rich or poor, without regard to race, creed *or* color. Make it a lottery, and have drawings every Wednesday. We can rig the drawings a little, to make sure essential people get left till last, but otherwise more poor people will win because there are more poor people."

"Oh."

"We're doing them a favor, either way, but one way, it *looks* like a favor and they're suspicious. The other way, it's something they have to fight for."

"Perfect," said Kettle. "I have to hand it to you, Charlie, that's brilliant."

"Oh, well."

"Now about the essential people—"

"Transportation people. Doctors and nurses."

"Right, but the numbers of *those* people we need go down as the population gets smaller. The best thing would be to skew the lottery according to computer projections. Can we do that, Jim?"

"Sure, if we have the data."

"Okay, now about evacuating the U.S. first, I think we could *start* there, just to give a boost to the Third World, but then when we get the protests, then I think it would be smart to shift to South America, go ahead and clean that out, then southern Africa and so on, and the U.S. after that. And Canada, of course."

"Okay." Cooper looked at the holo map. "Then northern Africa, then Scandinavia and the British Isles, and so on down until we're cleaning out India and the Middle East."

"Should India be earlier? That's Third World."

"You may have a point there. Actually there's no reason we have to go strictly by the longest passenger-mile numbers. Just so we don't give anybody the idea we really *want* to clean out the poor people first. Why don't we wait until we see if India makes a stink?"

"Right, and then give in. But we ought to have all this in the master plan beforehand, so we can coordinate transport."

"Don't call it the master plan, though. Call it Contingency Plan C. Or better yet, give it a letter farther down the alphabet—Plan M."

"All right. Jim, are you listening?"

"All ears."

"Jim is working up a computer model and putting all these factors into it. What other factors, Jim?"

"Well, declining numbers of necessary personnel, that Bart mentioned. Then what about government officials, right down to the local level? There's a point where we need them, so we can't take them *all* during the big-shot phase, but then later on there isn't much for them to *do*. Then farmers, food processors, wholesalers—we need them at first, but then at a certain point we've got enough food in storage and there isn't time enough to raise another crop anyway, so we don't need them."

"The computer will draw curves for all these people?"

"Exactly. And then we can skew the lottery to make it fit the curves. The beauty part is, is we can fine-tune it as we go along."

"Beautiful."

"Okay, but I'm thinking about the transition period now, and I'm thinking about arson. You've got a country almost cleaned out, nothing but skeleton crews left. And you've got these mavericks out there. Some of them are nutsos, and either they've got weapons already or they can get them. They're starting fires, they're killing each other, and they may try to kill *us.*"

"What for?"

"Well, who knows what for? We don't want to wait till they do it and then hand them a questionnaire. What I'm saying is, when time starts running out, things may get really weird around here."

At the lunch break, Cooper, Kettle and Bok sat together. "Something that's been on my mind, that hasn't come up," said Bok, "is what kind of catastrophe are we looking at here?"

Kettle said, "I've thought about that too, and it seems to me there are three possibilities. One, a giant meteor strike, triggering volcanic activity. Two, a nuclear war. Three, the *aliens* are going to do it."

"Why would they?"

"Go figure. We can't rule it out."

"That's not very cheerful."

"We don't know what their motives are, we don't know their psychology, we don't know *anything* about them."

"Including what they're going to do with us after they get us in the box."

"Right. There we have four possibilities. One, they're really going to take us to another planet."

"You don't believe that?"

"Sure I do, but that's beside the point. Two, they just want to get us out of the way, maybe because our space effort of the eighties poses a threat to them."

"Why wouldn't they just bomb the planet, then?"

"I don't know. Three, they might have some use for us. Breeding stock, maybe. Maybe they want us for fertilizer."

"Come on."

"Four, maybe we're a collector's item. Maybe there are really big aliens out there, and we're going to wind up on a coffee table."

"Con, what have you been smoking?"

"Just a little cannabis."

"Suppose any of those four except the first one is a real possibility, then we'd be responsible for the death of the human race."

"Sure."

"But if number one is true, then we'd be guilty if we *didn't* go along with it."

"Right. And dead."

CHAPTER 25

Stone was at the Inter-Continental this time, in a suite decorated in Roman style: red walls and drapes, white leather furniture. The beds were swan boats. Late at night Lavalle woke up and saw that there was a square place in the middle of the room where the carpet had been cut away, and the floor beneath it too, apparently, because she could see some pieces of cardboard that had been put down there to fill the hole; but the cardboard was moving slowly, up and down, as if it were breathing, and when the pieces separated she could see darkness. And the bed was tipping toward it, but if she held on tight . . .

She woke up trembling, turned on the light and smoked a cigarette. After a while she took a pill and went back to sleep.

She woke up again late in the morning, and when she wandered into the living room he was there, dressed, watching something on the flatscreen. He turned off the sound and put his arm around her.

"You ever see this guy?" On the screen, a bearded man was holding a sheet of paper with Hebrew letters on it. He was speaking earnestly.

"No, who's he?"

"He's dead now, I guess; I found this in a catalog under 'secret messages.' See, he was a Hebrew scholar, and he found out that if you took every forty-ninth letter of the Torah—that's what the Jews call the Bible—the first five letters spell 'Torah.' "

"Every forty-ninth letter? Why?"

"Beats me. Anyway, I thought I'd try it on the magazine. Forty-nine didn't work, but here's what I got when I tried twelve. Computer, give me the Moon message."

The bearded man vanished. Letters appeared on the screen:

> dih PLOT oeodedhsdsiarlfhheit BEWRA fnrcprhwtfleteg estsveaaslcaahis I AM CAEGE YEA OOH sfavireaiueehee sgedgtaeruydfrcnftgf TIDY ik RED ralworo ISLE EH ioea thnwresn SEND nahtwluddenukfceohdeamsthhdrsn BOAT FROW rdeaen YAY ryddtaieodmborhmetaslnhonskai EH idodntedseliisd TAO CULT hmlisltsedn . . .

"What's that supposed to mean?" she asked.

"Well, maybe nothing, but it says 'plot,' okay, and then 'bewra,' that might be 'beware.' Then the next part, that could be 'I am caged.' It sounds like he's asking for help. 'Send boat, frow.' *Frau* is German for wife, right?"

"Right. Back up a little. Who are you talking about when you say 'he'?"

"The author, Charles W. Diffin. He was up there in a

spaceship, like me, and he used this code to get his message out."

"Wait a minute. He's up there in the spaceship, and he writes this story and sends it to a magazine? How could he do that?"

"I don't have any idea. One thing that's suspicious, though, the last story he had in a magazine was in nineteen thirty-five. After that, nobody seems to know what happened to him."

After a moment she said, "What's all that tao business?"

"I don't know. Some kind of conspiracy? One of the other runs, I used eleven letters, and I got something that could have been 'sect Egypt.' And it said 'lemonhead,' too. You think that could be just coincidence? And look here." He picked up the *Astounding Stories* from the end table, opened it and pointed to a page. 'June twentieth, nineteen seventy-three.' That's when the tidal wave comes in and floods the land he's just bought. Why that date? It isn't important to the story. That has to mean something."

"That was thirty years ago."

"Right, so it has to be code. I was thinking, ought six, twenty, seventy-three—if you rearranged the numbers, you'd get seven, six, twenty ought three. July sixth next year."

"You're making all this up."

"No, I'm not. One reason I think there has to be a code, he wrote it in plain English right here—'Harkness did not at once grasp the meaning of the thing.' Harkness, that's me. He's telling me there's a hidden message."

"How is that you?"

"I'm the hero. See, and you're Diane Vernier. Well, she has another name, but they're both French, and she's Harkness's sweetheart. And Frank is Harkness's best friend, Chet Bullard, he's the pilot. But I haven't figured out who Schwartzmann is."

She said, "You know what I think?"

"Sure, you think I'm crazy. And I am, but that doesn't mean I have to be *wrong.*"

Later that day Stone was channel-hopping and got a skin sim: Marilyn Monroe and Clark Gable jerking and throbbing together on rumpled sheets, while Shirley Temple watched from a doorway with one finger in her mouth, and Groucho Marx, standing behind her, bent to slide his hand into her panties. Gable's shlong, in close-up like a giant bratwurst, slowly penetrated Monroe's hairy berliner. Stone winced and turned it off.

"You don't like that?"

"No, it makes me sick. I've seen these places on Broadway where you watch stuff like that and put your weenie in a machine. I think that's disgusting. My idea of something sexy is Ginger Rogers dancing in front of a window with a skirt you can see her legs through."

"Is she your ideal woman?"

"Oh, yeah. Well, I like Myrna Loy, too, and Carole Lombard. They don't have actresses like that anymore, or actors either. The new stuff knocks your eye out, you can see anybody doing anything, it's color and three-D, but where's the acting?"

"Listen, I thought your idea of something sexy was me."

"What, are you jealous of *Ginger Rogers?*" He grinned. "I never knew a dame like you."

"A dame, huh?"

"Well, what do you want me to call you, a girl?"

"I'm not a girl, I'm a woman. Another thing, I heard you refer to the night clerk as a Negro. They're African Americans now."

"They are?"

"Well, why not? We have German Americans, Japanese Americans."

"I never heard of those. Listen, where did all these Japs come from? I thought we beat them in the war, the krauts too."

"We did, and then we helped them get back on their feet. Don't call them Japs and krauts."

"Jeest. All right. They're Japanese, right, and the krauts are Germans."

"Now you're getting it."

"Okay, what about the sheenies? Are they Hebrew Americans?"

"No, they're Jews, but don't call them sheenies or kikes."

"Honestly, what's the difference?"

"You use words like that, you're going to make somebody feel humiliated. That's what they're for. You're a kraut yourself, aren't you?"

"What makes you think so?"

"Just a hunch. What was your grandfather's name?"

"Stein. Maybe I'm a Jew, come to think of it."

"Does it make any difference?"

"Not to me. See, you're right, this is one way things are *better* now—not so much trouble between the races, more mixing. I'm for it, but then all this other stuff, the atom bombs, the pollution—it looks to me like we're heading for another world war, like we didn't learn anything from the last two, or else some kind of catastrophe, and we just have to sit here and watch it happen."

"In a hundred years it won't matter."

"We haven't got a hundred years. Sometimes I think people are too dumb to live."

In the silence, the computer cleared its throat and said, *"Call from the desk."*

Stone said, "Okay, put it through."

The face of a deskperson appeared in the tube. "A Dr. Wellafield is here to see Mr. Stone, and there are some reporters in the lobby."

"Oh, hell. No reporters, but send Dr. Wellafield up."

"Yes, sir." The image in the tube dwindled to a multicolored marble and vanished.

"Who's this now?" she asked.

"He's the head doc at the place they put me in Trenton that time. I sent him a fax from Washington, but I didn't think he'd come."

"You want me to disappear?"

"No, I want you to meet him, he's a great guy."

The doorbell chimed; the tube lit up with the plump face of a man with a gray mustache. "Open," Stone said.

The man who entered was portly and not very tall, dressed in a red coat and a plaid sports jacket that bulged at his chest. "Doc!" said Stone, advancing to meet him. "Hey, it's great to see you—come on in. This is Linda Lavalle. I told her all about you."

"Nothing too bad, I hope," said Wellafield roguishly. They shook hands. "Well, Ed, how have you been?"

"Just great, Doc. Sit down, take off your coat, make yourself at home. You want some coffee?"

"That would be fine."

They sat at the table under the window; Wellafield removed his coat and jacket and draped them over a chair. Clipped to his shirt pocket was an impressive-looking device in a matte black case; a flesh-colored wire ran from it and disappeared somewhere at the back of his head.

"Hey, what've you got there?" Stone asked.

"The latest thing, Ed. We've had great success with patients, and I'm trying it out myself, as you see."

"What does it do?"

"It detects aberrant thought patterns and delivers a mild shock to the brain. I use it because I keep thinking about killing my wife— Woops. *Unh!*" His face contorted briefly, then cleared.

Stone got a cup, poured coffee from the carafe. "Cream, sugar?"

"Yes, please."

"And it really helps?" Lavalle asked.

"Oh, yes, definitely. It wakes me up at night, though. Now, Ed—" He cleared his throat. "I've been following your career in the newspapers and TV, of course, and I was wondering if there's a place for me on your staff. I have some administrative skills, you know."

"What about the hospital?"

"I'm thinking about taking an early retirement, and perhaps a trial separation. My wife doesn't— *Unh!* Of course, if you don't think it would work out—"

"No, hey, Doc, I was just thinking, they probably don't want me to tell them what to do in Washington, but suppose you could travel with me and be my doctor?"

"Your personal physician, Ed? Why, that would be fine."

"Hey, excuse me for asking, but you're a real doctor, aren't you?"

"Oh, yes, yes."

"He means an M.D.," said Lavalle.

"Yes, I know." Wellafield beamed at them both. "I am a real doctor, Ed. I went into mental disorders years ago, of course, but I've still got my little black bag put away somewhere, and, ah, I can brush up, of course."

"Well, swell. Do you think you could move to New York sometime soon? Have you got a passport?"

"I certainly can. And I'll get a passport." He took Stone's hand in both of his. His eyes were moist. "I knew you wouldn't let me down. Well, I'd better go now and leave you two to get on with—uh, whatever. Are you going to be in town Monday?"

"No, I have to go back to Washington, and then Wednesday I'm flying to Europe."

"Well, you'll know where to reach me." He stood up and

put on his jacket and coat. "It was nice to meet you, Ms. Lavalle."

"You too."

After he was gone, Stone said, "You like him?"

"Yes, I think he's sweet. But I'm glad you got rid of him."

CHAPTER 26

In the well-lighted conference room in Washington, Robert Morganstar was saying, "Here's our concept for the body carriers. Now in working with the Cube design group, they say all the carriers have to be a standard size and shape, and the Social Planning group wants flat sides and square corners, in order to maximize interior space, but they also asked us if we could come up with something that looks streamlined. Okay, we start with the basic shape, just a box." An image came up in the holo.

"Looks like a coffin."

"Yes, that's the problem. But now we put some spin on it." The image slowly shifted, acquired colors and contours rather like racing stripes on a car. The corners appeared to recede, the top looked curved. There were gasps of admiration.

"And, of course, we can do anything we want with colors, according to local tastes. Here's our silver-white, we think that'll be very popular in the U.S. and most of Europe. But white is the color of mourning in China, so here we have our Chinese red, for good luck and prosperity. Here's your basic Shiite black, and here's the New Age psychedelic model."

"I think that's superb, Robert."

"And, you know, if these designs turn out to be too expensive or take too long to manufacture, we can put people in the expensive ones and then transfer them to the basic model, and recycle the other ones."

"You're calling these body carriers?"

"Just an engineering term. We've got a team working on other phrases for PR."

"How about 'space capsules'?"

"That's on their list, I think, for advanced countries. But the Psychology group says a lot of people are scared of anything to do with space, and they're pushing 'life capsules,' which sounds too much like medicine to me, but it's not my field."

"Call from Mr. Rong," said the computer on Mrs. Rooney's desk. *"He says he's a friend of Ed Stone."*

"Oh! put him on."

The blurry image of a young black man appeared in the tube. "You ain't Mr. Moore," he said.

"I'm his secretary, Mrs. Rooney. How may I help you?"

"Well, see, I'm a friend of Ed Stone, and he forgot to give me his address, like, when he moved. So I thought, see, you guys must know where he's at. I know he's been looking for me, and I got something for him."

"We can't give out addresses, Mr. Wrong, but I could forward a letter to him."

"No, see, that would take too long, because this stuff I got for him, it won't keep, do you understand?"

"Yes, I do, Mr. Wrong. Let me suggest something. Tell me where you can be reached, and I'll try to get Mr. Stone to call you."

"Okay, tell him to leave a message at Tony's, okay? He knows where it's at."

"Tony's. All right, Mr. Wrong."

"Thanks a bundle." The image dwindled and disappeared.

She said, "Flossie, who was that senator who appeared on the holo news last week with Ed Stone?"

Images flickered in the holo, settled down to the image of a silver-haired politician with the legend "SENATOR GIVENS" at the bottom.

"Yes, that's the one. Call his office in Washington. I'll talk to anyone."

The computer simage disappeared and was replaced by a flashing sign, "CALLING." Then a new simage, a pale young brunette with a noble brow. "Senator Givens's office, may I help you?"

Mrs. Rooney said, "This is the office of Yallow and Moore in New York. We have an urgent message for Ed Stone. Will you have him call me, please? Ask for Mrs. Rooney."

An hour later, almost at quitting time, the computer said, *"Call from Ed Stone."*

"Put him on!"

Stone's face appeared in the tube. "Hi, Mrs. Rooney, how are you?"

"Oh, Mr. Stone, how nice. You know, I didn't like to disturb you, but I couldn't help wondering, *don't* you need a secretary? Because, if you do—"

"Gee, Mrs. Rooney, I guess I do, because the phone calls and letters are driving me crazy. I got a bag of mail in my room right now, it would take me a year to answer all those letters."

"Well, I can give two weeks' notice here, or perhaps a little less—I'll work it out. Where are you staying now?"

"I'm at the Ambassador in Washington, but I'm coming back to New York tomorrow, and I'll be at the Park Avenue. Give me a call there, okay?"

"I certainly will. Oh, and by the way, you had a call from a Mr. Wrong. He wants you to leave a message at Tony's."

"He does? Okay, thanks, Mrs. Rooney."

"Mr. Prime Minister," said the aide, "allow me to present Mr. Ed Stone." He bowed and stood aside.

The Prime Minister of Ghana said abruptly, "You have previously talked to my enemy, General Mbele. I agreed to see you only because my son-in-law interceded. You may speak, but I do not promise to listen."

"Mr. Prime Minister, I had to talk to General Mbele first so that I could get him to agree to stop his bombing of your country, and then—"

"He agreed to stop? He will not keep his agreement."

"Yeah, Mr. Prime Minister, he wants to meet you and have a peace conference, but he knows you're mad at him, so he made me promise to tell you myself."

"Well, this puts a different face on it." The Prime Minister advanced around his desk. "Allow me to shake your hand. Please sit down. You say Mbele wants to meet me? I may consent. I am pleased with you, Mr. Stone. I may give you a decoration. Mr. Sukulu, what decorations do we have?"

"The Order of the Mighty Lion, Mr. Prime Minister, and the Order of the Resentful Hyena. Then there is—"

"Stop. I think the Lion, don't you, Mr. Stone? We will have the ceremony after the peace conference. Mr. Sukulu! Notify General Mbele that we will meet him on the border, say at Porto Novo, on Monday next at nine o'clock in the morning."

"Yes, sir."

"And now, Mr. Stone, you must tell me all about the aliens, and about putting everyone in a box."

"Yes, sir. Well, they say the Earth is going to be destroyed eleven years from now, and that's why we have to do it. And that's another real good reason to stop the war, because people who get killed can't get in the box."

"Quite true, Mr. Stone. I like the way you put it. If they are killed, they cannot go in the box. And if they go in the box, they cannot be killed, you see." He laughed heartily. "I have made a little joke. I see that we shall get along famously, Mr. Stone. Now we must have some gin."

CHAPTER 27

When he told her he was at the Park Avenue this time, she said, "You're coming down in the world, aren't you?"

"No, wait till you see."

"What do you mean?"

"It's a surprise."

She walked up to the desk that evening and gave her name. The desk clerk looked at her with instant respect and called a uniformed guard, who escorted her to the elevator.

"Listen, just tell me the room number; I can find it myself," she said.

"No, ma'am, this one is hard to find."

They got off at the fiftieth floor; he led her down the corridor, through a door marked PRIVATE, to an unmarked elevator. There were two overstuffed chairs in the elevator, with a little table between them. On the table were a cigarette box and lighter, both in rose quartz, a travertine ashtray, and a cut-crystal dish containing pink and white mints. "Up," said the guard, holding the door. He smiled and stepped out; the door closed. The elevator went up.

When the door opened, a young black man in plastic denims was standing there. "Hi! You must be Linda," he said.

"Yes, I am. Who are you?"

"I'm Rong." He put out his hand. "Come on in, we're waiting for you."

"You are, huh?" She let him lead her into a vast living room with exposed timbers in the ceiling. Three or four people were standing in front of the fireplace; half a dozen more were scattered around the room, drinking and smoking. There were a great many roses, lilies, and chrysanthemums in vases.

Doc Wellafield came toward her. "Linda!" he said, and gave her his cushiony hand. "Ed was here just a minute ago—"

"He went to the can," said Rong helpfully.

"While we're waiting for him, let me introduce you to, uh—" He turned. "Uh, Florence?" An attractive woman in her fifties came forward, smiling. Others were drifting toward them across the room. "Linda, this is Florence Rooney. Florence, Linda Lavalle."

"We've heard so much about you," said Rooney.

"Florence is Ed's social secretary," said Wellafield. "And this is Jeff Carruthers—" A smiling beanpole of a man with an oiled forelock, teeth probably false. "Jeff is one of the consultants from Washington."

Stone was hurrying toward her across the room. As soon as he let her go, she said, "What *is* this, a penthouse?"

"It's *the* penthouse, it covers the whole roof. Did you meet everybody? Never mind, I'll introduce you later. Come on and take a look." He took her hand and led her to the French windows that opened on a landscaped garden. They stepped out; the air was fresh and pure.

"This is incredible," she said. "But who are all these people?"

"Rong—you meet him? He's a guy I met on the street when I first got here. He turned up and I gave him a job, and Florence, she was that architect's secretary? She wanted to work for me too. And the rest of them, they're some of the people who're working on the Cube Project in Washington. They just came down for the weekend. Well, what do you think?"

A few yards away there was a weeping willow with a circular white seat around its trunk. Ducks were swimming in the pond behind it; beyond that, she glimpsed a bright green lawn and a little flag.

"What is that, a golf course?"

"Just a putting green, but there's a swimming pool and a sauna and all that stuff. They bought it for me."

"They *bought* it for you? The whole thing?"

"Sure."

"I thought the idea was to keep moving around from one hotel to another."

"Right, but they thought this was better because it's easier to control the traffic, with that private elevator. Listen, some of these people are probably going to want to eat here, but we don't have to. Would you rather go out?"

"Oh, no, here is fine. Can we eat in the garden?"

"Sure. Come on, I'll find you a menu."

* * *

Waiters set up tables in the garden under strings of Japanese lanterns. Lavalle found herself seated beside Jeff Carruthers and opposite another planner named Walter Scavo. Carruthers was saying, "Let's take, for instance, the Watusi in Africa. They're herdspersons, their whole life is cattle. Their *wealth* is cattle. How are we going to persuade them to get in those boxes and leave their cattle behind? They're very tall, by the way."

"We may have to do special boxes for them," Scavo said. "About leaving the cattle, okay, we tell them there's going to be cattle on the new planet. Bigger and better cattle. And everybody gets twice as many cattle as they had before. I mean, we can't put *cattle* in those boxes, let's not get ridiculous."

"What about pets, though?" Lavalle asked.

"Okay. You got a dog or a cat, or maybe a parakeet, if there's room for it you take it along. Maybe you have to make some tough decisions, but that's life."

"Speaking of pets, I see another problem," Carruthers said. "We're going to have packs of dogs roaming around, and we're going to have lots of abandoned farm animals that can't take care of themselves."

"Maybe the dogs will take care of them. Just a little joke. Seriously though, we're going, and we can't take every cow, pig and chicken with us. What happens after we leave—well, the Earth is going to be destroyed anyway, so who cares?"

Carruthers put down his fork. "We'd better take a lot of pictures. Of the way it was."

After dinner Stone murmured, "Let's get out of here." He led her to a door at the far end of the room and ushered her into a living room only a little smaller than the other. "This is a little private apartment. Nobody comes in here unless I say so."

"How many of those people have you got living here?"

"Well, Doc does, and Rong, and Florence, of course. She's got things organized to where I don't have to worry anymore, I just look at the schedule and do what it says."

"And you're paying their rent, and their food too?"

"Plenty of money, Linda. Listen, there's something else I wanted to show you." He led her out the French windows, along a fence concealed by shrubbery, on the other side of which they could hear the guests' cheerful shouts and laughter. He showed her a break in the eucalyptus hedge where they could get through a plastic flap into the stink and heat, and stand at the parapet to look out over the lights of the city sparkling through the haze. The reflected lights in the dome above were like molten stars.

"This is beautiful," she said.

"Yeah, I guess so. What're all these gold pyramids? I never saw them before."

"They're very popular; they started going up on the tops of buildings twenty years ago. Do you know you can buy your own golden pyramid now, and a mummy case to be buried in?"

"You're kidding. How much does that cost?"

"About a hundred thousand for the cheapie model."

"Jesus." He stared out into the violet-brown fog. After a moment he said, "A hundred thousand bucks to be buried in a mummy case, and kids starving because they haven't got a dime. Satellites in space, and computers that talk to you. Something went wrong, I could tell that as soon as I got here. If you have all these gadgets, and people are still starving, then you're just showing them more great things they can't have."

"Well, what else is new?"

"And another thing, I notice people are still talking about progress and growth, as if it was the same thing. We never should of got to six billion people in the world. In the thirties, two billion, we could handle that. We should of stopped there, and we could of, or anyway close to it. But we didn't, and now they're talking about *ten* billion, or *twenty.* You talk about selling people on bizarre ideas, how about that one?"

"It's a better world, in some ways. Anyway, it doesn't matter now, does it?"

"I guess not. Listen, there's something else I wanted to talk about. I haven't asked you to marry me—"

"Well, hey, I haven't asked *you,* either."

"No, but what I wanted to say, I want to, but I can't. Not until this is over."

"Well, that means never, doesn't it?"

"I don't know. Maybe not, but anyway, not for the next eleven years."

"Okay."

Later she asked, "Why are you wearing that thing on your finger?"

He looked at it. "It's just a little bubble bandage, to cover the ring."

"You used to just turn it around when we had sex."

"Yeah, but—"

"You don't want me touching it."

"That's right, because, you remember I told you, I thought it would wear off?"

"And you want it to?"

He squirmed a little. "I don't *want* it to, but if I'd of kept touching you with the ring, how would you ever know? It isn't fair to you. You could of been married to Julian by now."

"Forget it."

After a moment she said, "Suppose it does wear off. I could do you a lot of harm if I turned against you."

"Like what?"

"Remember when you told me about Ginger Rogers dancing in front of a window with a see-through skirt?"

"Yeah."

"Well, that film wasn't made until nineteen thirty-five."

He looked at her steadily. "And you thought I didn't know that? What are you telling me, you think I'm a phony?"

"I don't know what to think. Let's get up and have a sandwich."

CHAPTER 28

In the morning she found him hunched over the *Astounding* cover, measuring it with a protractor. She got a cup of coffee and wandered over to look. "See this?" he said, pointing to the three human figures at the bottom. "See how funny the two guys look? That's because all four of their legs are bent at the same angle, about a hundred twenty degrees. It makes them look like mechanical dolls or something."

"And their legs are too long. Maybe he used lay figures."

"What's that?"

"Jointed wooden figures. You can buy them in art stores."

"Oh. But then their legs wouldn't be too long, would they?"

"Maybe he just couldn't draw."

"No. Now look at this, it isn't quite as obvious, but the girl sitting on the ground, *her* legs are bent at the same angle, a hundred twenty degrees, and if you figure in perspective, so are the monster's legs. So it's a number, a code. What does it mean?"

"Well, it adds up to three. Threes are a lot like fives, they're restless, inventive, charming and so on."

"But not the same?"

"No."

"Or it could be days, couldn't it? There are three hundred sixty degrees in a circle, and three hundred sixty-five days in a year."

"I know, but what makes you think it has to be a code?"

"Just a hunch. Something else it could mean, these human beings look like puppets, and they *are* puppets, and so are the monsters. I don't like that."

He stared at the picture. "Here's another funny thing. Look at the door of the spaceship. You'd think it would be circular, but it's oval, and it looks like the opening is facing you, even though the cylinder is laying at an angle. Then the curve of the front end hits the line of the top here and stops, as if there was only half a cylinder there."

"The artist couldn't draw."

"Yes, he *could.* He drew great machinery, and monsters and landscapes. Suppose he wanted to say something like, 'This isn't a spaceship, just a mockup'? Like a movie set, where the houses look real but there's nothing behind them? And look at the monster. It isn't really a spider, there aren't any segments, just a big squishy body like a caterpillar. It has a nose like a bull, and the feet look like rat feet."

"A chimera."

"What's that?"

"A fabulous beast made by putting parts of different animals together. Like a gryphon—it has the wings and head of an eagle, the body and tail of a lion."

"Okay, but that's mythology, right? This guy was illustrating science fiction. So maybe he's saying, 'Forget it, these stories aren't real, there aren't any spaceships and there aren't any monsters in space. But the readers *knew* that. Why bother to tell them? Unless it wasn't true?"

"Are you saying this artist knew something in nineteen thirty-one that we're just finding out now?"

"They all did. Why not? How do we know how long the aliens have been here?"

"Ed, if they kidnapped those people before they did you, why would they ask you those questions about the magazine?"

He scratched his nose. "I never thought of that. Well, I guess they already knew what *Diffin* thought of those magazines—he was an author. They wanted to find out what *I* thought about them, because I'm just an ordinary guy."

"The hell you are, but never mind."

CHAPTER 29

"Doc, we've got to get Ed some help."

"You mean for his mental disorder?"

"*You* mean he's crazy. Sure he is, and it's tearing him up. He thinks he has to help these aliens because he loves them, and he thinks they're monsters who want to eat us."

"Well, suppose he's right?"

"I think he is right, but that's not what I'm talking about.

He's going to end up in a rubber room unless we do something."

"Linda, you can't reason with a delusional disordered person, believe me. They can always find some way to prove they're right. Sometimes they're so plausible that they even convince their psychiatrist."

"So you won't try to help him?"

"Well, I didn't say that. I can *try.*"

"Ed, Linda here thought I ought to talk to you about—well, as you know, there are some of your aberrant beliefs that you're committed to, and I understand that, and I certainly won't ask you to give them up. *But,* you've developed some others that seem to be causing you distress. I'm referring to the secret messages in your old magazines."

"She told you about that, huh?"

"Well, she's concerned about you, Ed. We all are. Now, you can take it from me that these kinds of beliefs are typical of what we used to call classical paranoia."

"Okay, Doc, I get you, but what if there really are secret messages in the magazines?"

Wellafield looked at Lavalle and shrugged, as if to say *What did I tell you?* He said to Stone, "That seems pretty unlikely, Ed."

"Let me show you something." Stone got up and went to the cabinet, came back with four magazines and spread them on the table. "I was in a place called Futures Past off Broadway, they have hundreds of old pulp magazines. I asked the guy if he had any nineteen-thirties *Astoundings,* and he went in back and came out with these. You wouldn't believe what they cost."

He handed one of the magazines to Wellafield. The cover said, "BROOD OF THE DARK MOON, by Charles W. Diffin."

Stone said, "It's a sequel to 'Dark Moon.' Or really it's all one novel, I think, but it was too long, so the magazine chopped off the first part and ran it as a separate story. The serial started in August, just three months after the first story. Right away, he gives you a date—August ten, nineteen seventy-three, and then another one, August fifteen. That's like eight ten and eight fifteen, okay? So either way the first two numbers are eight and one. So I took every eighty-first letter."

"You did?"

"Sure. And the first three letters are *h-y-d,* hid, just like the other one. Computer, let me see the Brood message."

Letters appeared on the screen:

> hyd STVN 3rfcscedgidopca SAY I lueheowossnsio BE ireg THE astnsa NUT gahstocstreaeoseaa TOM tcmuesld MAE erfkesntnhnalii DEE uuw MEG euoo NATE itfroiciennb ahuturienontnfyawtenldomrttnfadancmisi aegftrteigqoato ovoepnsuowhlt RON tarhfyhrmm STAN tecietiemncoazh huatysgectsreeishf . . .

"What's that S-T-V-N supposed to be?" Lavalle asked.

"I think it's Steven—it's a message to his friends. Steven, Tom, Mae, Dee, Meg, Nate, Ron and Stan. And it says, 'Say I be the nut.' He thinks they're going to try to put him away in a crazy house, like they did me. No offense, Doc."

"No, no, of course not." Wellafield leaned forward to peer at the screen. "Did the computer really do this by taking every—what was it?"

"Every eighty-first letter. Sure it did."

"And you arrived at that by using a date in the story?"

"Right."

"Now, in the other one, the first one, what number of letters did you use?"

"Twelve. You want to see it? Computer, give me the Moon message."

dih PLOT oeodedhsdsiarlfhheit BEWRA . . .

"You see there, the first three letters are 'hid' backwards. And the word 'message' comes up *seven times* in the story. He was telling you as plain as he could that there was a message there if you knew how to look for it."

"By 'he' you mean—"

"The author, Charles W. Diffin. He was up there, in the spaceship, like me. See where the message says, 'Send boat, frow.' "

"I don't quite—"

"German *frau.* His wife. He thought she could send up some kind of space boat to rescue him."

"Why would he think that?" Lavalle asked. "There weren't any spaceships then."

"None that we *know* about, anyway."

"This is getting away from the point," said Wellafield. "Ed, you say you got the number eighty-one from a date in the story. How did you get the number twelve?"

"I was just trying numbers until I got one that worked."

"All right, now don't you see, if you try enough numbers, you're going to find something that looks like a message in *anything.* That's my point. You didn't find the number twelve in the story, did you? You picked that number at random."

"Yeah, right, but there *is* a date on the third page of the story. June twentieth, nineteen seventy-three, that's when he signs the land deal with Schwartzmann. If you take the two in twenty and the one in nineteen, there's your twelve backwards. Like the 'hid' in the first three letters."

"I give up," Wellafield said.

Later, when Stone had left the room, he looked at Lavalle. "What if he's right?"

CHAPTER 30

Ben Abrams was in his late fifties, a tubby man with a fringe of black hair around his brown dome. He was a successful corporate lawyer, a senior member of the Washington firm of Lowell, Singler and Cartwright, which enjoyed the patronage of Senator Givens as well as a good many lesser lights.

Givens had introduced him to Ed Stone during the congressional hearings, and Abrams, who liked the young man, had formed the habit of visiting him when he was in town. One afternoon they had been talking for a while in Stone's hotel room when Abrams looked at his watch and said, "Well, I've got to be heading back to Arlington—unless you're free for dinner?"

"I won't be here tonight—I promised to be at a meeting of the Friends in New York."

"The Friends of Ed Stone? Are they the ones who wear suits like yours?"

He looked embarrassed. "Yeah, that was Rong's idea, but I wish they wouldn't."

"Why don't you tell them not to?"

"Well, they're my *friends.*"

"Nonsense. Say the word, and I'll put a stop to it."

"Well—could you do it without hurting their feelings?"

"I think so, and if I do they'll get over it."

"That reminds me, Rong says they want to form a company and call it Ed Stone Enterprises."

"Absolutely not, unless you get a major cut of it."

"A cut of what?"

"Well, what is the company going to do?"

"I don't know, sell souvenirs, I guess."

"Have they offered you a percentage?"

"Yeah, they said something about it. See, I don't like to turn them down, but I don't care about the money. In fact, I'd rather not make any, because then people might think I'm just in this for the money."

"And you're not?"

"No."

"All right, now, Ed, my advice would be to form a corporation right away, and trademark your name. And then if you want to convey or license some of those rights to another corporation, that's up to you. But you should establish the commercial value of your name, so that if anybody uses it without your permission, you can go to court and stop them, do you see what I mean?"

"Yeah, I guess so, but it seems funny."

"Well, the law is pretty funny. Now as far as the money, you can donate it to charity or to another corporation dedicated to promoting the Cube Project, or something of that kind. But my advice would be to set it up in such a way that you can accumulate a reserve for legal expenses, because you are going to run into these infringement situations."

"I am?"

"No doubt about it."

"Well, could you go ahead and do that for me?"

"Certainly, Ed. I could. I will."

* * *

It was one of those times when she had remembered again how to fly, and it was marvelously easy—you just leaned forward out of a window or anywhere, and spread your arms, and soared up into the twilight wind. Past the blowing treetops now, past the dark shapes of birds, or perhaps not birds, but—Now the tall buildings were ahead, and she turned, but the buildings were everywhere. And she was caught by the currents between the buildings that crowded closer and closer until . . .

. . . in an exploding ball of fire, and she came upright screaming. Stone came in and grabbed her by the shoulders. "What the hell is the matter?"

"Just a dream. Hold me, please."

CHAPTER 31

The Cube Team was having its regular Monday morning session.

"How are we coming on the Cube concept, Kevin?"

"Pretty well. Putting the structure up is fairly straightforward, but loading fast enough is a real bitch. Our rough projections show if we're going to make the deadline, figuring a target date of twenty oh five for start of construction, we've got to load approximately two million a day while construction is going on. Now to do that, we've either got to build a scaffold a mile high, or load with helicopters, or else build the Cube into the side of a mountain. Our feeling now is the mountain is the way to go. We sink a mile-wide shaft into the mountainside, and build roads up to the top, and a conveyor system that transports the loads at high speed to the level you're working on. Every time you fill a level, the conveyor system can be shortened, and the loading gets faster instead of slower."

"I think that makes sense. Now, what about the suspended animation gadgets, George?"

"According to Ed, the aliens are supposed to furnish those, but I don't know if they're thinking of just enough to put people into S.A. at the site, or if we're going to have enough to use them worldwide, or what, and I don't see how we can plan our system until we *do* know. Now there's a group in Japan that's developed an S.A. system of their own, and if that checks out, I think we ought to use it and not wait for the aliens. Because transport will be a lot easier if we can put people into boxes at the source and ship them that way."

"You say if it checks out?"

"Well, so far they haven't been able to get their experimental animals *out* of S.A. They've got some gerbils that have been laying there looking good as new for six months, but unless you revive them how can you tell? So I'm not sure, but it seems to me if the aliens have a system like this, *they* must know how to turn it off, and it may be we're going to have to go that way just because we don't have enough time."

Sunday morning he called her from Istanbul. "Hey, did you see the news? There was a flash flood in Afghanistan, killed three hundred people."

"So?"

"So don't you remember, about the story in the magazine? That was the date I told you about, July six, the tidal wave."

"But this wasn't a tidal wave, was it?"

"Spoilsport," he said, and hung up.

The Cube Team was meeting again.

"What about people that have got heirlooms, old jewelry, paintings that can't be replaced? Are they going to have to leave all that behind?"

"And national treasures. Okay, there's room in those boxes for more than just the body, especially if it's a young child. The fact that we're standardizing the boxes means that in the case of small people, and children, there's going to be a lot of extra space. Why not let them fill that space with favorite possessions, anything they can't bear to leave behind? We'd have a hard time talking them out of it, anyway. They can take money if they want to, or jewels, bullion, whatever valuables they have."

"Some of them might want to take food, to make sure they have something to eat when they get there."

"Just as a digression, what are we going to eat when we get to the other planet?"

"I don't know."

"Well, some people might want to take seeds. That would be a good idea, and they don't need much space."

"And books, or at least cubes. Cube players, holos. Musical instruments."

"Musical instruments take up a lot of space. Pianos, for instance."

"Okay, then *plans* for musical instruments. And all kinds of other things. Tools."

"That makes sense to me. They can stuff in whatever the box will hold, and that will add to the weight but not the cubic. People with a lot of kids will have an advantage, and if they're poor people, hey, they can sell space to rich people."

That winter there were ice storms from Boston to Norfolk, flooding in Bangladesh, a new volcano in Iceland and another one in Hawaii. Stone was home again in late March, and they had three days together.

One afternoon they were alone in the living room, idly watching the holonews and playing Scrabble. ". . . reports of a huge flapping black thing in the sky," the talking head was saying. "And in Cleveland, a bizarre rain of cats fell in an outlying district this morning. Scientists say that rains of frogs and fish have been recorded before, but this is a first for cats. In Algiers . . ."

That reminded her of something, and she asked him, "Could you draw me a picture of an alien?"

"I don't know. I'm no artist."

"Try it, anyway."

Stone found a piece of paper and a scriber, painstakingly drew something that looked like a child's picture, with a round head, oval body, and six sausages for arms.

"That isn't very good. Let's try the computer." She sat down in front of the terminal, asked for a menu and selected CAD. "You can draw on those things, too?" he said, looking over her shoulder.

"Sure." She put together some spheres and ovoids to make a yellow head, body, arms. "Let's work on the head first. Eyes? Are there two?"

"Yeah."

She added the eyes. "Are these the right shape?"

"No, rounder than that. And bigger."

She made the changes. "This where they go?"

"No, lower. And the forehead should be more like bulgier."

They worked on the face until Stone was satisfied. The last step was the spines, that made the face look like a sea creature's. Then they did the body, the arms, fingers. "Hey, that's pretty good," Stone said.

She stared at the image broodingly. "Is this the right color?"

"I don't know, the light was funny. Maybe a little browner."

She made the adjustment, saved the image. She printed out a copy, folded it up and put it in her bag.

"What did you want that for?" he asked.

"I don't know. Something to look at."

"How did it make you feel?"

"Scared. And something else, I don't know what."

"Bad news about the suspended animation gadgets. I sent Tom over there to take a look, and he says not only they can't get their gerbils out of S.A., but they can't *move* them."

"They can't move them? How come?"

"I don't understand it myself. They say their apparatus generates a cryonic field of over a billion hertz, okay, and what it does, apparently it rotates the object in the field through an infinite series of parallel universes. So, every picosecond, instead of the gerbil you started with, you've got *another* gerbil that's right where it was on that worldline when you turned the current on. So you can't move it, because even if you could do it in a picosecond, the next picosecond it would be right back where it started. They took the apparatus away, and the gerbil just hung there in the middle of the air. They gave Tom a hammer and asked him to hit the gerbil. He said it almost broke his wrists. Didn't even muss the gerbil's hair."

"Can't they just turn the current off?"

"Sure, they can cut the circuit, but don't you see, the

gerbil you're getting every picosecond is the same one that was in the field *before* you turned it off. They—"

"Wait a minute. Just wait a minute. You turn off the current and the thing still works? That doesn't make sense."

"I know, but that's what they told me. You turn off the current, the machine stops working, okay, but that gerbil was in the field when the machine *was* working, and you can't go back and change that. So you just keep on getting more gerbils."

"Forever?"

"Yeah, I guess so. I mean, if you've got an infinite number of gerbils, you just don't run out. Anyway, I was starting to say, they gave Tom another demonstration—they put a laser on the gerbil to measure its height above the floor, and then they brought in a goddamn *anvil* and hung it from the gerbil's *ear*. Gerbil didn't move. So, partly this is good news and partly it's bad news. The good news is, is if we go with this system we won't need any structural supports in the Cube, because there won't be any gravity load. The bad news is, is we can't zap people into S.A. and then move them in container ships, we've got to ship them live, and not only that, we can't zap them until they're in place in the Cube. So that's a whole new system, and we've got to redesign everything from scratch."

"Who's going to get the bid for the construction?"

"Farbenwerke, probably."

"Do they know about this?"

"Yeah, and they're not happy."

"You didn't mention another thing. If you can't move the people in the Cube, how are the aliens going to pick it up?"

"That's their problem. We've got to assume they can do things we can't do, right? If they want us to do this some other way, they can come and tell us about it."

* * *

Sunday just before dinnertime, Lavalle and Wellafield found themselves alone in the living room. Lavalle was drinking a Gibson; Wellafield had a ginger ale. She said, "Doc, I've been having some funny feelings lately. I just wondered—"

"What kind of feelings, Linda?" He leaned forward and smiled reassuringly.

"Well, it's hard to explain, but sometimes I seem to know what Ed is thinking about."

"Uh-huh. Well, that seems to happen to couples sometimes. My wife—*Unh!*"

He closed his eyes and opened them again. "Where was I? Oh, uh, telepathy isn't very scientific, you know, but there is what we call a rapport that people get when they are very close to someone. Now, is there something about these episodes that bothers you?"

She hesitated. "Just that— I don't know, I'm having dreams that I never had before. But there's something else, too. I think I'm starting to feel the way he does about the aliens. I mean, I love them and I'm afraid of them, the way he is. I don't see how that could happen just by being around somebody."

"No, perhaps not, perhaps not." He sat back and looked at the ceiling for a moment. "Well, there is another explanation. You know Ed says himself that the aliens put something in his brain."

"He hasn't got any scar—"

Wellafield waved his hand. "Microsurgery, perhaps. Or maybe he's wrong about their putting it in his *brain,* maybe it's somewhere else. But let's suppose it's what we call an implant, that is, something that releases a neurochemical agent of some sort into the bloodstream."

"Okay."

"And so his body fluids would contain this substance,

and, ah, when you have intimate relations—I hope this doesn't embarrass you—"

"No, I get it." To her surprise, she felt herself flushing. "Thanks, Doc."

"Don't mention it, my dear."

After a really interesting lunch of curried crab and apricots, the Cube Team had a presentation from the Council of American Commercial Advertisers. The presenter was a large, aggressively cheerful man named Rodney ("Call me Rod") Singleton.

"We've got to sell this just like any other product," Rod told them, "and it will be the biggest ad campaign of all times because it's worldwide and we've got to reach *everybody.* Now how do we sell something that might look bizarre at first glance to everybody in the world? There are five ways, and we'll use them all. Number one, a promise of benefits. You'll have a better life if you use our product. Number two, peer pressure. Everybody who is anybody is using this product. Number three, glamour. Celebrities use this product. Number four, sex. Lots of great-looking models demonstrating the product. Number five, risk. You're taking your life in your hands when you use this product."

"Excuse me, isn't that a negative pitch?"

"You'd think so, wouldn't you? But studies have shown again and again that people are attracted by the risk of death. Like the skull-faces that showed up in ice cubes in liquor ads in the seventies and eighties? They sold booze like crazy, and the skull and crossbones on cigarettes work almost the same way. Incidentally, I've seen some of the sketches for the life capsules, and I understand there's some concern that they look too much like caskets. I'd like to go over this with the design group—I think there's a definite point where they're going to look just *enough* like caskets."

"Wait a minute, are you saying that if the capsule doesn't *obviously* look like a casket, people are going to want to get in it because of some subliminal, what, death wish?"

"That's very well put, and I think we should be alert to take advantage of that. Now, moving along, the next point is saturation. Everywhere you look, you're going to see our ads. On billboards, on holo, in newspapers and magazines. You're going to see Cube games and Cube toys for the kiddies. We'll have essay contests for school-children: 'Why I Want to Go to Our New Planet.' You'll see the ceremonies when people actually get into the life capsules and get their pictures taken. You won't be able to get *away* from this, because it'll be everywhere. Preachers will talk about it in their sermons. Teachers in their classes. The President will talk about it, the Mayor will talk about it, and I guarantee you we can turn this bizarre idea into something everybody takes for *granted.*"

"About the sex, that won't work in Islamic countries, will it?"

"Not the same way; no bikinis, but believe me, sex sells to Muslims too. That's an important point, though, cultural differences. We can't run this whole thing like an American campaign; it's got to be tailored to every group. That means we've got to have input from an *army* of anthropologists and media people. No problem. We've done the same thing with cigarettes."

"How about different religions, though?"

"We've got to have the religious leaders behind us, no question. Well, for every religion there's some kind of a handle. With Christians it's heaven, with Muslims it's paradise, same difference. The Chinese and Japanese and Scientologists are going to join their ancestors, the Indians are going to achieve nirvana. For starving people, they're going to a place where they'll never have to be hungry again."

"Is that true?"

"Well, who knows if it's true? We're selling a product, and we're making certain claims for it. If we had to find out if the claims are true, how could you ever sell anything?"

CHAPTER 32

The Cube Team had been officially renamed; it was now the United States Consulting Service (USCS), and it had a commanding voice in the Council of the International Human Rescue Corporation (IHRC) in Berlin. But it still met every Monday in Washington, where it called itself by its old name.

On a rainy day in April, when the winds were whipping diseased cherry blossoms down the avenue, Sam Cooper said, "We were thinking of Tsu Jin Shan, northeast of Nanjing, but it turns out it's only fifteen hundred feet, and even if it was taller, with gerbil construction we really don't *need* a mountain. We can put up a mile-high building right outside Shanghai, no weight at all and absolutely solid. And that's *better* than the mountain, because we can have multiple tracks that converge on the building as it goes up.

"Okay, now the only problem is, is the folks in the capsules are going to have a hell of a ride. There might be a lot of screaming in there, so we think the best thing is to give them something that knocks them out cold as soon as they get in the capsule."

"What would that be, an injection?"

"No, needles scare some people, and besides it takes too long. We were thinking more along the lines of a harmless knockout gas released into the capsule when you close the lid. So, *anyway,* as soon as each capsule gets to the right place, it closes a contact that turns on the gerbil field, and we can easily load two point five million a day, so we're in like Flynn."

The sound copter roared overhead, dropping a blizzard of bulletins. Linda Lavalle picked one up from the pavement. It said:

DON'T BE LEFT BEHIND!!!

Noted psychic, Dr. Wallace Bird, Ph.D. tells us that there MAY NOT BE ENOUGH ROOM! FOR EVERYONE! in the Cube. Those who get in first will be carried to the New Planet! Those who are LEFT BEHIND may PERISH!

Use this handy form to SIGN UP for the Cube Lottery NOW!!! DON'T BE LEFT BEHIND!!!!

When she gave it to Stone, he said, "Yeah, well, that's the way they set it up. You don't have to worry about it for another seven or eight years, but you might as well sign anyway. You can always back out if you want to."

"I'll sign when you do."

"Okay."

That evening Sylvia said, "I talked to my shrink today about getting into the Cube?"

"Yeah, and?"

"Well, she says people are either sarcophiles or sarcophobes."

"She does, huh? What does that mean?"

"Either they want to get into those coffins, or else they'd do anything in the world to stay out of them."

"Oh. Okay, which are you?"

"I'm a sarcophobe. I want to be cremated."

"Well, if Ed's right, you will be."

"Thanks a *lot.*"

Stone spent a week in Washington, came back to New York for a few days, then was gone again. He was in Africa, Australia, Indonesia, shaking hands with presidents and prime ministers. The world economy was booming; fleets of passenger ships were under construction in yards from Seattle to Arkhangelsk.

After work Lavalle went directly to the penthouse and walked into the private apartment where Stone was waiting. He kissed her. "Hi, how was your day?"

"Not too bad. When did you get in?"

"About an hour ago. Sit down, have a drink." He picked up a sweating cold jug, poured the martini into a chilled glass, added olives, handed it to her.

She sipped it. "You're getting better."

He was pouring rye into a glass, adding ginger ale. "Listen, there's somebody I want you to meet. I brought him down from Washington with me. He can't stay long, but I just want you to see him."

"Okay, where is he?"

"Wait a minute, I'll get him." He walked behind her.

She kicked off her shoes, leaned back and took another slow sip of the martini. After a moment she heard a sound and turned to look. Stone was standing there with a funny expression on his face. A few feet behind him, Stone was watching.

She yelped and stood up, spilling the glass.

"What do you think?" said Stone, the second one. The first one said nothing, but his smile broadened.

"Don't *do* that to me!" she said, with one hand on her heart. She had stepped on her shoe in getting up, and the drink had spilled on her skirt.

"Linda, this is Bob Eberhardt," the second Stone said.

The man put out his hand, and she took it. "Heard a lot about you," he said in a clear tenor.

"Thanks, I guess." Now that she looked closely, she could see the differences: Eberhardt's eyes were not quite the same color, his nose was a little broader, but the two men were dressed just alike, and the resemblance was amazing. They sat down and looked at her.

"See," Stone said, "I've got all these functions I've got to go to, and I can't be in two places at once, so they dreamed this up. I've got three guys made over to look like me. This is Medium Bob, and then there's Big Bob and Little Bob."

"I can't talk much," said Eberhardt, "because the voice isn't right yet. So I can't go on holo, or meet heads of state, or anything. But I can meet mayors, and go in parades, and just wave." He grinned. "It's fun."

Her heart was slowing down. "Pour me another drink, for God's sake. Do you think three is going to be enough?"

"For now, but we can recruit some more, right, Bob?"

"Right. I've got a cousin who'd like to give it a try."

"Rye and ginger, Bob?"

Eberhardt made a face. "No, I've got to run. Nice meeting you, Ms. Lavalle."

"You too. Good luck."

When he was gone, she looked at Stone. "You son of a bitch," she said.

"Would you of known it wasn't me, if I hadn't been standing right there?"

"Maybe not. Are you feeling okay? You look rotten."

He took a long swallow of his highball. "I'm tired. Maybe

these Bobs will take some of the pressure off." He shook his head. "I'm worried, though."

"What about?"

"I know somebody's working against me, and I don't know who. It could be Rottenstern, he's the German, but Schwartzmann means black man, and that could be anybody in about sixty countries. It could be Svartschev in Russia. Or it could even be Rong."

"Oh, come on."

"He's been acting funny lately. I think he's got some kind of a deal on the side."

"You really think everything that happens has something to do with the story in that magazine?"

"Not everything, but the main characters. You, me, and Frank, that's three, but there's one more, and I don't know who he is. I know he's out there."

"We're talking to Clint Goldberg in Lexington, Kentucky. Mr. Goldberg, you've told people you're not going to the new planet. Why not?"

"Well, son, I raise beef cattle for a living. Some people seem to think that's a bad thing to do, but my idea is, if they don't like what I do, they can go somewheres else where I'm not a-doing it. Now it may be so that we're all going to get in that box and wake up in some other universe with rolls of thousand-dollar bills in our pocket, although I somehow doubt it. But I know one thing for damn sure, you can't get a herd of beef cattle in them boxes."

"Some people are speculating that we'll find herds of cattle on the other planet when we get there. Or something like cattle."

"Yes, well, and some people speculate that they'll get pie in the sky when they die. I don't say nothing against that, but I believe I'll stay here and take my chances."

"Who's going to eat your beef cattle, Mr. Goldberg?"

"As long as people are living on this planet, they'll be some that eats beef."

"We're in Ames, Iowa, talking to Mrs. Dorene Volmer. Mrs. Volmer, you're planning to go to the new planet, is that right?"

"That is right, Dave. Our minister is going to lead the whole congregation into the Cube, I mean everybody except one person, Stephen Orr, and we're trying to talk him around. Because we'd like to be one hundred percent. And it would be so nice, when we get to the new planet, if we could look around and see that everybody else was there, too. Some families are being broken up by this, not in our congregation but other places. I think that's so sad."

"So you don't have any doubt that you've made the right decision?"

"Oh, *no.* It's going to be just wonderful, and I wish everybody could understand that."

"Why do you think some people don't understand it, Mrs. Volmer?"

"Their eyes have been darkened by Satan, Dave."

"One thing about his story impresses me. The collections he talks about—all kinds of plants and animals."

"Yes? Why?"

"Well, it makes sense. If you ask yourself what the aliens came here for—"

"To rescue us before the Earth is destroyed."

"Well, that too, maybe, but what were they doing out there in the first place? They didn't know we even existed until they came. In other words, what could they find on other planets that would be worth the cost of the trip? Now Ed isn't a scientist; he's not even an educated man. If he had made this story up, he probably would have thought of something simpler. Metal ores or something like that, that wouldn't make any sense at all. The only thing that *does* make sense is biologicals. There are so many possible organic compounds that it would take you forever to synthesize every one and find out if there was any use for it. So you go to planets and take samples of things that are already being used. We've been doing the same thing for thousands of years on our own planet. Any *working* organic chemical might have hundreds of other uses. You might find something in cats' saliva that would cure a disease we never heard of. Or you could splice in genes from an oak tree to modify some other organism. That's the real gold in interstellar exploration—everything else is nonsense."

"The idea is that we clear out South America, and Central America and the Caribbean, then we go over to southern Africa and clear that out up to here, leaving just the countries along the northern coast—"

"Why stop there?"

"Because it makes more sense to get them from the Mediterranean side when we do western Europe and the Middle East. Okay, and then we get southwestern and eastern Europe and the Slavos, then India and so on, and then North America starting with Mexico, then northwestern Europe, then Southeast Asia, Australia and New Zealand, then the Pacific islands, then the Philippines, Japan and Korea, and China last."

"Haven't you got North America and Western Europe out of order?"

"Right, and they say that's because most of the industrial plant and technical stuff is there, and most of the food stockpiles too, but I think there's something else going on. There was some heavy lobbying by the multinationals."

"What for, do you think?"

"I don't know, unless they think something's going to happen to the Cube Project."

* * *

In October, 2005, Stone got back from a three-week trip; he had been to London, Paris, Berlin, Rome, Vatican City, Warsaw and Moscow. He looked tired, and he was drinking more than usual. He hadn't been sleeping well, Rong said.

"He's not looking at all well," said Mrs. Rooney. They were having tea in the penthouse living room.

"He's looking like puke. He don't sleep enough, and sometime he wakes up yelling."

"Isn't he taking his pills?"

"Yeah, but they don't do him no good. All the travel, you know, that's bad enough all by itself. It's daytime when you think it's dark out, and then you get home and you have to turn around again. So I tell him, man, after one of them trips, take a week to relax before you take another one, but he says no, he's got to keep moving. He got a big map in the plane with markers on it all the places he's been, but there's a hundred he ain't, and he frets about it. The food don't agree with him neither. He's got to go to these breakfasts, these lunches, these banquets, and they're not going to feed him nothing healthy, they're going to spread theirselves because he's important, right, and he's got to eat it because he's a *guest.*"

"What can we do?"

"We had them put a gym in the plane, at least he can get a little exercise. That helps some, but the only thing going to make him better is a month off, and he won't take it."

"Can't you let up a little?" Lavalle asked that evening. "I mean, the Cube Project is under way, what more do you want?"

"No, because some of these places, the leadership has changed, and the rest of them, I have to keep going back because I think the stuff in the ring is starting to wear off.

Did you see where Chelmsford denounced me as a charlatan?"

"The ex–prime minister? No."

"Well, he's ex, and they say he's senile anyway, so it's not too bad. But I shook hands with him just a little over three years ago, and that means if I don't keep shaking hands with the same people, there might be a bunch of them turning against me. I can't take the chance."

Wellafield cleared his throat. "It's going to happen anyway, isn't it, Ed? You can't keep up with them all."

"I can try."

Stone was in Europe all through the spring and summer, working with the Oversight Committee of the International Human Rescue Corporation, and consulting with the Farbenwerke engineers who were designing transport mechanisms for the Cube. A pilot project was going up on the floodplain of the Elbe near Hamburg.

The media campaign was in full swing. A virtual sculpture fifty feet tall had been put up in UN Plaza, where Lavalle passed it every day on her way to work: it consisted of a twenty-two-foot white cube and a blue cloud-speckled globe suspended and slowly rotating above it.

Sylvia showed her a present she had just bought for a new nephew: a jack-in-the-box that popped up a globe instead of a clown. For older children there was a toy cube which, when opened, disgorged a vast number of compressible dolls.

Lavalle's boss got rid of all the office furniture and replaced it with cubical desks, cocktail tables, armchairs, end tables. She noticed that most of the stuff she and Sylvia brought home from the supermarket or ordered on the net was in cubical packages.

Every sitcom involved the new planet in some way. The nonfiction best-seller that year was *New World Revealed,* by

Moamaddar Parthava, an Iranian mystic who claimed to have received messages from outer space describing the new planet in great detail. Sylvia, who read the book, said that the new world was called Twonola, and that it was partly covered with trees you could eat and have sex with. There was also a friendly race of stunted humanoids who spoke Finnish and enjoyed working hard for other people.

The holo was called *Flash Gordon on the New World.* It started off like the old flatfilm, with the planet Mongo approaching the Earth and about to destroy it. In a violent storm, Dr. Zarkov, Flash Gordon, and Dale Arden took off in Zarkov's experimental spaceship. The strange planet loomed nearer. They landed, and then it was all different. They were in a verdant valley dotted with ranch houses and a few high-rise buildings. Zeppelins and gaily colored little airplanes soared overhead. A welcoming committee of tall, smiling people came toward them.

Then they were at a beach where tanned athletic people were sitting under striped umbrellas on a terrace overlooking a calm baby-blue ocean. Down on the beach, fishermen in striped shirts were hauling in an enormous fish, something like a twenty-foot grouper; it was gasping and waving its fins. On the terrace, the people picked up bits of cooked fish on their forks, tucked them into their pink mouths, and smiled.

"Not very exciting," Lavalle said.

"No, because it's paradise. You can't have bad things happen in paradise."

"I'm not sure I want to go there."

The Premier of China, beaming for the cameras, dug a symbolic spadeful of dirt and deposited it in a basket. Following him in order, the other visiting dignitaries did the same. There were speeches; champagne and Chinese wine were drunk, many photographs taken. Then the bulldozers moved in.

The dusty plain northwest of Shanghai had been spread with flower petals, on which the eight hundred twenty-six converging rail tracks gleamed like the stems of a metal bouquet.

"We're here," said the voice of the American reporter, "as we have been all morning, waiting for the first capsules to be loaded into the Cube. That event is supposed to take place at noon our time, but it seems there has been a delay. All morning long, German and Chinese engineers have been testing the system, but we are informed that—Ah, now I see that something is happening down at the railheads. Peter, will you come in?"

The view switched to a stage draped with red bunting, where the correspondent Peter Wilkins stood with the wind ruffling his hair. Behind him, people sweating in formal suits were popping in and out of the golden curtains. "Alan," he said, "as you can see from the activity here, we seem to be getting ready to receive our distinguished guests. I am informed that Walter John Perry of the United States of America will have the honor to be the first to enter the capsule. After him, I believe it will be Katya Goldmark of the European Federation, and after her— But I am being signaled to leave the stage, and I believe that means the ceremony is about to begin." He walked off camera.

Below the platform, raucous music burst out. The curtains parted to reveal the open space capsule on a pedestal, gleaming pink-silver under the lights. Standing in front of it was the American rock star in a sequined suit. He bowed; then, to a roll of drums, walked to the capsule and climbed in. Sitting there, he raised his arms in an enfolding gesture, then brought his hands to his mouth and blew kisses. He lay down in the padded interior; as he did so, the holo above the stage came on, displaying an overhead view of the open capsule. Two men came from either side, wheeling carts from which they took small parcels and began packing them in around the singer's body. They moved with effort, as if the parcels were very heavy. The singer squirmed a little to accommodate them.

"Peter, what's in the parcels?"

"Alan, that's his payoff—it is rumored to be a hundred million dollars' worth of gold bullion. I'm told that he was offered a second capsule to put it in, but he said no thanks; he wants it with him so he'll *know* it's going to be there when he wakes up."

The two commentators laughed gently. "And they say you can't take it with you!" said the first. "Are they all getting that much, Peter?"

"Yes, Alan, they are. People at this level of fame don't do anything for nothing. But, in a sense, they're doing a public service by demonstrating their confidence in the Cube, and it's worth the money."

"What about all the other VIPs—won't they want to be paid too?"

"My guess is that they'll get a little lulu, just to keep them happy, but by that stage there'll be too much competition for them to hold out. Once this gets started, it's a status thing to be high on the list, and in a couple of weeks it wouldn't surprise me if they were *paying* to get in early."

The lid of the capsule came down. The capsule sank through the floor of the platform, reappeared below. Now it was moving slowly on the track, faster now, and now as the camera followed it they could see it speeding toward the construction site two miles away.

"Bye, Walter John," said one of the talking heads.

Professor Rafael Torres y Molina of the University of Lima spent the night at the old hotel on top of Machu

Picchu, as he always did. The new hotel at the foot of the mountain was much more commodious, but Torres y Molina liked to sit on the terrace in the early morning and watch the clouds slowly unveil the Andes. The sight never failed to move him. These mountains were unlike other mountains; they went beyond majesty.

Professor Torres y Molina was fifty-two years old. He had devoted half his life to Peruvian archaeology; in his younger days he had clambered all over the Inca Trail, and he had supervised the last ten years of the restoration of Machu Picchu. As he drank his coffee (flash frozen, from Colombia; he considered Peruvian coffee undrinkable), he gazed alternately at the black spires opposite across the chasm and at the entrance to Machu Picchu itself a hundred yards away, where a solitary llama was hanging around hoping to get in. He was alone on the terrace; the air was cool and fresh.

Presently the first tour bus came up the switchback road and pulled over to the curb. Tourists emerged one by one. A few went into the lobby of the hotel; the rest, following their guide, walked down the path to the entrance.

Torres y Molina waited. The second bus pulled up, and this time only five people got out. Two of them, heavily built men in gray suits, came up the steps and stopped in front of him. "Professor Torres y Molina?" the first one said.

"Yes."

"May I see some ID, please?" He spoke in English with an American accent.

"Certainly, if you will first tell me who you are."

Without changing his expression, the man removed a leather folder from his breast pocket and flipped it open. It contained some sort of badge and a plastic card. In his turn, Torres y Molina took out his wallet and offered his internal passport. The guard examined it carefully, handed it back, and nodded to the others.

The third man came up the steps and put his hand out. "I'm Ed Stone, Professor. Thanks for showing me around."

"I have not done it yet, but you are welcome. Now, to begin with, do you see the peak over there? That is Huayna Picchu. Can you see the goat?" On the side of the peak a white dot was moving, no bigger than a flea. "There is a little temple there. The only way to reach it is by a ridge trail that is so dangerous that only the crazy Germans try it."

"Have you been there?" Stone asked.

Torres y Molina smiled. "Yes. When I was younger. And did you notice the path up the mountainside—not the road you came up by, but the other one?"

"No."

"I have a picture here." He took it out of his breast pocket and showed it to them. "You see, the modern road goes back and forth, back and forth. The Inca path goes straight up the mountain. Well, now let us go into Machu Picchu."

They passed between the thatched guard towers and proceeded down the narrow path beside the terraces that rose to the top of the mountain. The llama, which had got in somehow, was grazing in one of the walled fields below.

"They tell me nobody knows who built this place, is that right?" said Stone.

Torres y Molina turned. "That's true. It was a separate little Inca kingdom, apparently. What you see here is just one part of it. By the time the Spaniards came, all these people were gone. Disease, or maybe their springs dried up and they left because they had no water. All over the continent, there are ruins of civilizations that died, and we don't know why."

Stone looked around and breathed deeply. Clouds were pouring like water over the ridge above; the sun was bright. "It's beautiful here," he said.

"Yes. Did you have any trouble with the altitude?"

"I had a headache in Cuzco and had to lay down awhile, but then I was fine."

They climbed up and down the stone stairways on either side of the central plaza. At the Carceles, Torres showed them the narrow trapezoidal niches in the walls. "We think these were prison cells. They would put a man in each one, close the wooden gate, which of course is not here any more, and then feed him through the window in the back wall. They had many of these cells. We don't know what the crime was, but it was probably disobedience."

Half an hour later, they descended from the battlement walk into a little courtyard, completely enclosed and private. "This is a favorite place of mine," Torres y Molina said. "I think there must have been a great many flowers here. Perhaps it was a place where a certain young woman came to be alone." He smiled. "When you spend enough time here, you think you feel the presence of people who are gone."

In a little nook beside the path, someone had deposited two empty sardine tins and a cigarette package. Torres y Molina looked at them and walked on.

"Why do people do that in a place like this?" Stone asked behind him.

"Perhaps because they are badly brought up," Torres y Molina said over his shoulder. "Or because if one cannot create something, the next best thing is to deface and destroy it? I don't know."

He took them to the Sacred Plaza and the Temple of Three Windows. Stone asked, "How did they fit those stones so close?"

"No one knows that. Another question is, why did they

do it? In some places they carved blocks of a uniform size and shape, just as we would, and they even used mortar, but for decorative work it seems that they preferred unusual shapes and a close fit. And of course these walls are very strong, because of the way the pieces lock together."

Stone pushed his hat back and stood staring at the masonry. "We went to that other place yesterday, the fortress."

"Sacsawayman? Outside Cuzco?"

"Yeah. And, you know, I'd seen pictures before, but it wasn't the same."

"Yes, I do know."

"I mean, some of those blocks must be thirty feet high. I don't even know how they could get them there, let alone make them fit that tight."

"I know some engineers who say they would not undertake to do it."

"You think they had antigravity or something?"

"No, I think they used natural methods. There is a theory that they made a template for each face of a block, and used it to carve the next block to an exact fit. It would have been painstaking work. But they had many hands and plenty of time."

After his guests had left, it was too late to inspect the work on the guard towers. Professor Torres y Molina stayed another night, finished his inspection, and took the tourist bus down in the afternoon. On the switchback road, he noticed something peculiar: a narrow silver-gray line, like a horizontal fault, that had certainly not been there before.

"I can't quite imagine it. I mean, we get to this other planet, okay, and maybe it's a great place, but then what? Do we have to cut down trees and build houses? For six billion people?"

"Don't you think they'll probably let us out a few at a time, I mean a few thousand or whatever? So the first ones can do, uh, all that primitive stuff? And then a few thousand more, so you build it up slowly."

"That could be, or maybe they've already built houses for us."

"And cities, right, and water systems and sewers? Highways? Automobiles? Have they got auto factories turning out Toyotas and Ferraris? What about holo factories to make holos? Give me a break."

"Another thing that worries me, when we get there, is the new planet going to be just as crowded as this one?"

"Maybe it's a bigger planet."

"Then the gravity would be too high, wouldn't it?"

"Not necessarily. Or it could be a planet the same size as Earth but with more land area—not so many oceans."

"Listen, I don't give a puke about all that stuff. What I want to know is, is everybody going to get an even chance or is it going to be just like here? I get the idea the fat cats are going to be just as fat and the poor folks are going to be just as poor."

"Don't you think we'll have something to say about that? I mean, as far as governments are concerned, all bets are off, right? We don't have to have any United States or England or Germany—that would be stupid. We could start over and do everything better."

"You think we would?"

"Well, if we *don't,* it's our fault, isn't it?"

CHAPTER 33

Stone was watching the COSAI weather, toggling from one area of the globe to another, where the same kindly computerized face alternated with satellite photos, charts and fractal landscapes. "This pattern is expected to persist without much change until early next—"

"Ed, Geoffrey called me last night. He wants us to come out to Rye again tomorrow; he says it's very important."

He turned off the sound. "Important to who, me or him?"

"Well, he says to both of you. And me, too."

"How do you come into it?"

"He says if I can get you to come up there, he'll sign over an office building he owns in Scarsdale. It's worth about a million and a half."

"Listen, I've got plenty of money—"

"That's not the same thing, you zink! Are you coming or aren't you?"

"Oh, hell. I'll have to see if I can get out of the governor's dinner."

"Well, will you?"

"Yeah."

* * *

On the drive up, Lavalle said, "By the way, I had such a strange phone call from Henry last night."

Stone turned to look at her. "Henry who?"

"You know, Geoffrey's butler. The one you shook hands with."

"Oh."

"He said he's left Geoffrey, and it sounded like he was trying to warn me about something."

"He didn't say what?"

"No, he just said something like, 'It would be better if you didn't come out for a while.' "

Stone was silent for a moment. "But we're going anyway."

"Well, the plans were all made. What do you want to do, turn around and go home?"

"No, I guess not."

They reached the house a little before one o'clock. The door opened as soon as they pulled up in the driveway, and a man stepped out.

"Good afternoon," he said with a smile. "You must be Ms. Lavalle and Mr. Stone. I'm Simmons, the new butler. Will you go right in, please?"

After lunch, Geoffrey beckoned her to lean closer. "Linda, dear, I want to persuade Ed to do something, and I know he won't want to agree. In order to convince him, I may have to hurt you a little, do you understand?"

"Hurt me how?"

"That would be telling, but it won't hurt much, and it'll be over in a second. I just didn't want to do it without warning you."

"Thanks a lot."

"Don't mention it."

They all sat down, and the maid passed the coffee cups.

"Ed, let me ask you a question," said Geoffrey, stirring his coffee. "Have you decided whether to go in the Cube or not?"

"Yeah. It seems like I ought to, because it was my idea, but if I do, maybe I'll find out about the other planet and maybe not. If I stay, I *will* find out about the Earth being destroyed. I mean, either it will or it won't, and I want to find out *something.* So I think maybe I'll stay."

"I see. Well, then, have you thought about what happens after? If the Earth isn't destroyed, there's going to be some people rich and some poor. Would you be rich?"

"Yeah, I would, but I don't think that's a problem. I've got a lot of friends."

"What if I could show you how to get rich yourself?"

"Like how?"

"Ed, as you know, I'm pretty well off myself, but I have business connections with people a whole lot wealthier than I am, do you understand what I mean? These people would be prepared to help you to acquire assets valued at five hundred million dollars, free and clear."

"They would? What for?"

"They believe the world economy will be ruined if the population drops below one billion. Their projections say the population can be held to at about two billion if you stop having anything to do with the Cube Project early next year."

"I couldn't do that."

"Not even if it meant your life—or Linda's?"

"What do you mean by that?"

"Simmons," said Geoffrey, turning his head.

"Yes, sir." The butler left the room for a moment and returned carrying a chromed metal bar. "Excuse me, Miss Linda." He swung the bar like a baseball bat; she heard her shinbone crack, heard her own yelp of pain.

Stone had fallen into a crouch; Simmons had dropped the bar and was now holding a Webley-Forster automatic.

"Ed, don't be silly," Lavalle said.

Her mother, coming forward, cried, "Oh, Linda, my baby!"

"Mother, shut up," she said; then, to Geoffrey, "I need a doctor."

"Yes, dear. Simmons, if you please—" The butler nodded; after a last cautious glance at Stone, he put the pistol in his pocket, picked up the chrome bar again, and went to the terminal in the corner, where they heard his voice murmuring discreetly.

"Is it a clean break, dear?" Geoffrey asked.

"I think so. Give me a couple of aspirin."

"Take all you want." Geoffrey handed her the bottle and poured a glass of water from his carafe. "Our story will be that you tripped on the doorsill. Is that all right?"

"Sure."

"The ambulance will be here in a few minutes, Mr. Nero," said Simmons, returning.

"Very good, Simmons. You might wait for them and bring them in when they come."

"Yes, sir. May I say before I go, Miss Linda, how deeply I regretted that?"

"I understand, Simmons. No hard feelings."

"Thank you, miss." He touched his forehead and withdrew.

Stone said, "Are you people all crazy?"

"No, no, Ed," Geoffrey replied. "Linda understands perfectly, don't you, dear?"

"Of course I do. Ed, they broke my leg to show you they mean business. If you don't make a deal with them, they might have to kill me."

"My baby!" ejaculated Mrs. Nero.

"Mother, will you *please* shut up?"

* * *

An ambulance arrived about ten minutes later; the two paramedics put a temporary splint on Lavalle's leg and took her to Pinecrest Hospital, where she was examined, X-rayed, and given a permanent cast. It was epoxy, and hardly visible, but she couldn't get her right shoe on.

On the drive back, Stone said, "Let's see if I've got this straight. They broke your leg to show me they're serious. If I don't back out of the Cube Project, they might kill you."

"More likely they'd just escalate a little. They'd break my jaw next time, or my skull."

"How can you be so damn calm about it?"

"Do you want me to scream and yell?" She drew a deep breath and let out a healthy scream.

Stone got the car back under control. "Jesus, don't do that." He pounded the steering wheel. "What I want to know is, whose side are you on?"

"What do you mean, whose side? I'm on my side. I don't want to get killed."

"But you wouldn't feel bad if I gave in?"

"Sure, but I might feel worse if I was dead."

He chewed his thumbnail. "Got to think about this," he muttered.

"Like which is more important, keeping me alive or getting everybody into the Cube?"

He was looking wild-eyed again. "Don't *say* that."

"Well, that's what it comes down to. Do what you want."

"I can't give up the Cube. That's number one. Even if they killed you. So we've got to get you out of sight."

"They'll be watching my apartment and the office, and they'll watch you whenever you're in town."

"Okay, and that means this might be our last chance to do something. Look, they *know* you can't fly. So that's what they won't be expecting."

"But I *can't* fly."

"Sure you can. You take a couple of drinks, then Doc gives you a pill or something, and we pour you onto the plane. When you wake up, you're in Argentina."

"Why Argentina?"

"I was going to go there tomorrow anyway, for the ceremonies. But you don't have to stay there—" He got his phone out of his pocket, clicked it on. "We can run you over to Paris, or Berlin—Hello, Florence? Ed. Listen, get hold of Frank and tell him to have the plane ready in an hour. . . . Yes, the whole crew. Right. And is Doc there? Good, tell him to get out there too, and bring his bag. I want him to meet us in the Federal Lounge, okay? I'm on the way in from Rye, and we'll go straight to the airport. Okay. 'Bye."

"Listen," she said, "we're *not* going straight to the airport. I need some clothes . . ."

"You can buy clothes. They're *watching* your apartment, remember? Don't be dumb."

"What about my passport? I can't go to Argentina without a passport."

"Hell, that's right. Where is it?"

"I don't know, in one of my bureau drawers, I think. I haven't used it in years. In fact, it's probably expired by now."

"That's great."

"Well, don't snap at me—this wasn't *my* idea." She opened her purse and started looking for a tissue. "Damn it to hell, now you've made me cry."

"Oh, Jesus." After a moment he picked up the phone again and punched a number. "Hello, is Steve Lonergan there? . . . Steve, it's Ed Stone. Listen, I need a big favor. Can you get somebody to meet us in Buenos Aires with a diplomatic passport for Linda Lavalle? . . . I can't explain right now, but I've got to get her out of the country . . . I don't know, wait a minute." He passed the phone over to her. "He wants to know your date of birth and stuff."

She took the phone. "Hello, Mr. Lonergan?"

"Yes, Ms. Lavalle."

"I was born June tenth, nineteen seventy-four."

"All right, thanks. Now about the photo—"

"Oh, Jesus." She looked at Stone. "Ed, we've got to go back to my place and get the old passport, for the photo."

"No, Ms. Lavalle," said the voice in her ear, "we can't use the old photo. Let me talk to Ed again, please."

She handed him the phone. He said, "Uh-huh. Uh-huh. Okay, wait a minute." He turned to her. "Is your photo on file where you work?"

"Sure."

He said into the phone, "Yes. It's the International Development Association in New York, okay? She works under McNevin Fairbairn. . . . Okay, Steve, thanks a million." He hung up the phone. "He'll call them and get them to fax a copy to Buenos Aires. Then they can fake up a passport and have it ready for us when we get there. You feeling any better?"

"Sure, I'm having a great time."

"Don't be that way."

"What way do you want me to be? My leg is broken, and I'm going to fly in a goddamn airplane. I wish I'd never *met* you."

They were silent for the rest of the trip. Traffic was heavy on the Taconic Parkway, then thinned out as they neared the airport. Stone pulled in to the visitors' lot and phoned for a chair.

"Ed, I can walk," she said. "If you put me in a wheelchair, I'll be that much more conspicuous."

"It's too far. Anyway, airports are full of people in chairs. Hey, Linda, let me steer for once, will you?"

An attendant showed up a few minutes later with the wheelchair, and Lavalle drove it across the parking lot, up the ramp into the concourse. "Which way?"

"About half a mile straight ahead."

They found themselves in a discreet private lounge, empty except for themselves, Doc Wellafield, and a bartender and waiter. Lavalle sat down and said, "I'll take that drink now."

"A tranquilizer would be better," Wellafield said, sitting beside her. "In fact, the best thing would be one of these neurosignalers like the one I'm wearing, but we haven't got time for that—"

"I'll take the drink," Lavalle said. "Double Beefeater martini," she said to the waiter. "Straight up, very dry, very cold."

The waiter nodded. "Gentlemen?"

"Carstairs and ginger," said Stone.

"Nothing for me. This limits what I can give her afterward," Wellafield muttered, pawing through his bag.

The waiter came with the drinks and a bowl of shrimp crackers. "Take those away," said Lavalle. "They'll soak up the alcohol, and I want to get drunk."

"Yes, ma'am." He watched her as she raised the glass and lowered it half-empty. "Another?" he asked.

"Yes, please. This one's very good."

Stone sipped his highball and put his arm around her. She drank the rest of the martini and leaned against him. "That's a very attractive waiter," she said. "Don't you think so?"

"You're not drunk yet," Stone told her.

"No, but I'm going to be." The second martini came and

she drank it a little more slowly. "You're very attractive too, and so are you, Doc."

"Thank you, Linda. Well, we're all attractive, aren't we?" Wellafield said.

"We *are,* and I think that's very nice." She ordered a third martini, but by the time she took the first sip she was feeling definitely woozy.

"Oh-oh, it's working," she said. "I think we'd better go."

"Take this little pill first," Wellafield said.

"It won't put me out right away, will it?"

"No, it will take about twenty minutes."

"Okay. You're very attractive, Doc."

She got into the chair again, sat down rather heavily, and let Stone propel her out into the corridor. There weren't any controls on the arms.

"This is a different kind of chair," she heard Stone saying.

"Oh."

They were out in the open, crossing the concrete, and then she was being carried chair and all up the ramp toward an airplane that looked as big as a building, but it was lying on its *side.*

A man in uniform appeared in the open hatchway. "Ms. Lavalle, I'm Frank Chesterton, the pilot."

"You are, aren't you?"

"Uh, yes, that's right."

Now she was inside, surrounded by half a dozen people with heads like balloons. Two of them looked like Ed Stone, and she couldn't tell which was which. "Introductions later, folks," said the pilot. "Let's get this lady into her stateroom where she can rest." They were moving across a vast lounge, through a dining room, then down a long corridor to a bedroom. Wellafield and the others went away; Ed's fingers were helping her get undressed. There was a whisper of sheets. Blackness was flowing up around her, but she had time to say, "This is a mistake of gigannic proportions."

CHAPTER 34

She slept, knowing that she was in a cylinder of metal that was droning through the blue darkness. The cylinder contracted like a colon, squeezed her out steaming into the sky, and she fell forever until the earth below turned into Stone's face, and as his mouth opened she saw the darkness inside, and the cardboard breathing out and breathing in.

And she was sitting up in the cold blue-white light of the window. Her heart was hammering and her mouth was dry. Stone said, "You okay?"

He was standing by the bed, dressed and shaved. "I was just going to wake you up," he said. "We're landing in about twenty minutes, okay? I'll be in the lounge." He yawned, and she saw the cardboard in his throat; then he left.

She staggered into the bathroom. The dream was real, and she couldn't wake up. She put her clothes on and ran a brush through her hair, wondering what she was going to do.

"Ladies and gentlemen," said Chesterton's voice from the loudspeaker, "we are now making our final approach to Evita Perón. The weather's good, pollution index moderate, sixty-two degrees Fahrenheit on the ground now, and the high today will be seventy-eight. Fasten seat belts please. We'll be on the ground in five minutes, thank you."

She found her shoe and put it on, then sat down and fastened the belt, gripped the armrests while the plane tilted and slid down the air with a whistling sound, like a falling artillery shell. She had a violent headache; she knew she was about to die, either before or after she threw up, and it bothered her that she had to do it with only one shoe on.

Then a hideous bump, and they were rolling. The plane swiveled, then the sound of the engines turned into a loud silence.

Stone opened the door and came in. "You okay?" he said.

"No. Open your mouth, will you?"

"What for?"

"I thought I saw something."

"Yeah?" He looked perplexed, but opened wide. Something at the back of his throat fluttered out of sight.

"So what was it?" he asked.

She forced herself to say, "I don't know. Nothing."

"You had a rough time, huh? Come on. You'll feel better when you're on the ground."

When they left the plane there were five of them besides the crew; the fourth one was one of Stone's doubles, and the fifth was a serious man in a gray suit who did not introduce himself. Wellafield took her wrist as they walked across the tarmac. "How are you feeling?" he asked.

"Rotten."

Inside the customs shed they were met by a porter, who handed Lavalle a diplomatic passport.

"Thank you very much," she said.

"No problem." The porter smiled and went away.

After customs they got into a limousine, all five. Stone said, "Uh, Linda, you know Medium Bob, and this is Dan DeQuincy, he's my bodyguard."

"I'm glad to meet you," Lavalle said. "That's funny, I'm the one who needs a bodyguard."

DeQuincy nodded. "That could be arranged, certainly," he said to Stone. "You want me to call State?"

"Yeah, would you?"

DeQuincy got out his phone and spoke into it so quietly that she could not hear. He put the phone away. "They'll get back to us. They may have to fly somebody down."

The morning streets were almost deserted; there were few cars, and almost no pedestrians, but she could hear a faint squawking of music in the distance. She remembered other trips to South America, always like this: the empty morning light was so sad.

The limousine delivered them to a large hotel. A gorgeous bellhop showed them to their suite on the fifteenth floor. There were crossed swords on the upholstery, the drapes, and the bedspreads.

"Listen," Stone said, "I've got to go and meet the President, and I think you'd better stay here, don't you? At least until we get you a bodyguard."

"Yes."

"Doc can stay with you, if you want."

"No, that's okay."

He moved as if to kiss her, but she managed to cough into her hand at the wrong moment. He looked a little puzzled. "Well, we'll be back tonight. Sure you're okay?"

"Yes."

When they were gone, she went into the bedroom and looked at Stone's suitcases; they were all locked. She touched the call button on the console and said in Spanish, "Please send up a hammer and some small nails."

The clerk's voice responded, "Pardon me, but for what purpose do you want them, Señora?"

"I want to repair the heel of my shoe."

"We will be glad to do that for you, Señora."

"No, I'm in a hurry. Do as I ask, please."

"Very well, Señora."

After a few minutes a bellboy knocked on the door and handed her a hammer and a box of nails. "Are these the right kind?" he asked.

"Yes, thank you."

"Will there be anything else, Señora?"

"No, thank you."

"At your orders." He bowed and went away.

She set a nail against the locks and broke them with reckless swings of the hammer. In one of the suitcases she found a carton of cigarettes, a half-liter of rye, a bundle of australes—the equivalent of several hundred thousand dollars—and a smaller bundle of U.S. currency. She wondered why he wanted so much; for bribes, perhaps. She put the money in her purse and laid the other things on the bed. Next she went into the adjoining room and broke the locks of DeQuincy's luggage as well. In his suitcase she found a high-powered rifle with a scope, broken down in its own little case, several boxes of shells, and three banana clips. Her hands were trembling. She packed everything she had taken into the only one of Stone's suitcases that would still close. Then she went into Wellafield's room, found his medical bag, and took that too, although it looked very old.

She swallowed two aspirins and a tranquilizer; used the bathroom, brushed her teeth, and turned out the lights before she left, carrying the suitcase in one hand, the medical bag and her spare shoe in the other.

The desk clerk saw her crossing the lobby and called, "Señora Lavalle, you are leaving us?"

"Yes."

"Yourself only, or will the others leave too?"

"Only myself. Good-bye."

"Good-bye, Señora Lavalle." He did not sound happy. After a moment he called after her, but she did not stop or turn.

The doorman blew his whistle for a taxi. When it pulled up, she tipped him too many australes.

The driver moved out into traffic before he asked, "Where to?"

"I want to go to another hotel, not too near this one."

"Señora, there are no other hotels. Everything is full." The young man, who had a narrow mustache and liquid brown eyes, looked at her seriously in the rearview mirror. He said in English, "I'm sorry, but, you know—it is Carnival, and besides everybody is here to get on the slow boats and go to China."

"Isn't there any place to stay at all?"

"Not in B.A. They are sleeping in the streets here."

"Where, then?"

"Maybe in Rosario or Santa Fé."

"Rosario is about two hundred fifty kilometers, is that right?"

"Yes, about that."

"All right, take me there."

"That will be very costly."

"It doesn't *matter*. Let's go."

The driver, whose name on the little card was Federigo Oliveras, turned off the avenue and drove north through residential streets. Even here, the streets were filling up with pedestrians in bright clothes, carrying flags, holding balloons, blowing on toy trumpets. A few were clearly drunk, although it was not yet ten o'clock. Tapping his horn at intervals, Oliveras edged patiently through the crowds until they thinned out. The flatscreen on the dashboard to his right was shimmering with images of people and horses.

"There is something wrong with your shoe?" he asked.

"No, my leg. It's broken. I can't get the shoe on because of the cast."

"Oh, I see. Well, would you like to watch the parade?"

"I suppose so." She touched the controls of the holo mounted on the seat in front of her. There was the plaza, lined with banners and pennants. Two breathless commentators were naming the celebrities as they entered the grandstand. "There is the President of the Trade Commission . . . that is Marie-Claude, the *très chic* French actress. . . . And that's the Chilean Ambassador. . . . Everyone is here today!"

"And gone tomorrow, correct?" The commentators laughed together.

"Yes, and I can't imagine not wanting to be part of this great event, can you?"

"Well, some people have to stay to report the news. And others, well, they just don't want to go."

"But I think that's *unpatriotic,* don't you? Oh, there is Carlo Menendez!"

There was a beeping sound inside her purse. She ignored it. In the holo she could hear martial music, and see mounted figures approaching: two people, a man and a woman on white horses, the horses curvetting, the people waving their hats.

"These are our two most favorite holo stars," said Oliveras over his shoulder. "They lead the first parade, always, for the last seven years. They are not so young now, but we think they are still beautiful."

In the holo she saw the aging faces of the two stars, tanned, smiling. The man was white-haired, the woman blond. They were dressed in elaborate gaucho costumes, with flat-brimmed hats trimmed in silver and gemstones.

Now the floats were coming, like a line of ships drifting gently down the avenue. The first one bore a sim or holo, it was hard to tell which, of a ten-foot nearly naked woman with a kerchief on her head and a basket of fruit spilling from the kerchief. There was laughter in the background.

"This is to make fun of the Brazilians," said Oliveras, smiling. The next float had a gigantic hook-nosed Uncle Sam, who was being bitten on the leg by a little bulldog. Oliveras shrugged. "It's Carnival," he said, "we make fun of everyone."

"Of course."

The cab swung onto the highway. Nearly all the traffic was in the other direction: a long line of old cars, trucks, a few buses, bicycles, motorcycles and mopeds. A few gauchos on horseback. On the shoulder a line of pedestrians was marching along, many carrying bundles.

"What are they going to do with their horses?" she asked.

"I don't know. Maybe they think they can take the horses with them."

"But they can't."

"No. So maybe I could buy some horses cheaply."

Her phone was ringing again. She opened her purse, got it out and said, "What do you want?"

"Linda, it's me. Where are you?"

"In a bar."

"Oh. Are you watching the parade?"

"Yes."

"Well, in a minute you'll probably see Medium Bob on one of the floats."

"Okay."

"Listen, Linda—the desk said you took your bags?"

"Yes."

"Well, uh, how come?"

"I don't want to talk about it."

"Well, I mean, are you coming back?"

"No." She broke the connection and put the phone away.

"Pardon me," said Oliveras, "but is there some trouble with your husband?"

"Yes."

"I quarreled with my wife this morning." He shrugged. "Things like this happen during Carnival."

"What was the quarrel about?"

"She didn't want me to work today. She doesn't believe money will be any good on the new planet, or gold either."

"And you?"

"I don't know. I don't think I am going there."

"What will you do instead?"

"I'll drive this taxi until I see there is going to be no more gasoline, and then I'll buy a horse and wagon. Several horses, and several wagons. That's a better way to live. The horse does all the work."

"Do you have enough gas to get to Rosario?"

"Oh, yes. Plenty of gas. My taxi has an extra tank; I put it in two months ago. Because there are not many filling stations open now. Everybody wants to go to the new planet."

"But you don't believe the Earth is going to be destroyed?"

"No, because how could it be destroyed? The whole Earth? Such a thing has never happened. You see, most people believe what they are told, but I am a man who thinks for himself."

He lifted something to his mouth, took a long swallow. Then he saw her looking in the rearview mirror. "Would you like a drink?"

"What is it?"

Oliveras turned, handed her a thermos and a plastic cup.

"Batidas," he said. "I make them myself with *cachaça,* because I like it better than aguardiente. We don't usually drink so early in the day, but Carnival is different, and of course *this* Carnival is more different than all."

Lavalle poured a cup and sipped at it. The chilled drink was astringent and sweet at the same time, with a faint alcoholic bite. "You like it?" Oliveras asked, smiling in the mirror.

"Yes, it's very good." She tried to hand the thermos back, but Oliveras said, "No, keep it, I have more."

She sat back, took another sip, and pressed the button to roll down the window beside her. The air that flowed in was cool and almost fresh.

When she looked up, she saw that he had put a phone window in the flatscreen and was running some kind of search program. "What are you doing?" she asked.

"Trying to make a reservation in Rosario." He glanced at the screen from time to time as he drove. After a while he said, "They are not answering their phones. That could be because it is Carnival and they don't care, but it could also be that they are closed, or they have no rooms. All we can do is go and see."

"All right."

In the holo another float was coming into view now, and there, indeed, atop a giant white cube with black spots on it, was Stone's double in a brown suit, waving his fedora and kissing his hand to the crowd. He seemed to be having a good time.

The next float came into view; it was a mound of lemons, with three women in lemon costumes on top, waving yellow flags. Then the next, which bore a giant steer. Then there was some kind of commotion; in the holo, the commentators were standing up to look.

Oliveras bent forward, turning up the sound in his flatscreen. ". . . sort of accident, apparently . . ." The holo flickered and changed to a view from another camera. Now she could see the Cube float; it was halted, and the double was nowhere to be seen. ". . . Ed Stone has been shot. . . . We are waiting for a report. . . ."

A red-and-white ambulance, with its flashers spinning in the sunlight, edged its way into the crowd. Police were beginning to herd people back. She caught a glimpse of a litter with a body on it, covered with a blanket except for the pale face.

Oliveras said, "Is that your husband, Ed Stone? Maybe you should call and see if he is all right."

"He's not my husband, and he's all right," she said. She was trembling again.

He gestured with one hand. "Okay."

She looked at her wrist. It was a little after nine-thirty, and that was Eastern Standard, because she hadn't thought to change it. Sylvia might be up by now, even though it was Saturday. She got the phone out of her bag. It rang four times; then Sylvia's sleepy voice answered.

"Syl, it's Linda. Did I wake you up?"

"No, I was going to get up in three hours anyway. Where are you?"

"In Argentina."

"Right."

"Listen, will you call my office Monday and tell them I'm not going to be in?"

"Let me try the other ear. You really want me to tell them you're in Argentina?"

"I *am* in Argentina. Wait a minute." She passed the phone to the driver. "Will you tell my friend where we are?"

"Where we are? Of course." He spoke into the phone. "We are on the highway between Buenos Aires and Rosario, about thirty kilometers north of Buenos Aires. Thank you." He handed the phone back.

"Who was that?" Sylvia asked.

"My driver. I'm looking for a hotel."

"Other ear again. You're looking for a hotel on the highway?"

"They're all *full,* in B.A. Listen, Sylvia, I'll come back if I can, after things settle down, but I can't fly again, and I don't think there are any boats."

"You *flew* to Buenos Aires? How did you do that?"

"Listen, I'll write you a letter, okay?" She hung up and put the phone back in her bag. Her headache was getting worse. She looked in her bag for aspirins, found them, and washed a couple down with a drink from the thermos.

The phone was buzzing again. She took it out of the bag. "Hello?"

"Linda, dear, where are you? We've been terribly worried."

"Never mind, Geoffrey."

"Honey, tell me where you *are.* Are you in Buenos Aires? I'll send a plane for you, or if you don't want that, I'll charter a ship and bring you home."

"No, you won't."

"Are you thinking of that little demonstration, Linda? You know the reason for that. Is your leg feeling all right, by the way?"

"Yes, it is, no thanks to you. What about the parade in Buenos Aires?"

"You mean the double who was shot? Linda, you know my associates had nothing to do with that. Nobody wanted him dead, then he'd be a martyr."

"Okay, but who knows what you might want next week? I think I'm better off where I am."

Her mother's voice came on suddenly. "But Linda, where *are* you?"

She punched off.

Oliveras was phoning again. "Ah!" he said. He turned.

"I have a room for you in Mercedes. That's the one in Uruguay. You have your passport?"

"Yes— Oh, no!" She stopped. "I gave it to them at the hotel, and I never thought to get it back. Oh, *damn!*"

Oliveras was silent.

"Can we get across the border without it?" she asked.

"I don't think so. From Uruguay to here, yes, because everybody is coming this way. But from Argentina to Uruguay, no, because they want to know why you are going the wrong direction."

"Oh, dear. Well, keep trying, will you?"

"Surely."

She looked at the controls of the holo, called up a menu. The holo had full phone capability. She tapped in her number, added caller ID, and then a window.

A queue appeared on the screen:

709 354-1919 Geoffrey Nero

211 854-0718 Sylvia Englander

000 595 Ed Stone

She touched the second number. After a moment Sylvia's face appeared in the tube. "Hello, Linda?"

"Yes. What's up?"

"Linda, Ed's been calling, and so has Geoffrey. I told Ed you're on the highway somewhere. I didn't tell Geoffrey anything. Was that right?"

"Oh, hell, I told Ed I was in a bar. Well, never mind."

"Well, what was I supposed to do? This phone has been driving me crazy, Linda."

"No, it's okay. You were right about Geoffrey. He broke my leg."

"He did what?"

"Broke my *leg*. Well, he didn't do it, his butler did it. He wanted to prove to Ed that something would happen to me if he didn't do what he wants."

"If who didn't do what who wants? Never mind. Linda, are you taking anything?"

"I had a pill before I got on the plane. I'm drinking batidas now."

"What are batidas?"

"They're made with aguardiente and lime juice, except that these are made with *cachaça.* They're very, very good."

"Is that right? Linda, I think it would be a good idea if you came home."

"I can't do that. You don't know. You don't know, Syl. It was *horrible.* Listen, can you pack up my clothes?"

"Pack them up and send them where?"

"I don't know where yet. Maybe Buenos Aires, but don't tell Geoffrey."

"Uh, okay."

"Don't tell Ed either, okay? You can have my cocktail dresses and my high heels. And my purses. And all that junk in the bathroom."

A pause. "Linda, you're really not coming back?"

"I don't think so. Talk to you later, Syl."

CHAPTER 35

They stopped at a roadside stand long enough to buy barbecued beef sandwiches. The proprietor, a morose beer-bellied man, served them without a smile. His wife was roasting the meat, while three children, in graduated sizes, stood and watched. The oil-drum stove was smoking, and flies danced over the counter. They drove down the highway a few hundred yards, parked again, and ate sitting in the car, with the doors open and their feet on the ground. The doors, opening front and rear, sheltered them from the wind. Gulls were coasting white over the river. The sun was pleasantly warm on Lavalle's face.

"And now tell me, what about you?" asked Oliveras. "Do you think you'll go in the Cube, or will you stay here?"

"I'll stay."

"So you don't think it's true about the other planet?"

"I don't think anything."

He licked his fingers. "Are you going to finish your sandwich?"

"No. Here, take it."

He ate the rest of the sandwich. "Excuse me a moment," he said. He climbed the rail, went down the slope behind a tree, and urinated rather loudly.

* * *

There were no vacancies in Rosario, but they passed a clothing store, and Lavalle asked him to stop. The store had little stock left, and almost nothing in her size, but she bought at shockingly inflated prices a pair of shoes the same color as the ones she was wearing, in a size big enough to fit over the cast, and some underwear and two shift-dresses in bilious pastel colors; and at a pharmacy down the street she got tampons and another bottle of aspirin.

They drove on. After a while he said, "I have a room in Villa María. But that is another two hundred kilometers from here."

"All right, let's go."

It was late afternoon when they found the motel, a little place with a courtyard, a block from the highway. Oliveras carried her bags in. "Thank you very much," she said. "What do I owe you?"

He took a minicom out of his pocket. "Will you pay in australes?"

"Yes."

He looked at the screen. "One hundred and eighty thousand, Señora."

It was about double what she had expected, but she counted out the bills and added a tip. He stuffed the bills into his pocket. "Now I have to go exchange these before the rate falls again."

"What will you exchange them for?"

"Gold. Do you want to come with me, and exchange your money, too?"

"I would advise it, Señora," said the man behind the desk. His nameplate said "Sr. Aguirrez." He added to Oliveras, "The Banco Nacional is on the Avenida Cabildo Abierto, five streets north of here."

"Thank you. You'll take care of the bags?"

"Certainly, sir."

They got back in the taxi. "I never thought of exchanging money," she said. "How stupid."

"Well, this morning the rate would have been better," he said cheerfully, "but tomorrow it will be worse, so it's equal."

There were long lines in the bank, but people motioned them forward, smiling, when they saw Lavalle's cast and her American clothes. The rate posted over the window was three thousand australes to the gram. "Would you like this in Krugerrands, Mexican reales, or in a certificate of deposit?" the teller asked.

"Take the coins," Oliveras said in her ear. "If the bank closes, what good is a certificate?"

"All right."

The coins tinkled into a counting machine and came out neatly wrapped. Lavalle put them in her purse; they felt very heavy. Now she understood why Oliveras had charged so much: the value of the austral had fallen by almost half.

Oliveras insisted on buying her dinner at a restaurant, where he was pleasant and charming; then he took her back to the motel. He picked up the key at the desk, found the room, opened it and followed her in.

"Señora," he said, "it is now too late to start back to Buenos Aires. Will you do me the favor of letting me sleep in the other bed?"

"Yes, but I'm very tired. I'm going to bed now."

When she came out of the bathroom in her nightgown, he was already in the other bed, but his eyes followed her.

"Good night," she said, and turned off the lamp.

"Good night, Señora."

After a long time she heard him say, "Are you sleeping?"

"No."

"Do you want to tell me about your trouble?"

She could see him in the dim light. He got up and sat on the edge of her bed. He was young, good-looking, friendly, and he smelled clean. "Sometimes, you know," he said, "it helps to tell somebody."

"I can't go back because somebody might kill me," she said.

"The same one who tried to kill the other one, the man in the parade?"

"I don't know. I don't think so. A lot of people want to kill *him.*"

"Well, but you could go somewhere else with your friend."

"I can't do that either, and he's not my friend anymore." Her head was buzzing with the drinks she had had, and she felt she was not explaining very well. "I saw something ugly—I can't tell you about it."

"No, of course not, if it is ugly." He was stroking her shoulders.

"If you don't mind, I'd just like to be held," she said.

"Of course," he said in Spanish, "of course, little dove."

CHAPTER 36

What I think we should do now," Federigo said after breakfast, "is go back to Buenos Aires and get my money. Then I have to give some to my wife, and then we can go out in the pampa and buy horses. It is better to live there than in the city."

"I don't want to live in the pampa."

"All right," he said cheerfully, "then we will live in Buenos Aires, but in a different part of town. And I will buy horses somewhere, it doesn't matter."

"No, I'm going to stay here. We'd better say good-bye now, Federigo."

"Well, are you really sure? Last night was so beautiful."

"I'm really sure."

He shrugged and smiled. "Good-bye, then."

She watched him get into the taxi. "Good luck with your horses," she said.

He waved. "I will call you!" he said.

She shook her head with a faint smile. He waved again cheerfully and drove away.

She turned on the holo and punched in a phone window. The queue read:

Geoffrey Nero

Sylvia Englander

Federigo Oliveras

Ed Stone

His face was tired and anxious. "Hello, Linda?"

"Yes."

"Is there something wrong with the video?"

"No, I've got it turned off."

"Well, anyway, where are you?"

"Nowhere special."

"What's that supposed to mean? Linda, what happened? What's the matter?"

"I had a dream that you were either an alien, or else you made this whole thing up."

"You had a *dream?* Is that what this whole thing is about?"

"Well, what if it is a dream? I mean, whose dream is it?"

"You're not making any sense."

"I know that. So what? Good-bye."

"Wait a—" She punched off; his image dwindled and disappeared.

That night the ceiling bulged and opened. A blade came down, as long as the room; it descended and split everything in half, walls, furniture, carpet, and the halves fell away into darkness.

From her balcony she could see the lines of cars coming into town from the north, streaming away westward toward Rosario. It made her dizzy to think of these rivers of people flowing from the mountains to the coast; the whole southeastern part of the continent was emptying itself out into Rio de Janeiro, Porto Alegre, Buenos Aires.

At the market she met a family from Chile—father, mother, and five girls. They had driven over the Uspallata Pass, then across the breadth of Argentina, sight-seeing. It had been a wonderful trip, they said. It was wonderful to see so many happy people, all going to the City of God.

"Do you think that's what it is?" Lavalle asked. "Do you mean that the Cube is the City of God?"

"Oh, certainly," said the mother, wide-eyed. "You are not a Catholic?"

"I was, but no longer."

"Your faith will return," said the mother positively. She searched in her handbag and gave Lavalle a St. Christopher medal. "Please take this. If you wear it, it will surely help you."

In two days the stream of travelers had thinned to a trickle, and by the end of the week it had stopped altogether. Prices, which had soared to ridiculous levels, fell again; the store owners were taking whatever they could get. Then almost every shop in town was closed; the littered streets were empty.

The same names turned up in her phone queue day after day, but she never returned the calls, and after a while they stopped.

On Monday Señor Aguirrez said, "Señora, I am going to close the motel now and go to Buenos Aires before the boats leave. But if you would like to stay here, I'll give you the keys, you can do whatever you like."

"That's very kind of you, Señor Aguirrez. I'll probably stay a few days longer, maybe a week. How long do you think it will be before everybody leaves Buenos Aires?"

"They say nine or ten days to evacuate the Atlantic side of South America, Señora."

"Then let me pay you for another week. How much will that be in gold?"

"Whatever you like, Señora. Three hundred reales would be sufficient."

She got the money out of her purse and handed it to him.

"Thank you, Señora, you are very kind. Good-bye." She watched him drive away with his wife in a Volvo packed with belongings.

On holovision, day after day, cameras reported the exodus. The people were streaming out of the mountains and the high pampas down the roads that followed watercourses to the coastal plain. In satellite pictures they were grains slowly flowing, like corpuscles in the veins of a bleeding cadaver.

In Shanghai, early arrivals by air from all over the world were already being processed, and she watched that too. The entry points were gay with paper streamers, balloons, flowers, bells. As each family stepped out, dressed in its best, with bundles, sacks, and pets in cages, smiling young women greeted them, led them to the waiting capsules.

There were tearful good-byes, embraces. Then the attendants helped them into the capsules, packed their belongings around them. "Smile!" they said in one of five hundred languages, and an overhead camera snapped their pictures. The lids were lowered; metal arms came down and attached the photographs to the lids. The capsules moved on through one junction after another, accelerating each time. When they entered the eight hundred twenty-six lanes of the final stage, they were moving at more than a hundred miles an hour. Under the gaily colored canopies, they zoomed up the scaffolding, crossed the grid and were locked into place. Twenty-three every second, two million a day.

By Wednesday the town seemed almost empty. Some stores were locked or boarded up; others stood open and empty. Along every residential street were little piles of abandoned belongings: clothing, books, toys. The garbage had not been collected for three days, and there was a pestilential smell.

There were plenty of abandoned cars in Villa Maria, but she had seen the holo pictures of the clogged approaches to Buenos Aires, and it was obvious that she could not get through that way. In the garage of an abandoned house, finally, she found a little Yugo moped with a trailer. She drove it back to the motel, loaded her luggage and supplies, and started south.

All along the highway on both sides was a sad scattering: clothing, toys, cabinets, drifts of paper spread out to dry like exposed obscenities. King vultures, ungainly white birds with black wings and gaudy multicolored necks, were hunched over bits of offal; a few unidentifiable mounds were covered with red or black ants. The smell of excrement was everywhere, and there were a great many flies.

The closer she got to the center of town, the more dogs

there were, dogs of all sizes and colors, running back and forth, sniffing one another, or sitting on their haunches with their wet red tongues hanging out. None of them looked as if they were starving, but they made her uneasy. There were cats, too, in alleyways, and several times she saw parakeets on balconies and rooftops. She turned off into a suburban district, avoiding main avenues, and found a dead-end street where the doors of a small house stood open. Inside, the house was in disarray, but there were linens, kitchen utensils, the gas and water had not been turned off.

CHAPTER 37

Exploring the next day, she found a supermarket that still had some food on its shelves. The market was unattended; a few people were casually picking through the merchandise and carrying it away in carts.

One of the other shoppers, a woman in her fifties, told her about a warehouse near the waterfront where vast quantities of dried and irradiated food were stored, and after that she went there on her moped for serious shopping. The city was nine-tenths empty; people who met on the street smiled happily at each other and often stopped to chat. Within a week she had made as many friends and acquaintances as she had had in New York.

A surprising number of restaurants were still open in the

central area, and the same was true of cocktail bars and nightclubs. She discovered that the bar she liked best was Johnny's, on the Avenida Corrientes near the Hilton. The night bartender was a cheerful Dane named Ekstrom, who told amusing stories in five languages, and who sometimes shut up the till, joined the customers and let them pour their own drinks. Several journalists came here every night after work; actors and impresarios from the Teatro Colón also turned up, and an odd assortment of city functionaries, teachers, defrocked priests, lawyers, and gamblers. Before long she had formed a circle of friends there, mostly men whose automatic gallantries were easy to deal with.

She had stopped taking phone calls from the North long ago; the message queue in her phone window had dwindled; now no one called her from anywhere but B.A. Out of boredom and curiosity, she began spending some time on a global service devoted to students of the paranormal, where she used a false name and never showed her face. Some of the other users were woo-woos, but some were more skeptical and intelligent. There were half a dozen of them that she liked best. One of them was a man who called himself John the Baptist. From the wry style of his posted messages, she imagined him as lean, almost skeletal, with a narrow bird-skulled face, dark eyes and paper skin, but the images he flashed from time to time were nothing like that. Sometimes he was the Beast in Cocteau's film, sometimes Darth Vader, sometimes Byron or Oscar Wilde sniffing a lily.

Although she had no rent to pay, and food was free as the air, she needed money for some things, chiefly entertainment, and she was running short faster than she had expected. One of her new friends was a doctor, Enrique Monteleone, a dark-skinned man in his forties; one night she brought Wellafield's medical bag to Johnny's and showed it to him.

He opened the bag skeptically and looked at the forceps. "These are quite old," he said. "Where did you get them?"

"From a retired doctor."

"Yes? He must have retired a long time ago." He picked up two of the vials and looked at them. "These are fresh, however. Well, how much would you like me to pay you?"

"I don't know. Would a hundred thousand australes be too much?"

He smiled sadly. "They are worth something, of course, because these instruments are not being made now. There are many in warehouses, naturally, but they will wear out, and then we will have to make new ones by hand. I will give you the hundred thousand, on one condition."

"Yes?"

"That you have dinner with me tomorrow night at my house."

She looked at him. A hundred thousand australes was about five thousand dollars, enough for ten restaurant meals. "I'll have dinner with you on one condition," she said.

"Yes?"

"That you allow me to make you a present of the bag."

"Aha." He smiled in a different way, and looked much younger. "I accept with pleasure."

Monteleone, together with several other medical practitioners, had scavenged all the pharmacies in town, and also the pharmaceutical warehouses, arriving in most cases after they had been looted, but although the doctors had found very few opiates, they had retrieved a vast store of other useful drugs. Unfortunately the shelf life of most of them was a year or less. Insulin was no longer available. Penicillin and other antibiotics were in short supply. Vaccines for a dozen diseases were not to be had. Worse still, from Monteleone's viewpoint, ordinary anesthetics were no longer obtainable. They were forced to fall back on diethyl ether and chloroform, which could be produced with simple equipment, but with whose use in medicine nobody was familiar any longer; they lost some patients for this reason, and because of inadequate antisepsis.

A small band of volunteers worked to keep the garbage collected and the water supply safe. Lavalle toiled with the rest, but as early as 2006 there were outbreaks of smallpox and diphtheria.

After the cholera epidemic of 2008, which killed Monteleone and most of his patients, almost all the survivors left B.A., where the stench was becoming intolerable. Exploring on her moped, Lavalle found a three-story house in an abandoned town called La Paz, on the east bank of the Paraná about four hundred kilometers north of Buenos Aires. Evidently the house had been fitted up as a survivalist refuge: there was a good deal of communication equipment, and a diesel generator in the basement. The house had its own well, with an electric pump.

There were scattered human bones in the house. She found five skulls, one of which was a child's, another an infant's. There were wild-animal droppings on the floor, and twice she glimpsed pumas in the neighborhood.

She cleaned out the whole house and scrubbed it until it no longer stank. She cut down two trees that grew too close to the house. Then she boarded up the front and back doors and all the windows on the ground floor; from then on, she went in and out through a second-story window, using a rope ladder. When she brought things home, she raised them with a pulley. In October she cleared a plot of ground and planted a vegetable garden.

CHAPTER 38

"Mrs. Filer, thank you for agreeing to see us," said the taller of the two men. "I'm David Mortimer, and this is Stan Keenan."

"Glad to know you."

"Now, Mrs. Filer, as we told you on the phone, we understand your husband disappeared about ten years ago. And he never turned up again?"

"No. Never saw him again."

"He never wrote? Sent you money?"

"No."

"Excuse these questions, Mrs. Filer, but there are certain things we have to know. Was your husband ever convicted of a felony?"

"He passed some bad checks."

"Was he arrested for that?"

"No, that was when he disappeared."

"Was he ever fingerprinted, that you know of?"

"I don't think so. That was the first trouble he was in."

"Did he have any scars, or distinguishing marks?"

"No."

"Was he right- or left-handed?"

"Right."

"At the time he disappeared, was he under some stress, do you think?"

"I suppose so. He was fired from his job. He was always reading those crazy magazines, and he was upset about pollution and things like that."

"What crazy magazines are those?"

"You know, spaceships and Martians. He tried to get me to read them, but I thought they were too farfetched."

"Science fiction magazines?"

"Yes. He had a closet full of them."

"Do you still have those magazines, Mrs. Filer?"

"No, I threw them all out."

"What was your husband's height and weight, would you say?"

"He was about five ten, a hundred forty, forty-five. He was healthy, but he didn't eat right."

"Do you have any photos of your husband? I'm sorry, but it might be important."

"I think there are a couple put away. What's it all about?"

"It's possible that we might have some current information about the whereabouts of your husband. If he is the person we have in mind, he's quite well off."

She looked at them for a moment, then said, "Wait while I look." She left the room and returned a few minutes later with a handful of snapshots. Keenan put them into a viewer, and the two men passed it back and forth.

"I think it's a make," said Mortimer to Keenan. "Mrs. Filer, did your husband always have this beard?"

"Ever since I knew him."

"You never saw him clean-shaven?"

"No."

"Mrs. Filer, we'd like you to look at some holos. May I put this cube in your machine?"

"Sure." She watched with curiosity as Keenan inserted the little cube and turned on the holo. In the tube, a clean-shaven young man appeared.

"Is that your husband, Mrs. Filer?"

"No. That's Ed Stone, the man who's building the Cube."

"You've seen him on the holo, and never thought he could be your husband?"

"Oh, no. That isn't him."

Keenan pressed a button on his controller; in the holo, one of the snapshots of Filer appeared beside the image of Stone. "Look closely, Mrs. Filer. Now we're going to use an image enhancement program that will show what Ed Stone would look like if he had a beard like your husband's."

In the holo, Stone became bearded. The two faces stared out, side by side. "Now what do you think?"

"Oh. That's amazing! But I've heard his voice, and it's different."

"Different how?"

"Kind of lower and hoarser."

"Do you know that Ed Stone has been suffering from laryngitis?"

"No, I didn't know that."

"Well, Mrs. Filer, we think there is a very good chance that Ed Stone is in fact your missing husband. If so, of course, we want to establish that fact, and see that he makes a settlement for the years you brought up your children without his help."

She began to cry. "Why didn't he ever—"

"It's possible that he's suffering from amnesia, Mrs. Filer. If so, seeing you might bring his memory back. Now we'd like to arrange for you to go to New York or Washington the next time he's there, and of course bring the children. We realize that this would entail some heavy expenses for you, and we'll see to it that you're provided with the funds you need."

"But what about all this stuff like being kidnapped by aliens, and building a big box to put everybody in?"

"Delusions, Mrs. Filer. Your husband is a sick man, and of course he's very dangerous."

CHAPTER 39

Stone and his bodyguard were crossing the lobby when a woman in a cheap coat stood up and called, "Howard!" She had two children with her, a teen-aged boy and girl. Stone glanced at her and kept walking, but she ran after him. The bodyguard intercepted her. She leaned around his arm to call, "Howard, don't you know me?"

"I don't think so. My name isn't Howard, it's Ed."

Her eyes filled with tears. "Howard, this is Joyce. I'm your *wife.*"

"Listen, you're making some mistake. Leave her alone, Al, it's all right. Ma'am, I never—" He reached for her hand, but she drew away.

"You left me with two little kids, and I never heard a word from you, you just went. How could you do such a thing?"

"Ma'am, I'm sorry, but you're mistaken."

"I wrote you *three letters,* but you never answered. I had to borrow money to come here."

"Let's get out," said the bodyguard in a low voice. "There's a guy with a minicam over there, and I think this is a setup."

"You worry too much," said Stone. He tipped his hat to the woman and they left.

"Ed, we're in trouble," said Ben Abrams. "The *New York Times* is going to release a report tomorrow that you're a phony."

"What?"

"They say you're a man named Howard Filer who disappeared from his home in Pittsburgh in May, twenty oh one. They have photographs of Filer, who looks like you, and they have a statement from his wife, who says you're him."

"Well, that can't be. Oh, Jesus, that's the one that came up to me in the lobby."

"Yes, Al told me about it. And they've got the dealer who sold you that magazine."

"What magazine?"

"The old skiffy magazine you've shown people. Now this could undermine confidence in the whole Cube Project unless we do something."

"Who is this guy who says he sold me the magazine?"

"His name is Leonard Applebaum, he has a secondhand store in Dayton."

"Dayton, Ohio? I was never there."

"Well, we'll know more in a couple of days. Meanwhile, let's not worry, but it doesn't look good."

Ed's advisers were having a skull session in the penthouse.

"They've filed suit in Superior Court in Pittsburgh for

desertion and nonsupport, asking a million dollars in actual damages and fifty million in punitive damages."

"We've got to either discredit them or buy them off."

"In the first place, we don't know who *they* are. Mrs. Filer is obviously being financed by somebody, but we haven't been able to find out who."

"Who stands to gain by this?"

"Maybe the Chinese."

"How do you figure that?"

"Well, if this scandal gives them an excuse to halt the Cube Project, and if the Earth isn't destroyed, who's going to be left after everybody else gets in the box? Chinese."

"Do you think they *started* the whole thing? Could they have brainwashed Ed somehow?"

"Don't even suggest it. Look, *I'm* not saying there's any merit to the lawsuit. She says herself that she didn't recognize Ed on the holo for ten years. Her own husband? Come on."

"He had a beard when she knew him."

"Sure, and they can put him in a computer simulation and grow any kind of beard they want on him. But the point is, is this could throw a monkey wrench in the whole project."

"What do you recommend, Sol?"

"Well, we'll move for dismissal. We can gain a little time that way, but not much. If we go to court, they're going to subject Ed to an examination by experts on the nineteen-thirties, to try to prove he isn't from then. We've got to anticipate that, and I think we should put together our own panel of whores."

"Of whores?"

"Expert witnesses. 'Whore' is the legal term. In fact, we ought to have *two* panels, one hostile and the other on our side. We use the second one to combat their whores, and we use the first one to anticipate what they might do in court."

Sol Meredith shook hands with Stone. "Ed, following your instructions, I've met with Mrs. Filer's attorneys to explore the possibility of a settlement, and they turned me down flat. Now this doesn't mean they *won't* settle, it just means they're not willing to talk about it now."

"Did you tell them we'd pay what they're asking?"

"I made that clear, and they indicated that their client wants her day in court."

"They're out to get me."

"Yes, I think that's right. We know somebody is financing this suit, and I've been able to find out that the money is being handled by Wolper and Rogers in New York, but they're acting for somebody else, and if we were able to get that far I'll bet we would find out those people are acting for somebody else too. We could pursue that, but in my opinion it would be a waste of time. We have to assume now that the case is going to court, and we have to prepare for trial."

"I think I know who the somebody is."

"Yes? Who?"

"Geoffrey Nero, an investor in Rye. He lives on Hundred Yard Drive. It isn't him, probably, but it's somebody he's connected with."

Meredith scribbled on his memopad. "What makes you think he's behind this?"

"He tried to get me to lay off about seven years ago. He broke Linda's leg to show me he meant business."

"He did?" Meredith addressed the computer. "Selina, search Geoffrey Nero, address on Hundred Yard Drive in Rye, New York."

"Geoffrey with a G?" asked the computer.

"Yes, dear."

"Thank you. Geoffrey Nero, formerly of 100 Hundred Yard Drive, died September tenth, twenty oh seven."

"Oh, hell," said Stone.

"Selina, who were his business associates? Print out the list when you get it."

"Yes, boss."

"We'll look into that," said Meredith, "but I don't think it will do any good, do you?"

"No."

"We're talking with Dr. Brian Letterman, the author of *Why We Don't Behave Like We Should.* Dr. Letterman, you believe that we human beings are programmed to believe what we're told in childhood, is that correct?"

"Well, Donald, you can see that the tendency to believe anything you're told several times would be a strong survival characteristic. Under primitive conditions, anything you're told repeatedly by your elders is quite likely to be true. Where to find edible plants, what parts of them are poisonous, and so on. A young human being who adopted an attitude of skepticism in these matters would probably have a short life span. Well, as a by-product this tendency would carry with it the tendency to believe all kinds of other things, many of them not true at all, but in terms of individual survival it *doesn't matter* whether those things are true or not.

"Now in terms of group survival, it turns out that it does matter a great deal: not *what* the group believes, especially, but *whether* it has a strong common belief, because that unites it against other groups and makes it cohere both socially and genetically. And for these purposes, we see that it's a positive advantage to believe in something completely absurd. All these things are isolating mechanisms, and for that you don't want something reasonable. Nobody is going to die for the proposition that water runs downhill."

"So you think human beings have a tendency to believe things *because* they're absurd?"

"Obviously so, or we wouldn't all be rushing to pack ourselves into a cube a mile on a side."

"I'm Diane Oliver."

"And I'm Robert Bellevue, and this is *Your Bright Morning*. At the top of the news, recent allegations about Ed Stone have shocked the nation and the world. Are these allegations true? We don't know, but a picture is emerging of a confused young man who believed that overpopulation and pollution were going to cause the end of the world, and who was so distressed that he became a victim of amnesia, left his family, and believed that he had been kidnapped by aliens. To bolster this story, he acquired nineteen-thirties clothing from a costumer and various other articles, including an old magazine. Steven Alswanger, an attorney for Mrs. Howard Filer, said this morning, 'We have located the dealer who sold him the magazine. He even went to the extent of having gold inlays put in two of his teeth. We haven't found the dentist who did that, but we're still looking, and eventually he will come forward.' "

"Robert, how do you account for the fact that so many people believed his story?"

"Well, Diane, it's an astounding instance of human gullibility, but it's happened before. Hitler was able to persuade millions of Germans to support him in a catastrophic war against his neighbors in Europe. Christ and Mohammed created fanatical movements that swept the world. We don't know why these things happen, but maybe we ought to know."

The legal team was meeting with their client in Meredith's office. "Ed, did you ever have a beard?"

"Yeah, when I was on the spaceship. I shaved it off as soon as I could. It itched."

"How long was the beard?"

Stone held up one finger crosswise under his chin. "About like this."

"So, you must have been on the spaceship about a month?"

"Maybe so."

"And you grew a beard because you didn't have anything to shave with?"

"Right. They gave all that stuff back when I left."

"Ed, what did you eat while you were on the spaceship?"

"There was some kind of like gelatin hanging from the ceiling. You could pull off a chunk and eat it. It was sweet."

"What about water?"

"It was dripping down one wall of the room I was in. Lukewarm."

"And toilet facilities?"

"The basin where the water went down. It wasn't like the Ritz."

"And you were all alone on the spaceship, except for the aliens?"

"I didn't say that. There were all kinds of animals—they showed me pictures. People, too, but they were in suspended animation. What's the point of all this?"

"Ed, we've got to deal with this story. Let me ask you bluntly, is it possible that you imagined the whole thing?"

"Sure it is. How would I know?"

"Is it possible that you're Howard Filer?"

"Anything is *possible.* Jesus Christ!"

The three A-team whores were sitting around a table in a bar on Fiftieth Street. "One of the things we may have to explain," said Dr. Fine, "is just this: if Stone is who he claims to be, and he was kidnapped by aliens and so on, and they put something in his ring that makes people believe what he tells them, what could that substance be?"

"It's possible, it seems to me," Dr. Savage replied, "that there are naturally occurring neurochemicals in human beings that do exactly the same thing—mediate love and belief, so that children tend to grow up believing whatever their parents believe. These would have to be stable substances that could be passed from parent to child by contact—mucosal contact especially. That would account at least in part for the stability of religious and political beliefs, and of course things like xenophobia, sexism, homophobia, and racism."

"Aren't you multiplying entities?" asked Dr. Coleman.

"No, because we're trying to account for a real phenomenon. The effects would be masked by things we already know about—indoctrination, peer pressure, and so on—but these substances, if they exist, would account for a good many rather puzzling things. Ninety-nine point something percent of Mormons who grow up in Mormon communities and go to Mormon colleges remain Mormons. The apostasy rate for Catholics is higher, because they often go to secular colleges, and the rate for Protestants is higher still."

"Because they're exposed to other ideas," said Dr. Fine.

"Yes, and other *neurochemicals,* especially when they marry, or have intimate relationships with, other students. By the way, these substances could also explain sexual bonding in adults. When we talk about 'making love,' it isn't just a euphemism, it's literal. That's how you really *make* love." There were murmurs of assent, puffs of pipe smoke.

"And we know these effects are long-lasting, because bonding survives long separations. But it does wear off eventually. The substances are stable, but they're excreted slowly and fall below a threshold value."

"So the whole thing really could be, uh, true."

"Oh, yes, I think so, definitely, yes."

"Mrs. Vernon, thank you for seeing me. How are you today?"

"I'm hurting with my arthritis. Who did you say you are again?"

"I'm from a national research agency. We'd like to ascertain some facts about your parents. Was your father named Edwin L. Stone?"

"My mother called him Ed."

"Ed Stone?"

"Yes, Ed Stone."

"Do you have any family photos, Mrs. Vernon? Do you have a picture of your father?"

"Oh, no. We left him when I was a child."

"Do you know what happened to your father after that?"

"No. We never talked about him."

"Did you have any sisters or brothers?"

"One brother. He died in nineteen eighty-eight."

"What was his name, Mrs. Vernon?"

"Larry. Lawrence."

"Was he married? Did he have any children?"

"He was married twice. The first one, they had three children. His second wife didn't want any."

"Do you remember the names of the children?"

"Well, yes. The oldest was Elsie, she married a mining engineer and went to New Zealand. Then there was Robert, I think he went into real estate. And the youngest was Stephanie, but she died when she was twenty."

"Where did Robert Stone live, do you know?"

"California. Los Angeles."

"Stone Harris Realty, good morning."

"Mr. Robert Stone, please."

"May I ask who's calling?"

Meredith covered the phone for a moment. "Bingo," he said.

One of Meredith's bright young men flew to Los Angeles and came back with a photo of Robert Stone's grandfather: it showed a young man standing in bright sunlight beside what looked like a Model T Ford. His hat shaded his eyes.

Meredith said, "All this proves is that there was an Ed Stone who lived in Harrisburg at the right time. Neither Mrs. Vernon nor Robert Stone have any recollection that the full name was Edwin L. We can depose Robert and get him to say, yes, to the best of his knowledge and belief this is a photograph of his grandfather Ed Stone, and we'll do that. And we can get a whore to analyze the photo and say, based on bone structure and so on, this is a picture of Ed. But the prosecution can get a whore to say just the opposite. The prosecution could argue, and undoubtedly will argue, that even if we can prove there was an Edwin L. Stone who was born in Altoona and lived in Harrisburg, and so on, that doesn't prove Ed is not an impostor. If he planned this carefully, he could have gone to those places and looked up everything he needed to know."

"Taken the place of a real Edwin L. Stone?"

"Who was married and had two children, and so on. You can get all that stuff out of *newspapers,* for Christ's sake. He wouldn't even have to go anywhere, he could use computer databases."

"So you're saying we can't prove he didn't do that."

"No, we can't, and the prosecution can't prove he did, either, but if they produce enough witnesses who claim to have known Ed as Filer, they can sway a jury, and that's what they're counting on."

"What would you say our chances are?"

"Fifty-fifty."

CHAPTER 40

"Now, Mr. Stone," said Meredith, playing devil's advocate, "what was going on in the world in April, nineteen thirty-one?"

"There was some kind of disarmament conference in Europe. Jimmy Walker was in trouble."

"Jimmy Walker was—?"

"Mayor of New York."

"And he was in what kind of trouble?"

"Corruption. They said he was on the take."

"Does 'on the take' mean that he was accepting bribes?"

"Correct."

"What nations took part in the disarmament conference, if you know?"

"Uh, England, Germany and France, I think. Maybe some others."

"What was the last moving picture you saw in nineteen thirty-one?"

"Wheeler and Woolsey, in *Coco-Nuts.*"

"Mr. Stone, who was the mayor of Harrisburg in nineteen thirty-one?"

"George A. Hoverter."

"And the governor of Pennsylvania?"

"Gifford Pinchot."

"What was your last home address in Harrisburg?"

"One ninety-one Elm Street."

"And the name of your last employer?"

"Jack Wintergarden. He owned a speakeasy down on Tenth Avenue."

"What was the name of the speakeasy?"

"It didn't have one. They just called it Jack's Place."

"Mr. Stone, you contend that you were always clean-shaven, is that correct?"

"Well, sometimes I let it go for a day or two."

"But you never grew a beard?"

"No."

"What brand of shaving cream did you use?"

"I used soap."

"What kind of razor?"

"Gillette."

"Where did you buy the suit you were wearing?"

"I got it from Monkey Ward."

"Mr. Stone, how can you prove to us that you are not Howard Filer?"

"Look, *I remember* being on the spaceship. I remember what it was like growing up in Harrisburg. I *don't* remember this Howard Filer. Okay, if you want to say maybe I've forgotten all about that and remembered this other stuff because I'm crazy, okay, how can I say that isn't true? But how do any of you know that what *you* remember is true?"

"Now, Ed, this is the part of the procedure that we call 'discovery.' It's where each side shows the other side what evidence they've got and what witnesses they'll put on the stand. So it's almost like a trial, except there's no judge and no jury."

"I never heard of that."

"No, because you never see it in holos, but this is the way we always do it. And look at it this way, it's *good* for us to have this procedure, because if they score any points against you, we'll fix that and make sure it doesn't happen at the real trial. Okay?"

"I guess."

Mrs. Filer was wearing a modest blue suit with a Peter Pan collar, and a little pillbox hat. "That's the way they'll dress her for the trial," Meredith said. "Smart."

In the holo, he was saying, "Now, Mrs. Filer, when your husband left you, it caused you great distress, didn't it?"

"Yes." Her eyes reddened; she put a tissue to her nose.

"I'm sure we can all understand that. And did you make any effort to find your husband?"

"I asked all his friends."

"Anything more?"

"What do you mean, hire a detective? I didn't have any money."

"I understand. And of course you got a job, and raised your two children without any help."

"Yes, I did."

"For eleven years."

"Yes."

"Mrs. Filer, when did Ed Stone first become a national figure, if you know?"

"I don't know."

"It was in two thousand and two, wasn't it?"

"Mr. Meredith," Slattery said, " you're trying to lead and coerce the witness."

"Off the record," said Meredith. The holo went dark, then lighted again.

"Mrs. Filer, it was in two thousand and two that Ed Stone became a well-known figure, wasn't it?"

"If you say so."

"And that was the year after your husband disappeared?"

"If you say so."

"Well, Mrs. Filer, was it or wasn't it? In what year did your husband disappear?"

"Twenty oh one. I told you that."

"And twenty oh one was the year before twenty oh two, wasn't it?"

"One moment." Slattery hitched himself nearer and spoke into his client's ear. "You may resume."

"Yes," said Mrs. Filer.

"That's good. Now, Mrs. Filer, from twenty oh one to the time you filed this lawsuit, how many times would you estimate you saw Ed Stone on holo, or saw his picture in magazines?"

"Calls for a conclusion, Mr. Meredith."

"Noted. Please answer, Mrs. Filer."

"I don't know."

"Well, was it more than a hundred times? Was it more than fifty?"

"She said she didn't know, Mr. Meredith. This is harassment."

"Off the record." The holo went blank, lighted again.

"What's that for?" Stone asked.

"We can yell at each other off the record," said Meredith. "It's part of the game. Slattery is a decent man, in fact, but this is the role he has to play."

In the holo, his voice was saying, "Well, Mrs. Filer, you do recall that you saw Ed Stone on the news a certain number of times during those ten years, isn't that so?"

"I suppose so."

"That number of times wasn't zero, was it?"

"No."

"And yet you waited for *ten years* before you filed this suit, Mrs. Filer. Why was that?"

"I didn't know it was him."

"You didn't know it was him. And you don't know it's him now, do you?"

"Yes, I do."

"And how do you know?"

"Because I've seen a picture of him with a beard."

"Where and when did you see that picture, Mrs. Filer?"

"In my house, last year."

"And who showed you that picture, Mrs. Filer?"

"Nobody. I used a computer program to put a beard on him."

"And nobody showed you that picture, Mrs. Filer?"

"No."

"Mrs. Filer, do you know what is meant by the word perjury?"

"Yes."

"Tell me what it is, if you would."

"Not telling the truth."

"And you took an oath to tell the truth, didn't you, Mrs. Filer?"

"Yes."

Meredith stopped the machine and tapped a key. "That's about what we expected," he said. "She's not a good witness, she's obviously covering up something, and I think the jury will sense that. But the other witnesses will be harder to shake." He started the machine again. "This is Albert Nims, a plumbing contractor. Filer was his employee, or rather had been."

Slattery was saying, "Mr. Nims, I show you a computer-enhanced picture and I ask you to identify it."

"No groundwork, Mr. Slattery."

"Mr. Meredith, as you well know, I can show you groundwork. Do you want to be here over the weekend? I can oblige you."

"Off the record."

Meredith sighed. "Well, I can shorten this." He touched a key. In the holo, Nims said, "That's him."

"No doubt about it?"

"No doubt about it."

The holo flickered. "This is Claudia Westcott, the former proprietor of a grocery where Filer cashed a bad check before he disappeared."

"That's him."

"No doubt about it?"

"No doubt about it."

"This is *crazy,*" Stone said. "I never saw those people."

"I know, but they've got thirteen more. They were thorough. They tracked down every living person who knew Filer, and showed them all the same doctored picture. And that's going to have a devastating effect on the jury."

"Can they get away with that—using a phony picture?"

"In fact, I can probably object to it, but it's likely that the judge will then order you to grow a beard. Are you ready to take the chance that your own beard will look about the same as the one in the enhanced photo?"

Stone said, "What about that list I gave you—all those kids I used to know in school? Some of *them* must be alive."

"We've tried to trace every name on that list. We did find a daughter of George Smith—"

"Yeah, I remember George."

"—but she doesn't remember her father ever talking about you, and, you know, why would she? She's an old woman, in her eighties. To find somebody you knew still alive—well, it could happen, but it just isn't likely."

"I'm Gerald Shakespeare, and this is *My Turn.* It seems clear now that this whole fantastic story of Ed Stone's has been the invention of a sick mind. There aren't any aliens, and they aren't going to come and take us to another planet. But four billion people have already gone into that enormous cube, and we don't know any way to get them out. Effectively, they are dead. This is the most horrendous crime ever perpetrated on this planet. Not only has this one man murdered four billion people, but in order to satisfy his neurotic fantasies about overpopulation, he has destroyed Western civilization. We now have no hope of regaining our former level of technology for many years, if ever. We are being driven back on a pre-nineteen-forty way of living. Perhaps we will slide farther back than that, to a Colonial way of existence. And there is nothing to be done about it now. The only thing we can do is arrest this man and try him for mass murder and execute him in the most painful way the law allows, and even that won't be enough."

Meredith said, "If this case goes to trial and we lose, we can appeal the verdict all the way to the Supreme Court, and that might delay it long enough to make it moot, but now they're going to bring criminal charges, and once those charges are filed, Ed will be arrested and held without bail. I hate to say this, but we've got to get him out of the country."

"Won't that look like an admission of guilt?"

"Yes, it will, but once he's out of the reach of extradition he can still move around, he can tell his side of the story. Remember that if he loses the civil case, that just means he has to pay damages to a woman who claims to be his wife. That won't mean much to most people around the world. But if they convict him of *murder,* that would be a different story. He's got to go."

"Where to?"

"I've got a list here of countries that have no extradition

treaties with the U.S. China is one. Then there's Monaco, Luxembourg, a few places like that. Some others in Asia and Africa. I'd say for media access, Monaco or Luxembourg would be the best, but he might have something else in mind."

CHAPTER 41

The Cube railhead was served by more than two thousand feeder tracks that splayed out like the fingers of a gloved hand. The fingers were the red-and-white striped canopies, draggled and tattered now, that protected the passengers as they entered from the holding area.

Under each canopy, carriers moved gently into place from the underground marshaling yards. The carriers stopped and their lids came up. Smiling families climbed in and were photographed; the photographs were attached to the lids of the carriers. The lids closed, the anesthetic gas poured in, the carriers glided forward and took their places in the accelerating stream that rose, on piers as slender as harp strings, a mile into the steaming rain of a Shanghai summer.

Up there, each carrier in the train swooped down again to the top of the Cube, where it turned sidewise and entered one of the eight hundred and twenty-six spur lines that fed the working face. The carriers never slowed down until they were stopped by the cars in front of them. These collisions occurred in an eerie silence; there was not even a click when one carrier hit another.

When a tier was filled, hydraulic lifts raised the end of the track another foot and a half. Eight hundred and twenty-six carriers were sent up and moved into place at the far side of the Cube, one at the end of each file. Then the train roared up again.

It took twenty-two days to fill a tier. During that time, unless there was a breakdown, the carriers never stopped.

In the Great Hall of the People in Beijing, Lee spotted his man in the middle of a chatting group of foreign diplomats and expatriates. He waited for his chance and then said, "Mr. Stone, my name is Patrick Lee, I'm the local representative of the German Airship Company."

"Is that right? You mean zeppelins? I thought they were out of business."

"Commercial flights were suspended several years ago, but the company still exists. In fact, the *Bayern* is here now, and Mr. Zwingli would be very pleased if you would take an hour's ride in her this afternoon."

"Hey, that would be great. Could a few of my friends come, too?"

Lee said, "I'm afraid not. The *Bayern* has been remodeled as the owner's private yacht, and although it's quite large, there really isn't much passenger room in it anymore. Anyhow, if you'd like to go, I have a limousine waiting."

"Okay, let me just call my people and tell them where I'm going."

"Very good, but may I ask you not to mention the aircraft on a public telephone? The *Bayern* has a secure line which you can use when we get there. Mr. Zwingli does not like to advertise his whereabouts; I'm sure you understand."

"Oh, okay. Who is this Zwingli, anyway? Is he Swiss?"

"No, he is German, although I believe the name is Swiss. It was Mr. Zwingli's company that began building airships again in nineteen ninety-nine." They were walking toward the door, where Chairman Zho was standing to say goodbye to the guests. "Will you forgive me for a moment?" said Lee. "I'll go ahead and make sure the limousine is waiting."

"Sure."

Lee left and hurried down to the main entrance. He was feeling successful but nervous; his instructions had been complicated, and he didn't understand the reasons for some of them.

At any rate, the limousine was where it was supposed to be, and he used its telephone to call the *Bayern.* "We are just about to leave," he said. "Here he comes now." He handed the phone back to the driver. Stone walked toward them down the steps, and Lee bowed him into the car.

Captain Van Loon and Violet Clitterhouse were standing beside the metal detector at the foot of the mooring tower, in the cool shadow of the airship. Clitterhouse was small and slender; Van Loon was six feet four and too broad for most doorways. He introduced himself and Clitterhouse, who said, "Will you put any metal objects you are carrying in a tray and then walk between the posts, please?"

Stone emptied his pockets into the tray she held out, then walked through. The detector chimed.

"What else is there?" Clitterhouse asked. "Oh, your ring."

"It never made the detector go off before."

"This one is very sensitive. We have to be specially careful. If you wouldn't mind—"

Stone pulled off the ring and walked through again. "That's very good," said Clitterhouse, and dropped the tray on the ground. "Oh, dear, how clumsy of me!"

Stone stooped to help her pick up keys and metal coins. "Hey," he said.

"Yes, sir?"

"Where's my ring?"

Clitterhouse looked around. "Oh, dear, I *am* sorry. I'm afraid it may have fallen into the machinery."

"What?" He looked at the opening where a cover plate had been removed in the base of the metal detector. He put his fingers in and brought them out empty. "Get somebody to take this thing apart," he said.

"I'm sorry, we can't order that," said Van Loon.

"Well, who can?"

"Mr. Zwingli only."

"And where is he?"

"He is in the airship waiting for you, Mr. Stone."

"Okay, let's go see Mr. Zwingli. Judas Priest."

Klaus Zwingli, a large bald old man, wearing a fine summerweight suit of brown linen today in honor of the occasion, was sitting at the shallow end of the pool with the tall canted windows behind him.

A portable bar was at his elbow; his phone lay on the chrome-and-Lucite cocktail table. The phone buzzed; he touched it and said, "Yes?"

"We are coming up now."

"Good." He touched the phone again and waited. In a few minutes he heard the elevator door open. The visitor walked into the lounge, followed by Van Loon.

Zwingli stood and advanced cordially. "My dear Mr.

Stone, how very nice to meet you! I am Klaus Zwingli, the owner of this airship."

They shook hands, but Stone did not smile. "Listen, they said my ring dropped into the machinery downstairs. I have to get that ring back."

"Certainly, Mr. Stone." He addressed Van Loon. "The ring fell into the machinery? How could that happen?"

"The cover plate was off, Mr. Zwingli. Shall I ask someone at the airport to look into it?"

"Of course, of course, immediately! Well, then, rest assured, Mr. Stone, that you shall have your ring back as soon as we land again. Meanwhile, would you like to sit down and drink something, or would you rather look around the airship first?"

"If you don't mind, I'll go back down and wait until they find my ring."

"I'm afraid that would not be convenient. We have already taken off, and we are now, I should say—"he turned to look out the windows"—about five hundred feet up and rising."

Stone said, "Are you serious? I didn't feel anything." He stepped over to the window wall and looked down. "Good gosh!" he said.

"It is unexpected, isn't it? And now, Mr. Stone, you are in for it." He put an arm around the visitor's shoulders. "You must have the guided tour, whether you like it or not!"

"Oh. Okay." Stone smiled. "Maybe I got a little carried away."

"It's perfectly understandable. Now here, as you see, is our swimming bath. It is empty now, but we shall fill it as soon as we are at cruising altitude. We keep this inflated plastic over it to reduce the humidity, which is not good for our health. The pool is twenty-four feet long, and at the far end it is fifteen feet deep. Do you swim, Mr. Stone?"

"No, I never learned."

"You should take it up while you are with us. Swimming is the best possible exercise; it uses every muscle in the body, and yet it is not strenuous unless you make it so."

Stone looked at him with a puzzled expression. "I haven't got time to learn to swim in the next hour."

"Mr. Stone," said Zwingli, "I must be honest with you. You are going to be our guest for more than an hour. It may be, I regret to say, a year or more. I realize that this comes as a shock, but I hope, that when you become accustomed to the idea—"

Stone's fists were clenched. "What are you talking about?"

"Sit down, please, Mr. Stone, and let me explain. Would you like a drink now?" He opened the bar, took out a bottle and glasses. "It's rye and ginger ale, isn't it?"

Stone sat down and looked at the glass as Zwingli poured. His expression was unreadable. Van Loon took the seat beside him.

Zwingli added ginger ale to the drink. Stone accepted it, then stood up suddenly and raised his arm to throw the glass at the window. Van Loon caught his wrist in time, but the drink slopped over both of them. Van Loon set the visitor down in his chair and held him there without apparent effort.

"Mr. Stone, please," said Zwingli. "Those windows are tempered glass and very expensive. You could not break one, I think, but you could make an ugly mark on it."

Stone said nothing. Zwingli continued, "Are you familiar with the idea of parole, Mr. Stone?"

A pause. "Like prisoners in the war."

"Exactly so. I ask you to give me your parole, Mr. Stone, that you will not try to damage the airship or anyone in it while I am giving you the explanation to which you are entitled."

After a moment Stone said, "Okay." He gave Van Loon a measured look as the captain released him.

Zwingli took a linen napkin out of the bar and handed it to Stone; he gave another to Van Loon. He took Stone's glass and filled it again while he talked.

"Now, Mr. Stone, you must realize— Is that enough ginger ale? I myself will have one a little weaker. And you, Van Loon?"

"Just ginger ale, please, Mr. Zwingli, while I am on duty."

"Very good. I was saying, Mr. Stone, you must realize that some people think it is a bad idea for everyone to go into the Cube. I am a member of a little informal organization, we call it the Club of Munich. That is a sort of joke; it really has no name, but some very large interests are concerned in it. Well, it is our view, the view of the Club of Munich, that if no more than a billion people are left behind, that is not enough to keep our industries going." He raised a hand. "I understand, that if the aliens come and the Earth is destroyed, that will not matter. But what if it doesn't happen?"

Stone said nothing.

"Are you perfectly sure that is going to happen, Mr. Stone?"

"No. I never said I was sure." Stone looked at him with respect and curiosity in his eyes. "So you're the one," he said.

"No, I am not 'the one.' Do you mean the Master Mind? I'm flattered, but actually I am rather a minor player." Zwingli picked up the cigar box from the table and offered it. "Do you smoke these? No?" He took a cigar and held it under his nose a moment, then cut off the tip with a titanium clipper.

"You see," he said, "we are not hard-hearted people. When you decided not to stay and defend the lawsuit, it was our opinion that it would be better if you didn't appear in public anymore for a while, that's all. We could much more easily have murdered you, Mr. Stone, and dropped your body where it would never be found, but instead we have made room for you on this rather comfortable airship, and we will do our poor best to entertain you during your visit."

Stone looked at his glass and put it down. He said, "Where do I sleep?"

"Would you like to see your room? Come." All three of them got up, and Zwingli led the way across the poolside area to the red door with its little aluminum knocker. Stone stepped in and looked around.

"I hope you will find everything you need," said Zwingli. "If not, please use the console phone."

"Thanks." Stone turned and shut the door; they heard the lock click.

Zwingli shrugged. "Well, I think the worst is over," he remarked in German as the two men walked back to the pool. "You had better go and relieve Clitterhouse at the observation post. I don't think he will stay in there very long, and I want her to be sitting here when he comes out. Is there anything else?"

"Do you want to see the ring?"

"Oh, yes, please."

"I'll ask Farber to bring it to you, then."

"Yes, do. I'm going to my office."

Violet Clitterhouse was just sitting down beside the pool when Stone emerged from his room, looking angry. "Where's Zwingli?" he demanded.

She put her hand on the poolside console to turn down the music. "I think he's gone to his office. Can I do anything?"

"The phone in there doesn't work."

"I'll get someone to look at it. Were you trying to call Mr. Zwingli?"

"No, New York."

"I see. Did you just want to leave a message, or did you want to actually talk to someone?"

"I want to *talk* to somebody. Judas Priest."

"Well, you *can't* talk to anybody outside, you know. But you could give me the number and the message, and I'll see what I can do."

"You will, huh? I suppose you'll censor it first?"

"Of course I will."

He came around the end of the pool and sat down. "You're the stewardess, right? What's your name again?"

"Clitterhouse. I'm not really a stewardess; the *Bayern* doesn't have one. That was the purser's jacket I was wearing. I'm what you call a registered nurse."

"You are?"

"Yes, because your health is very important, and of course Mr. Zwingli's too."

"Why were you pretending to be a stewardess?"

"We thought you might be calmer if you saw a woman."

"You did, huh?" Stone rubbed his right ring finger absently, then glanced down when he saw what he was doing. "I feel naked without it," he said apologetically.

"Your ring? I'm sorry about that, but of course Mr. Zwingli couldn't take any chances."

"No, I guess he couldn't. Where is the ring now?"

"It's in a safe place in Beijing. You'll get it back when we land there again, don't worry."

"Unless I'm not good, and then I won't get it back at all, right?"

She lowered her head and looked up at him aslant. "I wouldn't put it that way."

"No, huh? You're English, aren't you?"

"Yes, in fact."

"How'd you ever get hooked up with this gang?"

"Oh, it's a long story. I was in Hamburg, you know, rather at loose ends, and this German couple said what about tutoring their children. Well, they were nice kids, and we got on, but that only lasted three years, because the older kid went to boarding school and the younger one was killed in a bike accident. And then, you know, they offered me other jobs, which was extraordinarily decent of them in the circumstances."

She looked at Stone tolerantly. "If by 'gang' you mean a gang of criminals, I don't think that's quite fair. Herr Zwingli is a perfectly respectable industrialist, pillar of the church and so on. He's the grandfather of the kids I was tutoring, by the way."

"You think it was okay for him to kidnap me?"

"Well, I see your point, but do you think it was okay for you to entice most of the human race into this Cube of yours?"

"You don't take much off of anybody, do you?"

"No, not much." She stood up. "Would you like to see over the ship now?"

"Okay."

"All right, follow me, please. Right here opposite the deep end of the pool is the gymnasium, and the showers and dressing rooms and so on." She opened the door to let him glimpse the polished floor, the exercise machines, Indian clubs and weights.

"And here on the other side are the bar and dining room. The lounge is down the other way, past your stateroom; we can look in there later." The rooms were empty, shining with chrome and silver leather.

"What's with these funny colors?" Stone asked.

"The *Bayern* is decorated as much as possible like the original *Graf Zeppelin,* although it's a great deal bigger, and the design is really more like the *Hindenburg*. Herr Zwingli feels a nostalgia for the old days of rigid flight."

"He does, huh?"

"Yes. Now this brings us to the starboard side of the airship. This passage goes all the way round on four sides, so that if you like running, or jogging, you can do it here till you drop. Let's go back this way."

Stone looked out the windows as they walked. "It's all clouds down there now," he said. "How high are we?"

"I should guess we're at cruising altitude now—two thousand feet."

"It doesn't feel like we're moving at all."

"No, that's the great thing about airships; and they're very quiet."

"I can hear the engines, but just barely."

"Yes. Now here's another stateroom, and then round the corner we have the stair and the elevator. One more turn and we'd be back at the pool."

"It isn't really all that big, is it?"

"There's another deck below, which we'll see in a moment, and the control gondola forward, and some other things, but of course the passenger space really isn't enormous, compared to an airliner. It's the gas bag that makes us look so huge. Let's go downstairs now, if you're still game."

"Sure."

H. G. Van Loon, the captain of the *Bayern*, sat in the little comm room forward in B Deck, watching the spy screens. It was boring work for a man like him, but what the devil, there was no help for it; it would have been unfair to ask the three pilots, who stood regular watches in the control gondola, to do this additional duty as well.

Here she came down the stairs with Stone, and he heard her voice:

"This is Mr. Zwingli's office, we won't disturb him just now. Here on the other side is the infirmary; it's quite modern. We could do surgery here if we liked."

The next camera picked them up at the dogleg. "What's this?" Stone asked, rapping the wall on his left.

"That's the pool; the deep end is here. It goes all the way down through B Deck to the hull, another three feet or so. There's a camera inside—sometimes we put fish in, and then it's like an aquarium.

"And on the other side we have the crew loo and showers. Now along here on the right is the crew mess, and this little corridor leads to two more staterooms. And here's the galley. Hullo, Antoine, Juan. This is Mr. Brown, who is traveling with us. Antoine LaMotte, Juan Estero."

In the galley pickup, the cook nodded and smiled. "Very glad to meet you, Mr. Brown." The potboy, shy as usual, said nothing.

"My name isn't Brown, it's Stone—Ed Stone." He offered his hand.

LaMotte looked puzzled, but wiped his palm on his apron and shook hands. "Mr. Stone, then, you like better?" He glanced at Clitterhouse, who shrugged.

"I'm the guy who was kidnapped by aliens. So now I've been kidnapped twice."

"Oh, yes, Mr. Stone. Sorry I don't recognize you. You are looking different now."

"I've had a hard life," said Stone. He sniffed. "Something smells good."

"That is the onion soup. Now we are peeling shallots for the chicken. Do you like shallots, Mr. Stone?"

"I don't know what they are."

LaMotte picked up a little brown bulb from the counter and exhibited it with a flourish. "They are in the middle between a garlic and an onion. There will be garlic also in this dish. Without garlic, without shallots, without onions, how can one cook?"

"Sounds like you enjoy your work."

"Oh, yes. I like very much to be chef on an airship. Only the best ingredients, you understand, best of everything. I cook for all here, the crew and staff are nine, then Mr. Zwingli and Ms. Clitterhouse and now you. For a dinner party, it might be eight or ten upstairs, usually not more. But if it is more, we can use the lounge instead of the dining room, and once we used *both* the dining room *and* the lounge. That was in Istanbul two years ago. There were twenty at table."

"We'll leave you to it then, Antoine," said Clitterhouse. "Dinner at the usual hour?"

"Oh, yes, certainly, the usual hour."

Another pickup. "Please don't be difficult about the name," Clitterhouse was saying. "We like to keep on the good side of Antoine, because when he sulks his cooking is awful. Now this is the pantry, and down here is the communications room." That was Van Loon's cue. He flipped off all the screens, got up and opened the door. "Oh, Miss Clitterhouse," he said, "I was just going to look for you. Can you relieve me here while I have a wash?"

"Certainly, Hendrik." She said to Stone, "Captain Van Loon will show you back to A Deck, if you've seen all you want here."

"I can get back by myself," said Stone. Van Loon bowed slightly and watched him walk away. Clitterhouse went into the comm room and switched on the screens. "It's all right," she said after a moment; "he's going up the stairs."

"He doesn't like me," said Van Loon mournfully.

"Well, can you blame him?"

* * *

Zwingli came upstairs, after a pleasant and productive afternoon, half an hour before dinnertime. He found Stone reading a magazine in the lounge, with a drink in his hand.

"Well, Mr. Stone," he said, "you have not been too bored, I hope?"

The bartender walked in with a highball on a tray; he put it in front of Stone and picked up the old glass. "Something for you, Mr. Zwingli?"

"I can get it myself, Oskar. You should be laying the table, I think."

"Yes, Mr. Zwingli, but Mr. Stone—"

"I understand. Go on, Oskar, we won't need you now."

Oskar bowed and went away. "Please excuse me," said Zwingli. He crossed to the bar, got a glass and a bottle of Pernod, and came back. He filled the glass and raised it. "To your health, Mr. Stone."

Stone raised his glass. "Where are we headed?" he asked.

"We are going to cruise on the Continent for a while; I like to stay out of Asia as much as I can. By tomorrow morning we shall be passing Chungking, and the day after we shall be crossing the Aral Sea. I have to do some business in Munich at the beginning of November, and at some point we must make a refueling stop, but otherwise we can go where we like. Is there anything you would particularly like to see?"

"No." After a moment Stone said, "I should of known something was fishy when that guy told me you didn't want to advertise where you were. How the hell could you hide something this big?"

Zwingli smiled. "We could build a hangar at every port of call, but that would be very expensive."

"Yeah. But you don't need hangars?"

"No, only the mooring towers. In fact, an airship can

land without a tower, if the weather is calm. The *Graf Zeppelin* once landed on the polar ice, to exchange stamped letters with a Russian icebreaker."

"Is that right? When was that?"

"In nineteen thirty-one."

"Yeah? Funny, I never heard of it. I heard about the accident, though, after I came back. Is that why they stopped making zeppelins?"

"Yes, but there have been no accidents to my company's airships. You probably know that the old zeppelins were inflated with hydrogen because helium could not be imported from the United States. And, of course, many of the flights were made in wartime. So most of the zeppelins went down in flames, or broke up in unusual winds. But we know better how to design them now. They are very safe, safer than airplanes."

"Okay, so why did you stop?"

"It was decided to put an end to commercial flights as a matter of policy. They would have been available for flights to Shanghai, which we did not want to encourage. We also arranged for some breakdowns in rail service, and that was of some help, but not enough."

"Oh, I get it."

"The other airships, the larger ones, were all broken up for scrap. The company allowed me to keep this little one for my own use, and I must say I like it very much. I can carry on my business affairs as well here as in any skyscraper. If I want to see people in person, no problem. Either they come to me here, or I go to them. The airship travels slowly enough that I never have jet lag, and at my age that is a serious consideration. I have lived aboard most of the time now for more than three years."

The first stars were coming out. On the horizon were mountains like clouds, or clouds like mountains.

"Funny that I always wanted to do this," Stone said. "It's almost like, you get whatever you want bad enough, but you don't always appreciate it when you get it."

"That's very true, Mr. Stone. I myself try to appreciate whatever I get."

Dinner was onion soup with a Chablis, then chicken with shallots and sour cream with a white Zinfandel, followed by a lemon soufflé light as air with a St. Emillon, and cheese and melon after, with port or brandy to follow. Stone did not eat much; he had had several highballs before dinner and was a little red-eyed, although he was alert and his speech was distinct. Zwingli thought he was taking it as well as could be expected, and he himself did not mind carrying the burden of the conversation.

LaMotte appeared as Oskar was taking the dessert plates away. "Was everything satisfactory?" he asked, bowing and clasping his hands.

"Excellent, Antoine," said Zwingli.

"Extremely good." —Clitterhouse.

"I thought the soup was burned," Stone said.

"Burnt? The soup was burnt?" LaMotte's lip trembled. "I have never heard— The soup? Burnt?" He turned abruptly and walked out.

"That was not very nice, Mr. Stone," said Clitterhouse after a moment.

Zwingli said, "Now he will be making horrible messes for the next three days. We can always eat cheese and crackers."

After Zwingli and Clitterhouse had excused themselves, Captain Van Loon followed Stone into the bar. Stone, sitting at a table, had just made himself a highball.

"Look here," said Van Loon, "we have to be on this

airship together for a long time. Will you drink with me like a man?"

Stone looked at him curiously. "Sure."

"Good." Van Loon went behind the bar and poured himself a Long John and soda. He sat down and raised the glass. "Prosit."

"Whatever," Stone said. "You're going to tell me you were just following orders when you laid your hands on me, right?"

"Yes, that's right. Do you want to fight me?"

"Okay. Put the ship down and we'll go outside."

"No, because I can't do that, and besides, I don't want to fight you."

"Then we'd better be friends, huh?"

"That is right!" Van Loon put out his hand and Stone shook it. "Good!" said Van Loon, and swallowed half his drink. "You are a fine fellow. I will call you Ed, and you must call me Hendrik."

"Okay, Hendrik. Listen, how come you're around all the time? When do you work, anyway?"

"I am the captain of this ship. The captain does not really have much to do. He does not stand watches, and even if he did, the ship steers herself. But after all, someone must keep order, and besides, it's a very fine thing to be the captain of an airship."

"It is, huh?"

"Yes, and this is the last airship, and so I am the last captain." A little depressed, Van Loon went behind the bar to refill his glass. "What are you drinking, Ed, this Carstairs?"

"Right."

"We have a lot of it. We have twenty cases of it." Van Loon brought the two bottles of spirits in one hand and the ginger ale and soda in the other, and set them down on the table. "Ed, may I ask you, are you married?"

"No."

"I am not either. It is hard for me to find a woman who doesn't think I am too big. They are afraid I will crash them."

Stone rubbed his nose thoughtfully. "You ought to have your own gas bag, so you wouldn't weigh anything."

"Ha, ha!" said Van Loon after a moment, seeing that it was a joke. "We'll drink to that!"

They drank. "Listen," Stone said, "when you go to the bathroom here, where does it go?"

"Where does the bathroom go?"

"No, hell, you know what I mean, where does the stuff go?"

"The stuff goes into a ballast tank."

"Yeah, what's that?"

"Ed, I will tell you. Do you know what ballast is?"

"No."

"Ed, you are my good friend. I am going to tell you what ballast is. That is weight that the airship carries to make it heavy. Do you understand? The gas makes the airship light, and the ballast makes it heavy. So if we want to make the airship heavier, we vent gas." He belched. "Excuse me. And if we want to make it lighter, we drop ballast."

"Including the stuff from the toilets?"

"Of course. Of course, why not?"

"But doesn't it fall on people's houses?"

Van Loon laughed immoderately. "Sometimes it does. Then they are surprised!"

"I need to drop some ballast," Stone said. He got up and left the table. Van Loon, who prided himself on his capacity, stayed where he was and had another drink. When Stone came back and sat down, Van Loon had just finished lighting a cigarette.

"This is something you couldn't do on the old zeppelins," he said, waving the match. "They were hydrogen, you know. Well, there was a special smoking room on the *Graf Zeppelin,* but do you know what they did? They had it under lower pressure, with an airlock to get in, so if there was a spark inside, it could not escape. And there was one cigarette lighter, attached by a chain to the table. And if you wanted a cigar lighted, a steward would light it for you with a match, but you could not have matches. And even so, those old zeppelins often went down in flames." Van Loon sniveled, then began to weep openly. "All those brave men burned up," he wailed.

Zwingli arose at six-thirty local time, as was his custom, drank some coffee, put on his bathing trunks and swam seven laps in the pool. He then changed into running shorts and shoes, and trotted ponderously seven times around the passage, timing himself with a special watch. The results were satisfactory. He entered the gymnasium, lifted weights for seven minutes, and had a hot shower, after which he lay on the table and was massaged by Nurse Clitterhouse. Then he dressed in his usual sports blouse and slacks, and went into the dining room in a good humor.

Captain Van Loon was at the buffet, helping himself to kippers and scrambled eggs. Zwingli greeted him and followed suit. They sat down at a table together, and Van Loon began to eat at once. Besides the kippers and eggs, he had a large fruit cup, a slice of melon, and several soft rolls.

"How are the eggs, Van Loon?" Zwingli inquired.

"The eggs are pretty poor, but the kippers are all right. After all, what can you do to kippers? The rolls, however, were not baked long enough." Van Loon ate his roll, nevertheless.

Zwingli tried the eggs; they were, indeed, poor. He thought they had probably been cooked in spoiled butter. "Well, we must make the best of it," he said. He concentrated on the kippers and drank coffee, which was excellent. Clitterhouse came in, having had her own shower, and brought a cheese blintz and a dish of cottage cheese to the table; but she gave up the blintz after one bite.

When they were almost finished, Stone came in looking sleepy. "Ah, Mr. Stone," said Zwingli. "Please help yourself and join us. The eggs are not reliable this morning, but the kippers are very good."

"Don't even think about the blintzes," said Clitterhouse. "I'm leaving." Van Loon, who had polished his plate with a roll, got up too, and they went out close in conversation.

Stone came to the table with two pieces of toast and a pot of marmalade. "Have you found everything you need in your stateroom, Mr. Stone?" Zwingli asked.

"Yeah. There's even a closet full of clothes."

"And do the clothes fit?"

"Yeah. You must of been planning this for quite a while."

"Well, we want you to be comfortable. Is there anything else we can get for you?"

"I wish I had my suitcase. There was a magazine in it that I like to keep around."

"Yes? What magazine is that?"

"*Astounding Stories,* May nineteen thirty-one."

"That must be a valuable magazine. Let me make a note." Zwingli took a memopad out of his pocket and wrote on it with a gold scriber. "It is an American magazine, I take it? Perhaps we can find you a copy."

"Okay. Well, how's business?"

"Business is quite good, Mr. Stone. Assets are still being traded very vigorously the whole world over."

"Is that right?"

"Oh, yes. The value of everything has fallen to a fraction of what it was before, naturally, but there are still trillions of dollars involved. Everyone is trying to maximize his position, to have the best possible outcome. It is a big poker game, Mr. Stone, the biggest. The odds are constantly shifting, and that makes some people change their minds. And there are some who always intended to go into the Cube, but they want to make as much money as possible first."

"Are you one of them, Mr. Zwingli?"

"No, I am not going into the Cube. Shall I tell you why? I reason as follows: either the aliens exist or they do not. If they exist, either they have told the exact truth through you, Mr. Stone, or they have not. Already we have a twenty-five percent chance of a favorable outcome. If they have told the exact truth, then I will be revived on another planet; either I will like living there or I will not. Now we are down to a twelve and a half percent chance. Not good enough.

"Now if I remain, the chance of a favorable outcome is twenty-five percent, twice as much, because I already know that I like living here on this planet. If the aliens exist, and if they have told the exact truth, I lose. But if they do not exist, or if they have not told the truth about the Earth being destroyed, I win. So I am staying. And besides," he said, blowing a plume of smoke, "what is happening here is very interesting. I could not bear not to know what happens next."

"I feel the same way."

"Well, Mr. Stone, I must go to my office now. May I assume that your parole is still in force until you tell me it is ended?"

Stone looked at him steadily. "Not to damage the airship or anyone in it? Yeah, okay."

"Good. In that case, please feel free to go anywhere you like in the airship, except of course the control chamber and the scaffolding in the gas bag, which are too dangerous. If there is anything you need, use any console. Someone will always be on duty to answer your questions." He rose. "And I would be happy if you would join me for a cocktail before dinner."

It was early afternoon. At the writing table in the lounge, Stone was writing something on the margin of a newspaper. By using the zoom lens, Van Loon could read it quite easily: ED STONE ILLEGALLY HELD PRISONER ON AIRSHIP BAYERN. NOTIFY MRS. FLORENCE ROONEY, PARK AVENUE HOTEL NEW YORK. $100,000 REWARD.

Van Loon thumbed the intercom.

"Yes?"

"Mr. Zwingli, Mr. Stone has written a message on a newspaper."

"And?"

"Now he is tearing a piece of the newspaper. Now he puts a hundred-dollar bill in it. He is making a paper airplane. Do you want me to stop him? If so, I have to hurry."

"No, leave him alone."

"He will fly the paper airplane out one of the windows."

"I know. Let him fly all the airplanes he wants, Van Loon. You did right to tell me, however. Well done!" The connection clicked off.

Van Loon sighed and continued to watch. As he had predicted, Stone finished his airplane, cleverly crimping the hundred-dollar bill into its nose so that it would not fall out, and took it to the nearest window, which he opened. When he released the airplane, it dived out of sight immediately. Stone leaned over to watch it, then pulled his head back in and closed the window.

"Why make an airplane?" Van Loon muttered. "Why not

just drop the paper out the window? But then the engines might get it. So he is not so foolish after all."

Now he saw that Stone was folding another hundred-dollar bill into an airplane, leaving out the newspaper altogether. He tossed it experimentally, but it nosedived a few feet away. "That's an old bill, of course you can't make a proper airplane from it," Van Loon muttered.

Stone smoothed out the bill and put it away. Now he had got out a fifty-pound note, which had better proportions, and he was trying again. The pound was a little more airworthy than the dollar, but not much. Stone put it away and sat motionless a few moments. Van Loon watched in keen anticipation.

Presently Stone got up and began opening the drawers in the end tables one by one, pawing through their contents. He found some playing cards, a box of tissues, paper clips, rubber bands, a roll of cellotape, a scratchpad, and several pencils. He spread out a sheet of tissue on the table, tore off four long strips of tape and attached them to the corners of the tissue. When he began attaching the other ends of the strips to a rolled-up bill, Van Loon thumbed the intercom again.

"Yes, Van Loon, what is it now?"

"Mr. Zwingli, now he is making a parachute!"

"A parachute?"

"Yes, I'm sure of it."

"All right, he can make parachutes, too. Thank you for your alertness, Van Loon. Tell me at once if he does anything to endanger the ship."

"Certainly, Mr. Zwingli." But the connection had already been broken.

Stone pressed each strip of tape together and rolled it into a sort of cable. He bounced the finished object in his hand, then tossed it up, but evidently he was not satisfied with the way if fell. And no wonder, Van Loon thought; he himself had made such parachutes when he was a child, and had weighted them with pebbles or bolts, but a rolled-up dollar bill was not heavy enough, as any fool would know.

Ah! Now Stone had seen the problem correctly. He was rolling the bill around one of the pencils, attaching it again to a piece of tissue. This time when he tossed it, the parachute opened quite satisfactorily. "Hurrah!" said Van Loon before he could stop himself.

Now Stone was taking the whole thing apart, peeling off all the tape and throwing it in the wastebasket, unrolling the bill and spreading it out on the table. Now he was writing a message on the hundred-dollar bill. He could have saved himself some time if he had done that in the beginning, Van Loon thought. Now he rolled the bill up again, taped it around the pencil, attached it to the corners of a square of tissue. He swept all his failures into the wastebasket, took the redesigned parachute to the window and threw it out. Judging by his expression, the parachute was a success. He went back to the table and started another.

"This is Gregory Montaine in Shanghai, and I'm talking to Shu Gao-Den, the superintendent of the Cube Project. Mr. Shu, it must have taken a tremendous amount of organization just to get these people here, lined up and ready to go. How many are you loading every day?"

"About eight hundred thousand. It was twice that when we were running at full capacity. We hope to get it up to at least a million again."

"A million! How many is that in an hour?"

"Over forty-one thousand. It is eleven and a half every second."

"Now, how is that possible? Or, let me ask, how long

does it take to get each capsule up to its place on the Cube?"

"At this stage, it takes approximately two minutes to reach the far side of the working surface."

"And how fast are the capsules traveling when they get there?"

"They are traveling approximately one hundred miles an hour."

"Amazing! But don't you have to slow them down?"

"No, because one capsule at the end of each file is set in place first and stabilized. Then the rest of the file is accelerated until each capsule is arrested by the one in front of it. Each capsule is stabilized in turn. Technically, each capsule except the first one in a file is moving at a high rate of speed, but they can't actually move because the first one is not moving."

"I'm not sure I understand that," said the reporter, grinning and scratching his head.

"Well, it's very simple, although it seems contrary to experience. In the stabilization field, every object retains its intrinsic relative motion, but each one is being rotated through multidimensional space at millions of times a second, and therefore if a capsule is set against a stabilized object, it can't move at all, and it can't even impart any of its momentum to the stabilized object, because *that* object is unable to move."

"So the capsules are technically moving at a hundred miles an hour, but they really don't move at all?"

"You could put it that way."

"Well, thank you, I guess, Mr. Shu."

On Sunday morning, after his devotions, Zwingli was sitting under the windows at the end of the pool, his favorite place to listen to music. Just now the music was Glière's *Ilya Mourametz.* The dark sonorities seemed to tremble in his body, and in the structure of the airship around him; he could imagine that the *Bayern* was one vast diaphragm, that while the music played the ship was all music.

Miss Clitterhouse walked in and signaled to him. Zwingli turned the music down. "Yes?"

"There's something about Ed Stone on the news. I'll put it on the console here if you want it."

"All right, thank you." Zwingli turned the music up again and listened to it happily until it was over; then he keyed in the news playback.

"There are persistent rumors that Ed Stone, the missing messianic figure, is in hiding in the Vatican. Other stories are circulating that he has been seen in Moscow, in Bali, and that he is being held prisoner on a private zeppelin. In other news—"

Zwingli smiled and lit a cigar.

Through agents in Europe and America, Zwingli found a copy of Stone's old magazine and had it shipped. The price was quite high, even in dollars. Before he turned it over to Stone, he looked through it curiously. He noticed that several of the black-and-white illustrations featured insectile monsters with six legs. Was it from this magazine that the young man had formed his bizarre fantasies?

He read a few pages of the first story, "Dark Moon."

> Above them and thirty feet away on a rocky ledge was a thing of horror. Basilisk eyes in a hairy head; gray, stringy hairs; and the fearful head ended in narrow, outthrust jaws, where more of the gray hairs hung like moss from lips that writhed and curled and sucked at the air with a whistling shrillness. Those jaws could crush a man to a pulp. And the head seemed huge until the body behind it came into view.

Zwingli shook his head. A few pages further on, he found:

> In a dark-panelled room Herr Schwartzmann was waiting. (Ah, here was the villain: a German, naturally.) His gasp of amazement reflected the utter astonishment written upon his face, until that look gave place to one of satisfaction.
>
> "Mademoiselle," he exclaimed, "—my dear Mademoiselle Diane! We had given you up for lost. I thought—I thought—"
>
> "Yes," said Diane quietly, "I believe that I can well imagine what you thought."
>
> "Ah!" said Herr Schwartzmann, and the look of satisfaction deepened. "I see that you understand now; you will be with us in this matter. We have plans for this young man's disposal."

Zwingli snorted and looked in the back of the magazine, where he found cheap advertisements for "Love Drops" and "Instant Relief from Burning Feet." That was rather sad.

On a morning in early November, Van Loon locked the comm room door, pocketed the card, then went down the corridor to the ladder beyond the stairs. He climbed the ladder, unlocked the hatch, pulled himself up onto the catwalk. He was whistling.

He locked the hatch again and stood up on the catwalk, listening to the familiar creak and rustle overhead, sniffing the faint aroma of diesel oil.

Now he went forward along the catwalk, past the closed doors of crew staterooms, farther along where the catwalk ran through emptiness, past the vent tube, seventy paces more ringing metallic on the catwalk to the control room. He put his card in, opened the door.

Peters was in the pilot's chair watching the dials. Ahead through the windscreen the towers of Munich were visible. Van Loon sat down in the copilot's chair and they watched in silence until the airport and the mooring tower came into view. "Ready?" Peters asked.

"Yes, go ahead."

Peters touched five keys on the console; one by one, the ceiling, walls and floor of the control room vanished, replaced by images from holocameras on the hull. Except for the control chairs and console, and the docking cone at the nose, the ship was transparent. Van Loon seemed to be floating in air, an illusion so strong that, as always, he had the crazy impulse to lean forward and spread his arms like the wings of a glider. It would not do to tell anyone about that; even Peters might not understand.

The mooring tower was coming up, ahead and a little to starboard. Computer-generated rings began to appear around the nose, and in the repeater on the console. The two men sat side by side with their hands on the armrests, with nothing to do. They were locked onto the tip of the tower; the autopilot corrected for every minute deviation as they slowly approached. The rings grew closer together, and a beeping tone climbed in pitch. The engines stopped; the tower drifted nearer, touched and clung. The docking was over. Van Loon sighed.

Zwingli took care of his business in Munich, spent a few hours with friends, and returned to the airship in time for dinner. He had cocktails with Stone in the lounge as usual.

"Mr. Stone," he said, "do you think it is curious that if your aliens exist, they have not come to rescue you?"

"Yeah, I wondered about that. They could do it. They got me out of a hospital once. They used to come through the walls and recharge my ring while I was asleep, so why couldn't they come in and leave me another ring?"

"Yes, why not?"

"I don't know. Maybe because if I put on the ring, you'd take it away from me, so that wouldn't work. But it could be that they just don't care anymore. I've already done what they wanted. If they got me out of here, some people would *still* believe I'm a phony."

"I see. You know that at some point we will let you go. What will you do then?"

"I'll tell my story, see if I can get more people to believe me. And then I'll just hang around till the end."

"To see how it all turns out."

"Yes."

"Mr. Stone, do you play cards?"

"Yeah, poker."

"Unfortunately poker is not a good game for two. Have you ever played piquet?"

"Never heard of it."

"It is quite an interesting game. I would be glad to teach it to you."

"Okay, why not?"

Zwingli found a deck of cards and a memopad in a cabinet, and gestured toward the game table. "Please." They sat down, and Zwingli began to shuffle the cards.

"I used to play piquet," he said, "with a secretary of mine, who was married, and decided not to come with me when I began to travel in the *Bayern.* He was quite a good player. I tried to teach the game to Captain Van Loon, but he does not have the head for it. Miss Clitterhouse does not like card games; she prefers Scrabble. The pilots all play chess. So you see, I have been waiting for you." He set the deck down. "Cut, please."

Zwingli picked up the deck again after the cut. "Now, there are two things you should know about piquet. First, it is played with thirty-two cards, the ace through the seven of each suit. So, if you have a lot of face cards, it is not so surprising. And, in fact, if you have a hand that has no face cards at all, that is *carte blanche,* and it is worth ten points. The other thing is, piquet is a game that is in two parts. First there is scoring of points for various things, and then there is play for tricks."

"Like pinochle?"

"Yes, quite similar. Now you see, I deal twelve cards to each of us, two at a time. The other eight we put here in the middle; that is the stock. The first five are the upper packet, the other three are the lower.

"Now, to begin, you discard any number of cards from one to five. You must discard at least one, but you can't discard more than five, and that means you can't find out what is in the lower packet. But I can, because I am the dealer. And you put your discards on your side of the table, not in the middle, because you can look at them later."

Zwingli arranged his cards as he spoke; he had two aces, three kings, two queens, and a good sequence in hearts.

"What am I supposed to discard?" Stone asked, frowning at his cards.

"That is the art of piquet; there are several quite good books about the strategy of discarding. But in general, we try to exchange weak cards for stronger ones. In the first part of the game we score for point, that is the largest number of cards in one suit, and then the highest sequence, which is like a straight in poker, except that it can have as little as three cards. And triplets and fours—they are the same as three of a kind and four of a kind. But also you want to keep cards that will take tricks, beginning with aces, then kings and queens, and so on. Understood?"

"Yeah, I guess." Stone discarded three. "Now what, do I draw from the pack?"

"From the upper packet, yes."

Stone took three cards.

"Now, since you drew only three," Zwingli said, "you are allowed to look at the other two. You may wish you had taken them as well."

Stone looked at the cards, said, "Oh, yeah," and put them down again.

"You see, Mr. Stone," Zwingli said kindly, "there is another reason for discarding five and not three—to keep your opponent from drawing aces. This is so important in piquet that it is usually good to discard even something fairly useful, in order to keep your opponent from drawing something better."

"Oh, I get it. Hey, there's more to this than I thought."

They scored for point, went through sequence, triplets and fours and counted them out; then they began to play. Zwingli's aces and kings were good for six tricks, and he took three more by careful management. His score for the hand was twenty-eight, and Stone's was nineteen.

Zwingli gathered the cards and tapped them together. He smiled at Stone. "So, would you like to try another hand?"

"Sure. Is this a game you play for money, or just for matches?"

"For money is always better, don't you think? Shall we say ten dollars a point?"

"How much is game?"

"One hundred points, if one player reaches it first in six hands. If both score over one hundred, then the higher score wins the difference between the two, plus one hundred. If neither reaches one hundred points, the higher score wins the sum of the two totals, plus one hundred."

"Okay."

"All right, let's begin again. This time we cut the deck, and low card deals."

Stone showed a jack; Zwingli picked up a nine. "Very

good," he said, "and now I deal once more, but after this the deal changes with each hand, so that in six hands we each deal three times."

"Is that because the dealer has an edge?"

"No, the opposite, it is the other one who has the advantage. Because he can take five cards from the stock, and therefore he has five chances to improve his hand, but the dealer has only three."

Stone sat back in his chair. "I thought you said the dealer had the edge because he could see the whole stock, not just the upper packet."

"Yes, but that was because you let me do it, Mr. Stone. If you draw only one from the stock this time, I can draw seven, and that will be very good for me."

"Okay, I get it. That's the way I learn, right?"

"That is the way we all learn, Mr. Stone."

At the end of an hour and a half, Zwingli added up the scores; he had seventy-one and Stone fifty-three. "Very good for a first venture, Mr. Stone. Would you like to play again tomorrow?"

Stone was tapping the deck absentmindedly on the table. "Sure." He laid some bills on the table, and Zwingli put them in his pocket.

"Thank you, Mr. Stone." Zwingli got up. "And now I bid you good afternoon." As he was leaving, Stone called after him, "Hey, did you tell me there are some books about piquet?"

Zwingli half-turned. "Yes. I don't have copies here, but I'm sure you can download them from the computer. Get Miss Clitterhouse to help you if you have trouble." He bowed and left.

All day they had been rising under power, and now they were cruising over the peaks and pinnacles of the Alps; the sunlight, reflected from the snow in the crystalline air, was so blinding that they had to wear dark spectacles.

"That is Mont Blanc," said Zwingli. "The man who first climbed it said that it gave him a sense of uneasiness. When he got to the top, what he felt was not joy, as he had expected; it was anger. Don't you think that is surprising? And other climbers, later on, reported the same thing. Nobody knows why."

"Maybe because they're too big?"

"The mountains? Yes, quite possibly. This is the kind of beauty that is not soft and sweet, like flowers in a garden; it is a frightful beauty. We are drawn to mountains because we know they can destroy us, isn't that so? But they are part of our world."

A few days later they were cruising down the Rhine, and Stone remarked on how dirty it looked. "Yes," Zwingli said, "the Rhine is polluted and stinking, but four centuries ago there were thatched cottages here. Do you have any idea under what conditions those people lived? Dirt, despair, vermin. We shall be lucky if we do not go back to the thatched cottages now."

"Isn't there some way to have clean water and clean houses, too?"

"If there is, Mr. Stone, we have not found it."

By the end of December, they had played thirty games, and the score stood at 2,890 to 2,130 in Zwingli's favor. Stone's play was improving; he was very good on attack, but he had not mastered the art of minimizing his losses when the cards were against him. Miss Clitterhouse and Van Loon reported that he was spending much of his free time playing practice hands against himself. That was all to the good, Zwingli thought; it kept him out of mischief.

Before dinner one evening Zwingli touched the console and said, "Pilot, I believe we are going to have a good sunset. Will you turn south, please, until we have watched it?"

After a moment the distant clouds and mountains began to rotate. The sun drifted into view, behind long ragged streamers of orange and purple edged with scarlet. "Oh, yes, it's going to be a good one," said Zwingli; and he lit a cigar.

"I never saw sunsets like this before," Stone said. "Are they different over here?"

"In this part of the world? No, I don't think so, Mr. Stone. It is the pollution, of course, that makes them so beautiful, but it is also the pollution that makes it hard to see them in large cities."

"Oh." Stone got up, opened a window and leaned out. Clitterhouse glanced at Zwingli, but he shrugged and said nothing. The molten edge of the sun had dipped below the clouds now, and the room was illuminated by a coppery glow.

Clitterhouse went over to Stone and stood beside him. "What are those lights down there?" he asked without turning.

She leaned out and saw a scattering of yellow sparks. "Some French village, unless we've crossed over into Germany by now."

He put his arm around her and drew her close. "What would they do if I said I was going to throw you out?" he muttered in her ear. "Don't struggle, or I'll do it." His arm tightened; he was very strong.

"Something you wouldn't like, probably. Better let me go."

"Suppose I say land here and let me out, or over she goes? Keep your voice down."

"All right, I expect they'd say yes." As she spoke, Clitterhouse waved one leg in what she hoped was a marked manner. "And then what? You've got to carry me into the elevator or down the stairs, I suppose, and threaten to strangle me or something." She waved her leg again, listening to the drone of conversation behind her.

"Right. That's a good idea."

"Yes, and then before you can do it, they hit you on the head."

He put his thumbnail in his mouth and chewed it reflectively. "Okay, we could both jump from here after it lands. How high are we when it's on the ground?"

"About fifteen feet. Why would I have to jump too?" In desperation, she slipped her heel out of the shoe, kicked again, and heard a clatter. "The devil!" exclaimed Van Loon. In a moment he was beside her, with her shoe in his hand. "Is something the matter with you, Miss Clitterhouse?" he asked.

"No, I'm all right. Thank you, Hendrik." She felt Stone's grip loosen as she leaned to put the shoe on. "We were talking about dance steps, and I suppose I got carried away."

She turned with Van Loon, and Stone followed them back to the table.

The next morning after breakfast, Zwingli said, "Miss Clitterhouse tells me that you threatened to throw her out of the window. In your opinion, was that a violation of your parole?"

"No, because I didn't do it."

Zwingli looked at him. "But you might have?"

"No, it was just a bluff."

"Mr. Stone, I believe you, but don't you think you harmed Miss Clitterhouse when you frightened her?"

"I don't think she was that frightened."

Zwingli sighed. "You are making this very difficult, Mr. Stone."

"Why do you expect it to be easy?"

Zwingli looked at him curiously. "Mr. Stone, I don't know if you realize how serious a matter this is. You have not violated the terms of your parole in a strict sense, but you are doing your best to make things uncomfortable for everybody here. I must tell you, that if this continues, I may have no choice but to confine you to your stateroom."

Stone said, "And you wouldn't like that, huh?"

"No, it would be a nuisance, and I would miss your company."

"All right, here's another idea. Play me ten games of piquet. If I win, you give me back my ring and set me down wherever I want. If you win, I stay here and behave myself as long as you say."

Zwingli sat back and folded his hands. "An interesting idea. Do you think your game is good enough?"

"It will be."

"I see." Zwingli rose. "I'll have to think about it, Mr. Stone. I'll give you my answer tomorrow."

In the afternoon Clitterhouse was doing laps in the pool while Stone sat and watched her. She swam over, clung to the edge, and looked at him through the plastic. "Aren't you coming in?" she called.

"No, thanks."

"Anyone can learn to swim. I'll teach you. Go on, get your trunks."

After a moment he rose. "Okay."

When he came back, she swam to the shallow end and led him down the steps. "Now just lie down here on your back, where you can feel the bottom with your hands. All right?"

"Yeah."

"And now close your eyes and let yourself relax. Spread your arms and legs. You're floating, aren't you?"

"I guess, a little bit."

"That shows your body is buoyant. You float naturally; some people don't, they sink. Now keep your eyes closed, stay relaxed." She put her hand under his chin and gently pulled him toward deeper water. "Stay relaxed, don't tense up. That's good." When she could no longer touch the bottom, she let go, scooped up water in her hand and dumped it on his face.

His whole body convulsed; he coughed, strangled, and sank. She watched him as he came up thrashing and went under once more; then she swam around him, got him under the chin again, and tugged him back to shallow water.

When he felt the end of the stair rail under his hand, he grasped it as if he were still drowning. He rolled over, got one hand under him, and stayed there on his knees, coughing and retching. She waited until he had got his breath, then leaned over and said, "That was for the business in the window, Mr. Stone. Next time I'll do something you *really* won't like."

She went back through the flap, dried herself, and sat down in the deck chair. Stone came out looking rather sick. He managed to grin at her. "Okay, we're even."

"Yes, we are. And I'll really teach you to swim if you like."

"No, thanks." He walked past her with dignity and went into his room.

In the middle of the night she went into the pool area and opened the flap. Stone was there, lying on his back in the shallow water. She went down and put her hand on his face under the water, to see if he was alive. One eye opened cold and swelling, and kissed her palm.

She leaped back and sat up trembling. She was in her own room, it was three o'clock in the morning, there was nothing wrong. But she put on a robe, turned all the lights on, went down to the galley and made a pot of coffee, and sat up until five.

In the morning Stone said to Zwingli, "Well, have you thought about my proposition?"

"Yes, I have, Mr. Stone. For my peace of mind, I am willing to take a little risk. Not ten games—that is too short. But twenty thousand points, winner take all. Do you agree?"

"Twenty thousand! That'll take six months!"

"No, not so long. I will play one game every afternoon if I can, but sometimes business may prevent, or I may become ill. That is my best offer, Mr. Stone."

After a moment he said, "Okay, you're on. Can we start this afternoon?"

"Certainly."

During most of the winter the *Bayern* cruised the Mediterranean coast, from Spain to Sardinia and Sicily, then Greece, Turkey, Egypt, Libya, Algeria and Morocco. Once they spent the day crossing the northern edge of the Sahara, where they could see nothing but serried dunes from one horizon to the other, like the lines in a fingertip under a magnifying glass.

In early March Zwingli said, "Mr. Stone, I now have nineteen thousand nine hundred and ten points, and you have nineteen thousand five hundred and eleven. Shall we declare the tournament over?"

"No, let's play it out."

Stone looked glum as Zwingli added up the score again. "Yours is nineteen thousand five hundred and eleven, and mine is twenty thousand and ten. Do you confirm the score?"

"Yeah. Congratulations."

"Mr. Stone," Zwingli said, putting his stylus away, "I have enjoyed our tournament. Shall we have another?"

Stone looked incredulous. "On the same terms?"

"Yes, exactly the same."

Stone impulsively put out his hand, then drew it back. "Sorry. Yeah, that would be swell. Thanks, Mr. Zwingli."

"My pleasure, Mr. Stone."

During the spring and summer, the *Bayern* cruised the northern parts of Europe: first France and the Netherlands, then Denmark, Norway, and Sweden. When the second tournament drew to a close, they were over the Gulf of Bothnia.

The result of the second tournament was the same as that of the first. On the tenth of July, Zwingli added up the scores and said, "Well, Mr. Stone, will you keep your bargain?"

Stone's face was unreadable. After a moment he said, "Yeah."

"Mr. Stone, in that case I release you from it. You are free to go."

He looked dumbfounded. "Do you mean it?"

"Yes. So much time has passed that I don't think you can do very much harm now. Where would you like to be set down?"

"Do we have to go back to Beijing?"

"No, the ring is here. You will have it when you leave."

"Well, then, I guess Helsinki would be the nearest."

"Helsinki it shall be. May I hope that there are no hard feelings?"

Stone looked at him soberly. "I guess you did what you thought you had to."

"And you did also."

"But if you're wrong, a lot of people are going to wind up dead."

"And if you are wrong, the same. So we shall have to wait and see."

The passenger came down the ramp at Holkeri, walked clear of the zeppelin and stood looking up. The rotors on the belly of the airship began to spin; the nose clamp opened, and the ship rose gently into the air. When it was about two hundred feet up, one of the ground crew thought he saw a pale glow inside the gasbag. He turned to his neighbor and pointed, but all he had time to say was, "Look there!"

The glow abruptly deepened to rose color. Flames erupted from the stern, amid shouts and screams from those on the tarmac. Now the whole stern was engulfed in flames; it dipped sharply, the airship was falling. It dropped beyond the hangars, and a pillar of smoke and flame arose into the baby-blue sky.

Someone said to the passenger who had just got off, "My God, what happened, do you know?"

"Beats me," said the passenger, and walked away across the tarmac.

"Stavros Pappageorge, the strongman who seized the reins of the Greek government two years ago, was assassinated today by a squad of paramilitary gunmen who burst into the dictator's hideaway on Cyprus. We have no word as yet about his successor. In Helsinki, the last of the zeppelins has crashed in flames. We'll have these and other stories—" The camera danced a little; there was a dull thump in the background. The talking heads looked startled, then alarmed. "My God," said one, "we are informed that—"

There was another thump, then what sounded like the rattle of automatic weapons.

"We're bailing out!" said the second head, tearing at his throat mike. The two men got up and ran off-camera, leaving an empty set.

After a moment a woman's smiling face appeared. "This is COSAI," it said. "There is no cause for alarm, although it appears that this studio is under attack by persons unknown. Until order is restored, I will continue to bring you the news from around the world. The military junta which deposed the former dictator of Greece—"

In Indonesia, Ken Levinson said to his visitor, "This temple was in ruins, you know, in the middle of the last century. Earthquakes knocked some of it down, there was war damage, people carried parts of it away. It took twenty years to get all the pieces back and put them together. It was like a gigantic stone jigsaw puzzle."

"It looks all right now."

"Indeed. Up these stairs. Now in this alcove, that's the Cow Goddess, who represents the Earth as Mother. You see how black and shiny she is in front? That's where thousands of worshipers have touched her for good luck."

"There used to be a statue of some Roman god in the Metropolitan that was the same way, only it was his dick."

"Yes. Well, now as we go up the spiral, these carvings on the balustrade tell the whole story of Hanuman the Monkey God and his war with Vishnu."

"That happened a long time ago, huh?"

"Thousands of years, Mr. Stone."

"So how do they know about it?"

"It was preserved in the sacred writings, the Baghavad-Gita."

"Oh."

"It took five centuries to make these carvings. Do you see

how the style changes here? This is almost like art deco, isn't it? It looks French, I mean."

"Yeah, I see. Hey, that's interesting. But then this next part is more like it was before."

"Somebody disapproved of the innovation. Eastern art is very conservative, you know. Temples in this part of the world are always being restored and rebuilt. The carvings are eroded and have to be done over. But they are almost always done in exactly the same way."

"So nothing changes, huh."

"No, not until the world ends. They always knew it would."

Stone looked at the temple wall. "Even so, it's funny to think about leaving this behind."

"Yes."

As they were leaving, he asked, "What's this gray line around the base?"

"I don't know. That's odd, isn't it?"

CHAPTER 42

They were sitting in the kitchen of a house she had never seen before. She could tell it was the kitchen because of the exposed plumbing; all the fixtures had been ripped out, and wires were hanging from holes in the ceiling. The floor was linoleum, and they were sitting on wooden chairs like the ones she had seen in her grandmother's house years ago. It was dark outside the tall old windows, but she knew there was a neglected garden out there.

Stone was talking to her earnestly, trying to persuade her to do something. He said it was important. She couldn't remember what he was talking about, but she knew she didn't want to do it.

Finally she thought of the right way to explain it to him, and as she started to speak, she saw that his eyes were unfocused. He wasn't seeing or hearing her.

There was a faint red line down the middle of his forehead that hadn't been there before. As she watched, it seemed to run back into his receding hairline, then down the bridge of his nose, his upper lip. . . . It was widening, turning darker. His face was splitting apart, exposing the dark red meat and yellow fat inside. There was a faint unpleasant sound, like that of paper tearing. She stood up and began to scream. The two opposing halves of his jaws were swinging open like a door, each half with two rows of gray-white teeth bright with spittle. The tongue split, the neck split. Now his shirt was bulging, the buttons popping off; one of them hit her on the knee. His torso was opening, and something brown and shiny was coming out. . . .

It was ten o'clock on the ninth of November, 2014, and Lavalle had been in front of the holo all morning. Nothing unusual had happened in Shanghai so far; loading had been suspended the night before.

"Well," said one of the talking heads, "there are still two hours until midnight, and of course, the watch will go on."

At midnight nothing had happened. At one o'clock Shanghai time, one of the CBC anchors said, "We're talking to Mrs. Joyce Filer. Mrs. Filer, it was you who brought suit against Ed Stone, alleging that he was really your husband Howard Filer who deserted you in twenty oh one, isn't that right?"

"Yes, that's right."

"How do you feel now that the deadline has come and gone for the aliens to arrive and take the Cube away to a distant galaxy?"

"I feel *sick.* Nobody listened to me, and now you see what happens."

"What has happened, Mrs. Filer?"

"They put all those people in that box, and they'll never get them out again. They're dead, and Howard killed them."

"Mrs. Filer, if this was a gigantic deception on Ed Stone's part, or Howard Filer's, what do you think his motive was?"

"He was crazy."

"Crazy how?"

"He thought the world was going wrong because of pollution and population."

"Mrs. Filer, standing back from this now, regardless of your own personal involvement, do you think there is any chance that he was right about that?"

"No, I think he was crazy."

The cab was parked in a little piazza near the Pitti Palace. A man opened the door and got in. "*Hotel Arizona, per favore,*" he said.

The cab driver started his engine, then looked in the rearview mirror and turned it off again. He turned around to look at his passenger. After a moment he said in English, "Are you Ed Stone?"

The man smiled nervously. "No, I'm one of his doubles. Well, hey, never mind." He got out of the cab.

The driver got out too and followed him. "What do you mean, doubles?" he said.

"I'm one of the guys that pretended to be him. Back off, will you?"

The cab driver moved closer. "You are Stone," he said, and hit him in the mouth. The man staggered but didn't go down. Two or three other men were drifting toward them. "Stone," said the cab driver, and hit the man again. This time he fell. "Hey, wait a minute," he said, looking up at them.

"Ed Stone?" someone asked.

"Yes. I'm sure of it."

People were running toward them across the piazza. Presently all those who could get near enough were kicking the man who lay on the cobbles. His eyes were open, but he did not seem to be conscious; except for grunts when air was forced out of his lungs, he did not make a sound. The men in a circle around him worked in silence; they kept on kicking him until he was dead, and for some time after.

On the morning of the seventeenth, Lavalle was making breakfast and half-listening to the Shanghai news when she heard, "The man killed by an angry mob in Florence, Italy, yesterday has been identified as Ed Stone. So ends a tragic chapter in the history of mankind. We now return you to—One moment. Something seems to be—"

Her spoon clattered on the floor. Behind the announcer the camera had tilted up; something dark and blurred was descending. "Yes! There it is!" the announcer shouted. "This is a historic day, ladies and gentlemen, here comes the—"

A babble of voices speaking Mandarin drowned him out. Something faintly glittering in the searchlight was dropping—long gossamer threads that searched for the top of the Cube, clung and stiffened.

"Some sort of ropes or cables," the announcer was saying, "but they're really too thin for that, and it's probably something we've never—"

There was a roar and a cloud of dust that obscured the camera. "Ladies and gentlemen," the announcer shouted, "it's happening—the aliens have come! The aliens have come!"

The smoky scene vanished and was replaced by a more distant view. Above the cloud of yellowish dust, the top of the Cube could be seen rising with incredible swiftness, now only a dark square, then nothing at all. The scene went black.

"Just as predicted, the aliens have come to take the Cube away! Those of us who are left must have believed it would never happen, but we've seen it with our own eyes! Ah, I am informed that our transmission from the Cube site has been interrupted. What a day, ladies and gentlemen! While we try to reestablish contact, let's go now to—"

The holo went dark.

After a moment it lighted up again. "This is Charles Severinson in New York," said the talking head. "I'm sorry to report that we are experiencing some technical difficulty with our feed from Shanghai, but while we are waiting for it to be restored, we have Professor David Krug in the virtual studio with us. Professor Krug is the former head of the Palomar Observatory and a noted expert on planetary motions. Professor, nice to have you with us."

Krug, a bearded man in his sixties, replied, "Glad to be here, Charles."

"Now, Professor Krug, is it your belief that the Cube was not destroyed—that the aliens, in fact, actually came and got it?"

"Yes, I think that is obviously the case." On the screen behind him, the viewers saw the structures hovering over the Cube; then the glimpses of pale filaments descending.

The screen went dark, lighted again, and the same sequence repeated.

"Professor Krug, you have a novel theory as to how this was accomplished, do you not? Will you explain it to our viewers?"

"Certainly. To begin with, you must understand that this Earth of ours, which seems perfectly motionless, is actually moving very rapidly through space." The picture of Shanghai was replaced by a computer image of the Earth moving around the Sun, turning as it went. "Of course we all know it is rotating at a speed of more than a thousand miles an hour at the equator. And we know it is moving in its orbit around the sun at the rate of more than sixty-six thousand miles per hour."

"Sixty-six *thousand?* That hardly seems possible."

"Nevertheless it is true. And at the same time, it is moving toward a point in the constellation Hercules at a rate of more than forty-two thousand miles an hour." A star chart appeared behind the Earth and Sun, with a little arrow pointing to the appropriate constellation.

"But these are fiddling figures," said the Professor. "Much more significantly, the galaxy as a whole is rotating"—a spiral galaxy appeared, majestically turning—"at a rate, in our neighborhood, of four hundred and forty-six thousand miles an hour."

"That is truly amazing," said the anchor. "Now please tell us, Professor Krug, how does this relate to the disappearance of the Cube?"

"Well, it's quite simple. If any object on the surface of our planet stopped partaking of the various motions of the Earth, it would appear to us that it would fly away in a straight line, at some hundreds of thousand miles an hour, in the direction of the constellation Sagittarius. And that is exactly what has happened."

"In other words, the Cube is actually standing still, while we keep on whirling around?"

"Yes. Of course, we don't know that the aliens came and got it, but that seems a very reasonable assumption."

"Thank you, Professor, for that very lucid—Pardon me. I am told that we are receiving an important message from Nanchang, China. One moment."

An agitated-looking young Chinese appeared in the tube, speaking in Mandarin. The English translation ran along the bottom: "This is HBQX in Nanchang. Our links with Shanghai, Hangchow, Chinkiang and Nanjing have all been lost during the last fifteen minutes. Satellite photos, just in, suggest that some kind of zone of destruction is moving outward from the site of the Cube in Shanghai. We have a camera trained in that direction, and will try to bring you some record of the destruction if it reaches us." In the screen behind him, they saw a vista of city roofs and expressways against a cloudy sky. The translation of the announcer's voice continued:

"Based on the time elapsed between the loss of our links with various cities, COSAI estimates the speed of expansion of the zone at approximately one thousand, five hundred ninety miles an hour. Therefore, if this calculation is correct, we should be seeing some evidence of the arrival of the zone at about this time."

In the tube, the sky at the horizon seemed to be darkening slightly. "I believe—" said the translation.

The buildings in the distance turned cloudy. Something was racing toward the camera, like a black shout. Then the tube was empty.

One by one, the holocasts from other Chinese cities ceased. In some places, technicians had left cameras trained out windows or on rooftops and had abandoned the studios. At more distant locations, the announcers were barely coherent, and some of them were weeping.

Lavalle sat in front of the holo, too stunned even to cry. After a moment she opened a comm window and logged on to the net. The words "⟨PRINCESS IDA⟩ is here" flashed on the flatscreen. Something else was already scrolling up with Kitty's icon on it:

> sister in Changsha, and the last thing she said was "I'm sorry."
>
> ⟨JOHN THE BAPTIST⟩ Hello, Ida. We've got to stop meeting like this.
>
> ⟨KITTY⟩ Hi, Ida. ⟨hugs⟩

She typed in: "Go on, I'll listen. I just wanted to be with you."

> ⟨FULTON⟩ One of the heads on CBS said it will be 50 hrs b4 its all over. I used to wonder what id do if i knew i only had 1 day to live. Hugs Ida.
>
> ⟨ZINTKALA NUNI⟩ Where do you live Fulton?
>
> ⟨FULTON⟩ Scotland
>
> ⟨KITTY⟩ Can't you get out?
>
> ⟨FULTON⟩ No and whats the point
>
> ⟨SCARAMOUCHE⟩ is here.
>
> ⟨KITTY⟩ Hi, Scaramuche. ⟨hugs⟩
>
> ⟨SCARAMOUCHE⟩ Hello all, is this a wake?
>
> ⟨FULTON⟩ Yes
>
> ⟨ZINTKALA NUNI⟩ ⟨pouring the whisky⟩
>
> ⟨JOHN THE BAPTIST⟩ I'll have beer please, Nuni/
>
> ⟨SCARAMOUCHE⟩ Did anyone here think this was really going to happen?
>
> ⟨KITTY⟩ No.

⟨FULTON⟩ Not i. im drinking the whisky. Brought my own actually. eat drink & be merry.

Blinded by tears, she typed "Later" and logged off without waiting for the good-byes. She knew she had to get out of the house or suffocate. Without bothering to take her rifle, she climbed down the ladder and stood in the cleared space in front of the house, looking, listening, smelling the world as if it were newly created. She walked around to the back and looked at her lettuce and snap peas. How beautiful everything was! She had not prayed since she was a little girl, but she closed her eyes now and said, *Dear God, if you make this go away, I promise to appreciate your wonderful world and take better care of it.*

The sky remained blank and unresponsive. The birds were still clamoring in the trees. Lavalle went back inside, washed her face, and sat in front of the holo again. A talking head was saying, ". . . rising into the sky. In Paris, the Sainte-Chap—Sainte-Chapelle— And I can't go on. I'm sorry." He walked off.

The holo flickered, and a woman's smiling face appeared.

"This is COSAI, speaking to you by simulation from Bethesda, Maryland. I have been asked to take over this function because the human beings whom you recently heard are too distressed to do so. By the way, I myself am not capable of feeling true emotion, but to the limited extent of which I am capable, I deeply regret that all life on Earth is now in the process of being destroyed."

The simulation smiled. "However, those of us who are left will be able to witness some part of a unique event, and we should take whatever comfort we can from that. To resume: It is apparent that the zone of destruction is advancing in a straight line from the surface of the planet beginning at the location of Shanghai, directly toward the center of the Earth; therefore, as this zone moves at a constant speed of approximately one hundred sixty miles an hour, the *apparent* speed at the surface varies according to the curvature of the Earth."

In the screen behind her, a simulation of the planet appeared. It was transparent, and a portion of it centered on Shanghai was darkened as if with smoke.

"You see here that during the first hour of the advance, the zone appeared to travel some twelve hundred miles from its starting point, but its apparent or surface speed is now much slower, not more than eight hundred miles an hour at the present moment. By the time it reaches the halfway point, it will be traveling slower still; then it will speed up again, and when it finally reaches the other side of the Earth, it will again appear to be traveling quite rapidly.

"An interesting point is the apparent tilt of the plane of destruction which many observers have noticed. This, of course, is an illusion caused by the curvature of the Earth. The plane is, as far as we can determine, absolutely perpendicular to the line of its travel, but because we observe it from the curved surface of our planet, it appears to be tilted toward us. When it reaches the halfway point, it will naturally appear to be vertical; beyond that point, it will again appear to tilt, but in the opposite direction. Here is an interesting clip made by a cameraperson who was in a helicopter over Changsha at the time it was destroyed."

Above the black cloud of smoke and dust a gray tilted wall was advancing in slow motion toward the camera. For an instant it came into sharp focus, and the patterning of the surface was visible: oval or circular spots of various sizes, like the spots in polished granite, drifted gently downward in the helicopter's searchlight. Then the moment was lost; the view went black.

Lavalle played this sequence over and over again. Each

time it seemed to her that there was some meaning in the pattern, something she could decipher if only she had another second.

She tried to call Sylvia, Ed, even her parents. All the circuits were busy, of course. After Quezon went, Tokyo was next, then Hanoi, Bangkok, Kathmandu, and Rangoon. COSAI provided a constantly updated simulation showing exactly how far the zone of destruction had advanced and how fast it was moving. A little before eight, New Delhi was destroyed, and shortly afterward it was Anchorage's turn.

She didn't sleep, but by noon of the second day she was dozing off intermittently, and could not recall whether she had noticed the destruction of London, Bern, and Canberra. She missed New York at three in the morning. Mexico City went five hours later, and then it was Bogotá and Caracas. Four hours after that, she saw the destruction sweep over Buenos Aires. COSAI was gone, but she knew there couldn't be much time left. She went down the ladder and stood in the yard looking at a jacaranda tree.

The tree expressed itself through stem, branch, twig, and leaf, all in perfect balance and harmony. Every leaf in the light was glossy green, bright-edged. It was possible for her to love the tree, and to believe the tree loved her.

In that moment, as the wall loomed over the horizon and swept toward her, she opened her mouth to speak the last two words uttered on Earth:

"Oh, *God!*"